PRAISE FOR CLAIRE McGOWAN

'A knockout new talent you should read immediately.'

—Lee Child

'A brilliant, breathless thriller that kept me guessing to the last shocking page.'

—Erin Kelly, *Sunday Times* bestselling author of *He Said/She Said*

'Absorbing, timely, and beautifully written, *What You Did* is a superior psychological thriller from a major talent.'

—Mark Edwards, bestselling author of *The Retreat* and *In Her Shadow*

'*What You Did* is a triumph, a gripping story of the secrets and lies that can underpin even the closest friendships. Put some time aside—this is one you'll want to read in a single sitting.'

—Kevin Wignall, bestselling author of *A Death in Sweden* and *The Traitor's Story*

'Hitting the rare sweet spot between a satisfying read and a real page turner, this brilliantly written book deserves to fly high.'

—Cass Green, bestselling author of *In a Cottage In a Wood*

'McGowan writes utterly convincingly in three very different voices and she knows how to tell a cracking story. She will go far.'

—*Daily Mail*

'One of the very best novels I've read in a long while . . . astonishing, powerful and immensely satisfying.'

—Peter James

'Funny and perfectly paced . . . chills to the bone.'

—*Daily Telegraph*

'Plenty of intrigue makes this a must read.'

—*Woman & Home*

'A brilliantly executed thriller with a haunting and atmospheric setting. Spine tingling.'

—*Sunday Mirror*

'A complex, disturbing, resonant novel that remains light on its feet and immensely entertaining.'

—*Irish Times*

'Page-turning.'

—*Guardian*

'Highly satisfying and intelligent.'

—*The Bookseller*

'Creepy and oh-so-clever.'

—*Fabulous*

'A fantastic and intense book that grips you right from the very first line.'

—We Love This Book

'McGowan's pacy, direct style ensures that the twists come thick and fast.'

—*The Irish Times*

'A riveting police thriller.'

—*Woman* pick of the week

'Taut plotting and assured writing.'

—*Good Housekeeping*

'A gripping yarn you will be unable to put down.'

—*Sun*

'A brilliant portrait of a fractured society and a mystery full of heartstopping twists. Compelling, clever and entertaining.'

—Jane Casey

'A keeps-you-guessing mystery.'

—Alex Marwood

'A brilliant crime novel . . . gripping.'

—*Company*

'A compelling and flawless thriller . . . there is nothing not to like.'

—Sharon Bolton

'Ireland's answer to Ruth Rendell.'

—Ken Bruen

'Enthralling . . . evoked wonderfully.'

—*Sunday Mirror*

'A superb, gripping & trenchant crime novel steeped in loss, pain and history.'

—Stav Sherez

WHAT
YOU
DID

ALSO BY CLAIRE McGOWAN

The Fall

Paula Maguire series

The Lost
The Dead Ground
The Silent Dead
A Savage Hunger
Blood Tide
The Killing House

Writing as Eva Woods

The Thirty List
The Ex Factor
How to be Happy
The Lives We Touch

WHAT YOU DID

CLAIRE McGOWAN

THOMAS & MERCER

Published by Thomas & Mercer, Seattle

www.apub.com

Amazon, the Amazon logo, and Thomas & Mercer are trademarks of Amazon.com, Inc., or its affiliates.

ISBN-13: 9781542007269 (hardcover)
ISBN-10: 1542007267 (hardcover)
ISBN-13: 9781542091336 (paperback)
ISBN-10: 1542091330 (paperback)

Cover design by Heike Schüssler

Printed in the United States of America

WHAT
YOU
DID

PROLOGUE

When it stops, she's lying on the grass with her face crushed into it. She can smell the green sap of it, feel the scratch of weeds against her skin. Her body comes back to her piece by piece. Her throat, wheezing and burning from where he choked her. He *choked* her. She can't entirely believe it, the feel of his hands around her neck, the panic of gasping for a breath and not finding it there, the weight of him pushing her into the ground. Her legs are cold and scratched, her feet bare on the damp grass. Her head aches, her mouth is dry. And there are other things wrong too, things she can't even begin to acknowledge. She opens her mouth and tries to shout but the words are gone, like in those dreams where you scream and scream and nothing comes out. He has taken that from her too. She tries to move, to get up, to show herself she's still alive, she's not hurt – oh, but she is – and a rip of pain tears through her.

The house is just metres away, at the other end of the large silent garden, but it may as well be miles, because no one heard this happen, no one saw, no one came to help. He has gone now, but she knows he won't be far, and despite where she is, despite the absurdity of it, all she can feel is a sudden fear that crushes her lungs and stops up her breath. He's still here somewhere. She has to get away. She has to get up, on her feet, get moving, get help. It is very dark. She blinks away the tears that have filled her eyes and sees that, in the darkness of the house, one yellow light has just winked on.

Chapter One

These days, now that everything is over, I often find myself thinking of the moment it all changed. The small slice of time when my life went from perfect, or, OK, not perfect but pretty good at least, to utterly ruined. Most of all I think about how my mind tried to pull away from it – *please, not now* – how I did my best, for a few seconds at least, to pretend it wasn't real. It was something I didn't know about myself, this capacity to stop up my ears, close my eyes. I thought I'd be the kind of person who sprang to help, called the police, made hot sweet tea for the shock.

But instead, when Karen came into my kitchen that night – staggering, trembling, her black jersey dress ruched up about her thighs, the bruises on her neck standing out like ink smudges from the newspaper – I wasn't ready. I stood frozen in horror, wishing we could scroll back time and keep that moment right before this, clean and unshattered.

Karen gave a gulping sob, as if even her voice had been scared out of her. And before my treacherous mind even had time to think, *please, don't tell us* – she said it.

'He raped me. He *raped* me.'

Jodi was there too, standing with the cafetière in her hand, kettle boiling, and it was her, not me, who had the courage to say: 'Who, Karen? What do you mean?'

And Karen said the name, and then she fell to her knees, dramatically, as if her legs were giving way. Her hair was bunched up, clumped as if someone had been grabbing it. A trickle of blood ran down her thigh, coming to rest on the slate tiles of my kitchen floor. Later, when the police were done, I would scrub it, but it would never truly shift.

I said before I was not ready to hear what Karen had to say, bursting into my kitchen and collapsing in front of me. But really, how could you ever be ready for a thing like that?

Earlier that day

'Do I have to, Mum?'

'Of course you do. What else would you do?' My to-do list was revolving in my head. *Beds, towels, after-dinner chocolates, Benji's room.*

Benji barely looked up from his iPad. Ten years old and he owned an iPad. I marvelled at that, sometimes, as I did with many things in my life. 'It'll be so boring. No one's my age.'

I hated that tinge of whining in his voice, the way his features, still smooth and acne-free, twisted into a frown. No one ever tells you that this is the downside of giving your kids everything you never had – they turn into spoiled little brats. 'Look, just eat your dinner with us and be polite and then you can do whatever you want. Watch a film or play on your iPad or something. OK?' *Good plates, ice cream from freezer, polish glasses.*

'What are we having?' His fingers never stopped, swiping, swiping, swiping at the device. I watched his eyes, the irises such a clear blue, jiggle along with it, and worried about screen time, attention deficit disorder, spoiling him.

'I'm doing tagine. Couscous, salad, that sort of thing.' Although now I'd planned the menu and ordered the Ocado shop and the lamb and vegetables were sitting in piles on the chopping board in front of me, I worried it was too easy.

Benji groaned. 'I *hate* Moroccan.'

I felt the words bubble in my mouth: *When I was your age I'd never even heard of Moroccan.* I bit them down. 'Benj. This is important to me, and to Dad. We haven't all been together, all us friends, since university. It's a special weekend. So how about you stop the poor little rich boy routine, huh?'

'Do I really have to share with Cassie?'

'You know you do. We don't have space for everyone otherwise.'

'But Cassie always wakes me up. She's on her phone all night, the light shines in my eyes.'

The list in my head was unravelling. I glanced at the clock – bugger, I had to leave in less than an hour. Why did I have to meet Vix today of all days? 'I'll tell her not to then. Is your room tidy for Auntie Karen?'

'Yeah.' He reached for the packet of Kettle Chips and I batted his hand away.

'You've just had lunch. Why don't you go and play, Benj?'

'Play what?'

I was sure at his age I'd been more self-sufficient than this. I had to speak to Mike about taking away his iPad. I added that to the mental list under *check loos, light candles*, and all the other things I had to do before they arrived. Why did I always run out of time? I offered a sop to my son. 'Listen. You know Bill, who's coming? He goes fishing all the time in Sweden. I bet he'll show you how, if you ask nicely.'

One blue eye cocked at me over the iPad screen. I had him.

'You'd like that, wouldn't you?' Mike had bought Benji a rod for Christmas but still not found time to take him to the small stream that ran past the side of the garden. I didn't think Mike actually knew how to fish, but Bill would. Even at university I remembered him catching a frightened grey tiddler off the back of a punt, using a prawn sandwich as bait. We threw it back, but I still remembered the thrill of it spasming on the wooden deck, Karen and Jodi and I screeching girlishly. Bill with the joint hanging from his mouth, always so cool but even him smiling a little, proud and surprised.

Benji snapped off the iPad and stood up from the kitchen table. 'I'll tidy my room then. I mean, tidy it better.'

I pulled him under my arm in a bear hug; he smelled of biscuits and shampoo. Not yet like a teenager, of feet and resentment, and that reminded me Jake would be here soon, that I had to think of things to talk to him about, a way in to the impenetrable teenager he'd become. Find out what he might like for his eighteenth birthday, fast approaching. At least I still had Benji for a few more years. 'You're a good boy.'

'Urgh, Mum.' But he hugged back. 'Where's Cassie?'

'Town.' I'd asked her to buy another candle and she still wasn't home. *Soup, bread, herbs for tagine, wine out to breathe . . .*

'Bet she's with Aaron.'

'Well, maybe they had homework . . .'

'They're not in the same *class*, Mum.' No, because Cassie's boyfriend was in the Oxbridge stream and she hadn't made it, and Mike and I were pretending it was totally fine, not an issue at all. A cloud of extra worries burst around my head like flies – how much time Cassie was spending with Aaron, what they got up to in that time, what if something had happened to her to make her late – and then the back door of the house, the one that led into the woods, slammed and she was here.

'Cassie?'

She sloped into the kitchen, and I noted how short her skirt was, how tight her vest top. 'What?'

She had a red mark on the side of her neck. Behind her in the hall, I saw someone – her boyfriend, Aaron. So tall already his head almost knocked into the antique chandelier I'd hung in the hallway. 'Hello, Aaron.'

'Hello, Mrs Morris.' He had lovely manners – of course he did. Just like his grades and his sporting ability and his clean, blonde good looks.

I worried for Cassie, with a boy like this. A boy who already knew he could have anything he wanted in life.

'How's school?'

'Oh, you know,' he said. 'Busy with exams. I'm going home to study now, in fact.'

'You wouldn't like to stay for dinner?' My offer was lukewarm and we both knew it.

'Oh, that's really kind, but Mum's expecting me. She's made fresh pasta.' And I was serving tagine, one of the easiest dishes there was. I found myself wondering, ridiculously, if it was too late to start again.

'Bye then, Cass.' He reached for her, and I wondered if he'd kiss her in front of me, but he just hugged her. Cassie held on tight, closing her eyes, clinging to him. She looked so frail next to his rugby-playing bulk. She'd lost weight again.

'Did you get the candle?' I asked, once Aaron had left through the door to the woods.

She plonked it on the counter, making the plates rattle.

'Careful. What is it?'

'Fig and orange. Smells gross.'

'Can you help me, please? I'm struggling here.' I pushed a lock of hair back with my forearm. It was boiling in the kitchen, with all four hob rings and the oven going. It was only June and already the summer was being talked of as record-breaking, a scorcher, hottest since records began. I'd looked forward to it – dinner in the garden, how Mediterranean – but now the heat seemed to press down on me like a lid, slowing my steps until I was hopelessly behind.

'Why can't Dad help?'

'He's in his office.'

'No he's not, he's in the garden reading the paper.'

'Well, can you ask him to check the table's clean, and wipe the chairs, oh and find some citronella, there'll be flies.'

'Ask him yourself, he's here.'

'Pick me some herbs!' I yelled after her, as she slunk out and Mike came in, holding the door open for her to pass.

'Smells good!' He seemed cheerful: a relief. He hadn't been keen on this weekend. It would be too much work, he said, and we didn't have space for everyone. A four-bedroom house plus a room over the garage, still not enough.

I took a moment to look at him, critically. If this was the anniversary of us starting university, that made it twenty-five years since I'd first seen Mike, across the cavern-like college bar. The easy stance he'd adopted, chatting, while everyone else squirmed and shouted in their awkward first-year way. Five nine, not tall, but enough for me. Some grey now in his dark hair. Today he was wearing a polo shirt and khaki shorts, a cotton jumper in a flaming scarlet colour, despite the rising heat in the garden. That was new, and looked expensive. Trying to impress, just like I was, in my own way.

'Karen texted me – apparently, you're not answering. They're getting a taxi from town.'

'Oh God, I'm not ready. Why so early?' I'd planned to pick them up later, on my way back.

He shrugged, reaching out to squeeze the sourdough in its paper bag. 'Guess she made good time. On the *Megabus*.'

I ignored his small jibe – it wasn't Karen's fault she couldn't afford the train fare. Although maybe if she'd done what everyone begged her to, from tutors to parents, and resat her Finals, she might have a degree and a better job than doing admin for the council. 'But I told her I had this meeting! Are the rooms ready?' I ran through it again in my head. Callum and Jodi in the spare room, Karen in Benji's, Bill in Mike's office over the garage, and Jake was insisting on camping for some weird reason of his own. Would it work, all of us piling in on each other?

Mike came up behind me as I stirred the stew, and squeezed my shoulders. 'You're so tense I could bounce ten pees off your back. Relax, will you. It's just our friends, not *Come Dine With Me*. Karen won't care if we're not immaculate.'

But I would. And Jodi was bound to notice, and say something that sounded innocuous, but which I would brood over for days after. 'Will they need lunch?'

'It's after two, I don't think they'll expect it. Cup of tea, bit of cake on the lawn, how about it? I'll hold the fort while you pop out.'

'But . . .'

'Ali.' Mike spun me around, hands on my shoulders, forcing eye contact. 'Look, there's no point in doing this if you don't enjoy it. Is there? So come on, love, take a chill pill, as Cassie would say.'

'She'd rather die than say something so naff.'

'Yes, because "naff" is such cutting-edge slang.'

I felt a small ease of the knot in my stomach as we drew apart, our hands moving to tidy and wipe and organise in a well-practised dance. He was right. They were our friends, they wouldn't expect perfection. It would all be fine.

Outside, I heard the sound of a car on gravel. She was here.

Chapter Two

'So what happened with—'

'My awful boss? Still awful. Last week he said we'll all have to reapply for our own jobs!'

'No way, that's outrageous. I'm sure that's illegal, isn't it, Mike? Mike?'

He shook his head, like a dog clearing itself of rain. 'What are you on now? I can't keep up. I'd need to record the conversation and play it back at normal speed.'

People had always said that about Karen and me, falling away from our chatter, puzzled at how we leapt from topic to topic like monkeys in trees, sometimes returning to a conversation we'd left pinned an hour ago, always seamless. I smiled at her over the table, thinking how young she looked in her tight jeans and vest top, identical to Cassie's. I was wearing a flowery Joules dress. Frumpy. Mum-like, even though it was Karen who'd been a mother first, at just twenty-five.

Karen rolled her eyes at Mike. 'We've got a lot to say to each other, that's all.' Now she lived in Birmingham and we were in Kent, I didn't see her as often as I'd like, and sometimes the need to talk to her built up inside me like a pressure hose, only to explode when we finally met. And I had to leave in – I checked my watch – five minutes. Bollocks.

'It's beautiful here, guys. You're so lucky.' Karen gazed round at the garden. What the estate agent called *mature and developed*, which had made Mike snicker, it was the main reason I'd lobbied so hard for this place. The back of the house, a late-Victorian red-brick, faced right into the woods, and the access lane from the front only went past three other houses. It was like being in the country, except the shops of Bishopsdean were only ten minutes away if you cut through the woods. Today, the garden was full of lavender and wild garlic and birds hidden in the trees, little statues poking out from nooks, their faces crumbled by rain. I averted my eyes from the pile of garden waste behind the shed – Andrej, our gardener, had cancelled on us the week before. Family emergency in Krakow. Never mind that. It was amazing that we had a gardener at all. We were lucky. We'd been here only six months and I still had odd moments of shivering pleasure, thinking – *I live here. This is mine.*

'Do you do all this, Mikey?' Karen asked, lifting a macaron to her hot-pink lips.

I laughed. 'You're kidding, right. Mike hasn't been near a lawn-mower since 1998. Andrej does it – totally dreamy Polish guy.'

'I would if I had time,' Mike said sadly. 'But when would I get that?'

'Still keeping you busy then?'

'You've no idea.' Mike's law firm had been bought out by Americans earlier in the year, and they expected him in the office late for New York calls and early for Japan. Most days he didn't get off his commuter train until nine.

Karen turned to me. 'Well, maybe Ali can keep you now she's doing so well. Saw you in *Good Housekeeping* this month! Very cool.'

'Oh, thanks.' A piece on sexting and checking your teenager's phone. I said I'd never look at Cassie's, because it would destroy the trust between us. There'd been a lot of comments online, some calling me deluded and a bad mother. I told myself any buzz was good.

'How did Cass feel about it, being in the magazine?'

I looked over to where Cassie and Jake swayed in the swing seat, side by side. Her long bare legs were hooked over the side. Jake had come dressed all in black. Black T-shirt, black jeans, black trainers.

Black curtains of hair over his face. It was hard to picture the sweet little boy he'd been, so anxious to please, always grabbing me round my legs when I looked after him while Karen was at work. But that was years ago, when we lived within streets of each other in London. Now, we were so far apart. When he'd arrived, I'd gone to hug him and he'd dodged me, and I scolded myself for how bad it felt. Jake was seventeen, with no dad, and clearly in the throes of teenage angst. He'd come out of it. 'Oh, she didn't mind. She knows it's an important issue.' The truth was, I'd been afraid to ask what she thought. These days, she was opaque to me – unreadable.

'We taped you off Channel 4 too. Well, with the box, you know. You really stood up to that little toerag.'

'Someone has to. It's disgusting, the way he talks. Rape jokes, in 2018!'

'Here she goes,' said Mike. 'Isn't there something to be said for free speech, especially in comedy? We don't live in Soviet Russia.'

'She's done really well,' said Karen gently. 'Don't be a dick about it, Mikey. Leave that devil's advocate shtick to Callum.'

'I know, I know. We're very proud of her.' He squeezed my leg under the table. 'She's turned that charity around as well. They were going to close the refuge before Ali joined the board.'

'Oh bugger, that reminds me. I have to go – sorry, Kar. I did say I had this meeting?' I was sure I had, so I didn't know why she'd arrived so early.

She flapped her hands at me. 'Go, go. We'll be fine here.'

'You're sure?' I stood up, but something held me at the chipped wooden table, the wrought-iron chairs we'd picked up in an antiques yard, the plate of pastel-coloured cakes and the floral-printed cups and teapot. It was moments like this I'd pictured when I imagined having a proper house, not the cramped terrace we'd been bulging out of for the past ten years. Crockery. Nice furniture. Friends to admire it all. And of course Karen, my best friend for twenty-five years. I knew that if I didn't go, I could sit and talk to her until it got dark, and the children went unfed, the work forgotten.

'I think we can manage.' Mike leaned forward and poured more tea for Karen out of the vintage china pot. It leaked, but it was such a pretty colour, yellow with blue flowers on it. For a moment, I considered cancelling, speaking to Vix on the phone instead, but this was a big deal. It was my job, albeit unpaid, and if I didn't do it, I'd just be a housewife who dabbled in journalism between dentist appointments and Sainsbury's trips.

'You know it's important, or I wouldn't . . . I'm sorry.'

She put her sunglasses – cheap off-brand ones that all the same made her look like a film star – down over her nose and flipped her long dark hair, the same length as when we were students, over her shoulder. 'Oh, we'll be fine. We were early anyway. Jakey just wanted to see Cass.'

I looked over at them again. Deep in conversation, the way Karen and I used to be, sitting in a coffee shop for four or five hours and never stopping. 'We should get them together more often.' But it was such a trek to Birmingham, and also, it was Birmingham. I invited Karen down all the time but she always pleaded work. I suspected she sometimes couldn't afford the fare. 'Does Jake have a girlfriend, anything like that?'

'Chance would be a fine thing. I'm hoping he's one of those boys that blossom at uni. Like you, Mikey.'

'Cheek! I was born blossoming.'

'Cassie has this boyfriend,' I said. 'Aaron. I'm not sure about him. His mother is the most God-awful snob.'

'Should get on with Jodi then,' Karen smiled, and I smiled too, feeling guilt mingle with relief as our feet once again found the common ground between us. She was still my best friend, even if we didn't see each other much, even if our lives had diverged. Even if I had this house now, which also gave me prickles of guilt now I saw it through her eyes, the lavishness of all this space, the Victorian brickwork and stained glass. Despite all that, time hadn't come between us. And I was proud of that, of keeping our friendship, of saving it from that odd cooling we'd had in the months after university. When the six of us had brushed against something dark, and come away intact.

I turned at the door and looked out. Karen and Mike, leaning across the table to each other, laughing about something, and in the swing seat, his daughter and her son, so wrapped up in each other they didn't even notice me leave. Hindsight is deadly. If I'd known then what was already happening, what would so soon engulf us, I might have taken a few more moments to stand there in the sun, and drink in all the things I was about to lose. But I didn't, and so I left.

Chapter Three

'Tell me one more time what happened.'

Despite the problem that had brought me to the police station on such a sunny day, I sort of liked myself in this role. Ali Morris, Chair of Bishopsdean Women's Refuge. A title, a purpose, after years of just being Mum, Mrs Morris, Mike's wife.

Vix, the charity's Director, had met me at the station, in a room they let us use at moments such as this, which happened more often than you'd like to think. She was a slight woman of no more than thirty, with cropped black hair and dark-rimmed glasses. The kind of person you'd expect to find living in Berlin or somewhere, not Bishopsdean. I'd never asked what her story was, because in this kind of organisation they're rarely easy to tell, or hear. We'd gone over and over the incident, figuring out what to do in response.

'He came to the refuge about three last night. Julie swears she didn't tell him where it was but I'm not sure I believe her. He broke the kitchen window and got in, found Julie in her room with the kids, got her by the throat against the wall.'

'The kids saw?'

Vix just nodded. 'One of the other women pressed the alarm and the police came. He had a knife. He – I think he was planning to use it.'

Whatever way we spun it, it was bad. 'You've got a press statement drafted?'

She nodded again, sliding over a piece of paper. Vix used to work in PR, so she was good at this type of thing. I thought, sometimes, privately, she wasn't so good at the empathy side of it all. She had a tendency to stick to rules, never allowing for the grey areas. The fact that the women usually loved the men they were fleeing from. I understood that, so I tried to make up for her.

The statement hit all the right notes. Always risky running a women's refuge, isolated incident, police response praised, restraining order filed. 'So what do you think?'

'I think it's a one-off. The police say they'll request a tag for him this time.'

So it was decided: we wouldn't be moving the refuge. It was a big decision, and costly as hell, but I felt uneasy all the same. If Paul Dean had found it, maybe other men would too. The other men the women there were hiding from. It was my call, ultimately, my responsibility. I nodded. 'Let's table a discussion for the next board meeting. Can I see Julie?'

'Don't you have that big reunion thing this weekend?' We were standing up, Vix straightening her grey shift dress. I felt bloated and mumsy in my florals. Unprofessional. I should have changed.

'Just two minutes? Please.'

Julie was in another room, a nicer one with a sofa and a toy-box. Her two kids played on the floor with the resignation of children who have learned to wait around in official spaces. The older one was pretending to read a picture book to the baby. 'Julie. I'm Ali, the Chair of the charity. I'm so sorry for what happened.' I saw Vix flash me a look – perhaps I shouldn't have said that, perhaps that suggested we'd done something wrong.

Julie had been crying, her make-up clumped round her eyes. 'I can't go back there. It's not safe.'

'I know. We'll see about getting you to a refuge in another town.'

'I swear to God I never told him. Maybe he asked Kaylee or some-thing, worked it out.'

I could see from Vix's carefully blank look that she highly doubted a three-year-old would let an address slip, but I just nodded. 'We'll get this sorted, Julie. God, you poor thing.' On impulse, and feeling Vix's disapproval, I gave Julie a hug, feeling the bones of her spine under her hoody, smelling her – stale fags and fear. She flinched, and I saw the ring of bruises on her throat, a necklace of hurt. There were memories surfacing in my head – wearing a polo neck on the hottest day of sum-mer, rubbing panstick on to tender skin – but I pushed them away.

'You shoot off, Ali,' said Vix, following me to the door. 'I'm sure you have cooking to finish.' A little pointed, or did I imagine it? I was over-sensitive about having been out of work for so long, I knew. Sometimes I saw slights that weren't there.

So I went, back to my tagine and candles, leaving Julie and her kids to cope as best they could with the fact that their father, her hus-band, had tried to hurt her. In the car, heading back through town in the sunshine, tense again as I worried about the weekend – we hadn't been together, the six of us, for over twenty years – I caught myself and remembered to feel grateful. This wasn't my life any more – spending a hot Saturday in the stale air of a police station, dependent on profes-sional kindness. I'd worked hard so it wouldn't be, and if I could help women like Julie get away from it too, it eased some of my feelings of guilt. As I drove back home, I was trying to be thankful for my life. It was mine, whether I deserved it or not.

Chapter Four

When I reached the house, I could see there was already a people-carrier in the drive behind Mike's BMW. Callum and Jodi were just arriving, unpacking cases and raffia bags with flowers and Tupperware poking out of them. I parked my Kia and dashed out. 'Sorry! Sorry, work emergency. I'm here now.'

Callum was also wearing shorts and a polo shirt, though they were Ralph Lauren. 'Work?' He stretched out his arms and I hugged him, feeling his solidity and strength. 'You've gone and got yourself a Saturday job, Al? What does Mike think about that? Mike who appears to be wearing some kind of orange jersey? Gone colour blind, mate?'

I saw Mike was annoyed. 'It's red, you divvy. Speaking of colour blind.'

I steered the conversation back. 'It's not work as such. You know I'm on the board of that charity.' Although I was working too, as a journalist, so I didn't know why I was downplaying it. And what business was it of Mike's?

Jodi nudged him. She was so enormous under her maternity smock (some kind of homespun broderie anglaise thing I thought was from The White Company, in shocking contrast to the tailored suits she normally wore) I could hardly reach her, so we air-kissed. She looked tired and pale, her limp fair hair scraped back. 'You do know, Cal. We watched her on the news, remember?'

'Of course. You ate that kid for breakfast.'

'That "kid" is almost thirty, and a rape apologist,' I retorted. Mike caught my eye. This was just Callum's way. His 'top bantz' hadn't changed since our university days, and working in corporate law seemed to make him worse. I reminded myself of his many kindnesses, the countless times he'd bought me drinks at college, waving away payment, knowing I was usually short. The thoughtful presents on every one of the kids' birthdays, that I had at first mistakenly thought were Jodi's work. 'Come in, come in. We're going to be a bit squashed up, I'm afraid.'

I felt a small pang at the way Jodi was standing, her hand on the curve of her back. So many years since that had been me. She said, 'Oh, it'll be fine. I'm so tired at the minute I drop right off. Finally I get what you and Karen were always on about! Where is she?'

'Getting changed,' Mike said, taking one of the bags. 'What have you brought us, Jod?'

'Just a few bits. You know how it is, nesting like crazy, getting ready for this bub.' The 'bub' set my teeth on edge, as did the fact she'd turned up with her own food – did she not trust me to cook? – but I reminded myself it had taken them fifteen long years and three ruinous IVF cycles, just to get to this point.

'You look great,' I told her. 'Glowing and all those clichés.'

'By the size of her, she must be having triplets,' said Callum, but he slid his arm around her, protective. 'Nice place you've got here, Mikeyboy. What's it worth – half a mill?'

We moved into the kitchen, cool and dark after the dazzling weight of the sun. 'Place up the lane went for 800k last year,' said Mike, and I saw the pleasure it gave him, to be able to speak those words so casually. He'd worked hard for this life too – all those late nights, coming in exhausted, not seeing the kids from one end of the week to the other.

'Jesus,' said Callum. 'And here we are stuck in a semi in Pimlico. Ah, Cassie my dear, hello.' Cassie had sloped in from the living room, and I wished fleetingly I'd thought to speak to her about what she was wearing. 'Looking more like your mum every year. Thank God you didn't inherit your old dad's looks, eh?'

'Hi Callum,' she said nonchalantly. She'd dropped the 'uncle', I noticed. 'Hi Jodi. Wow! When are you due?'

'A month, or so they say. I don't think I can get any bigger.' Jodi gave a small laugh.

Mike already had the fridge open. 'Beer, Cal? Jodi – I guess no wine for you?'

'Just water, please,' she said, in an exhausted way.

'Can I have some wine?' said Cassie, in a languid manner that suggested she drank all the time. For all I knew, she did.

Mike met my eyes for a moment. He shrugged; always more easygoing than me. I was too tired to have the discussion. 'One glass.'

Mike poured one out for her. 'Drink it slowly, Cass. If you like that, and you're sensible, maybe one day I'll let you taste the really special stuff I have hidden far away from your Uncle Callum's greedy grasp.' She smiled at him, her shoulders relaxing into his arm. If I'd said that about being sensible, she'd have flounced out of the room.

'Quite right too,' said Callum. 'Time she learned to appreciate a good vintage. Now, Jodi here, she still prefers a Chardonnay spritzer. She's a lost cause. What have you there?' He examined the bottle of Muscadet I'd bought, knowing Callum preferred French whites. 'Supposed to be a good little vineyard, that one.' I knew it was his way of saying sorry for needling me about the TV interview.

'Where's Jake?' I asked Cassie.

'Pitching his tent.' Oh God, his tent. Another spurt of anxiety – was this going to work, or would it all fall apart?

Jodi seemed to slump. 'Can we take our bags up?' A touch pointed, I thought. But there I went again, so tense I was seeing things that weren't there. These were our friends. All of us together for the first time in years. Well, once Bill got here. *Bill*. My stomach tripped itself up in an odd nervy way, some very old echo in my blood.

'Let's do that now.' I bent to pick up their wheelie-case, feeling something twinge in my back, and the passage of time suddenly left me dizzy. We'd been eighteen when we met, and now we were forty-three. Twenty-five years gone, lost like something dropping out of my pocket.

'No sign of Bill yet?' asked Jodi, lumbering up the stairs behind me.

I'd nipped ahead to make sure Benji had actually tidied up the apple cores and Minecraft toys he usually left strewn behind him. I saw, to my surprise, that the door of his room was open, and no sign of Karen or her things. Had Mike forgotten she was going in there? 'Not yet. He's biking down, you know.'

Callum came up behind us with the rest of the bags, puffing with the effort. 'Classic Bill. And is it true the porn actress has given him the boot? The thigh-high boot?'

'She's not a porn actress, Callum, for God's sake! She's an artist. And yes, I think Bill and Astrid are no more.'

'What a shame,' said Jodi, looking round the room. 'I really liked her when they came for our wedding. And we stayed with them out there once.'

Bill hadn't come to my wedding. Too expensive to travel from Sweden, he said. It still niggled at me that he'd made it for Callum and Jodi's two years later. Even though I understood why.

And then, just as I was thinking of him, a roar began on the edge of my hearing – a thrumming like a deep heartbeat – and Mike, shouting up from downstairs, yelled, 'That'll be Bill now.' I looked out the window and saw the motorbike draw up the drive, the figure in leathers perched on top, and I recognised the set of his shoulders, the long lines of his back, and something inside me relaxed. Bill was here. We were all here, together, and the party could start.

Chapter Five

As the night slid forwards, and the bottles of wine were replaced on the table in rapid succession, I relaxed more and more. I'd served up the tagine, and although Jodi had said, 'I do love Moroccan, so easy', everyone seemed to enjoy it. Benji had thirds. He was being sweet, answering Jodi's cutesy questions about school, and Cassie had even put her phone down and was chatting to Karen. Only Jake sat sullen, toying with his food and announcing a hitherto unmentioned vegetarianism. Poor Jake, his acne was awful. We'd taken Cassie to a private dermatologist at the first sign of hers, and here she was, smooth-skinned and perfect. Rich-girl skin. I imagined what my mother would say about that, and almost smiled. But I wasn't thinking about Mum.

'You see what I have to contend with,' sighed Karen, watching Jake pick at his meal. 'The teachers say he could be Oxbridge material, but he won't even apply.'

'Oh please. It's sooo bourgeois,' said Jake, sneering, and I tried not to smile, remembering how right-on we'd thought ourselves at that age. 'It's, like, a bastion of unearned privilege. No thanks.'

Karen leaned towards Bill, who was facing partly away from the circle as always, rolling what I hoped was just a cigarette. 'Maybe you could talk to him, Bill. You know, float the idea that he doesn't have to be an evil lawyer or a banker just because he goes to a good university.'

'You didn't even pass,' said Jake, snapping at his mother, and we all fell silent. The subject of Karen's failed degree – such a shock, when she was the smartest of us all, except for maybe Bill – was still contentious.

'What is it you do out there anyway, Bilbo?' Callum changed the subject. 'Cure herring, that sort of thing?'

Bill carried on rolling, placid, careful. He'd taken off his leathers and was in jeans and a jumper of some robust grey wool, despite the heat. He'd hardly changed at all in twenty years. Lanky, laconic, his brown hair a bit too long, though now it was streaked with grey. I'd made sure to sit on the other side of the table from him, because some part of my brain was thoroughly thrown by his presence, after all these years. Remembering that night. His hand on my face, his breath on my neck. But no, I wasn't thinking about that either. 'Bit of this, bit of that. Where we lived was sort of self-sufficient. I'd barter my labour for food, wood-chopping, driving, that sort of thing.'

'Sounds like a commune.'

'I guess it was a bit.'

'But tell me this. You and Miss Sweden are kaput, yes?'

Jodi frowned at Callum. *Be tactful.* But Bill never rose to Callum's banter, never had. In a strange way, they got on well. 'Sadly, yes, we broke up a few months ago.'

'How come, Bill?' said Karen. 'If you don't mind me asking.'

Bill smiled at her, the warm lopsided crease I remembered so well. There were always a few moments before he answered any question. I liked that. I liked the feeling he was thinking about what you'd said, considering it. 'I don't mind. She wanted us to have a child. Adopted, probably, though she thought it was worth giving IVF a whirl first.'

'Hardly a whirl,' said Jodi, rubbing her own belly. 'Bloody expensive. Heartbreaking, too.'

'I know. I told her that. Plus, as you know, she's older than us. But anyway it didn't matter because I don't want kids, adopted or IVF or anything.'

'Haven't changed your mind then?' said Callum, wiping his plate with sourdough. Across the table, I saw Cassie lift up her phone, bored by the conversation. Jake picked the vegetables from the tagine bowl.

'Nope.'

I remembered Bill at university, expounding on Malthusian population theory and global warming and the world our children were going to be born into. Of course, a lot of students say these things then change their minds, but I think I knew even then that Bill meant it. It was one of the reasons things had happened the way they did.

'So what will you do?' Karen asked. She'd changed into a low-cut black dress while I was out, so as she leaned forward I could see her cleavage, high and firm for a woman of forty-three. Of course, she hadn't breastfed Jake. 'Will you stay in Sweden? Can I have a cig, by the way?'

Bill shrugged, passed over the rollie he'd been making, sparking it for her. I turned away; I didn't like smoking in front of the kids. I was sure he had stronger stuff in his tin too, for once they'd gone to bed. 'I don't know. I thought I might stick around here. Go back up north, see the family and that. Bike about.'

Mike shook his head. 'Mate, I wish I had the time to do that. The bank have me by the short and curlies. I miss the kids all the time – and Ali, of course. It's tough.' He'd taken off the jumper Callum had mocked, but was still in his shorts and polo shirt – he'd tried to slope off and shower when I got back from the police station, at the worst possible time just when everyone was arriving, but I'd hissed that there was no need. And he'd put Bill and Karen in the wrong rooms. I reminded myself it didn't matter, that having a full house all weekend was not his idea of fun. He was doing this for me, after all.

Callum was saying, 'Tell me about it. I looked into shared leave for when this little one comes' – patting Jodi's belly – 'and I was summarily asked if Jodi had my balls in her handbag.' I tutted, but Benji had his iPad out and hadn't heard, I hoped. I'd have to send him to bed soon. Being together made the men regress, bantering and bawdy like schoolboys.

'That's terrible!' I said. 'And illegal.'

'Yes, well, they're not too sympathetic to this whole nappy-changing new-man thing. Looks like Jodi'll be doing the lot.'

'You're giving up work?' Karen raised her eyebrows. Jodi was a criminal lawyer, working with the very rich and very guilty. Her job had always defined her as much as her designer handbags and regular manicures.

'For a while,' she said, her hair falling over her face. 'It just makes sense. We don't want our baby raised by nannies. Not when we've fought so hard for this.'

'But . . .' Karen subsided. She flashed me a look – we'd discuss this later.

'It's bloody unfair,' Callum continued. 'It's like we're just sperm machines. Walking turkey basters.' I saw Benji's ears prick up at the word *sperm*.

'Don't tell me you're joining Fathers for Justice.' Karen rolled her eyes.

'I think parental leave is a real issue,' I said. 'I wrote a piece just the other day and . . .'

Mike groaned. 'Please, babe. It's too hot for feminism right now.'

Karen tutted. Jodi said, soothingly, 'Oh yes, tell us about the new career, Ali. It all came from the TV interview?'

'Well, not really new of course.' I'd been a journalist before having Cassie, for five years. 'I wanted to do something with my time now the kids are older, and there was a vacancy on the trustee board of the Women's Refuge here. So I joined, and then the chance came up to debate domestic violence on Channel 4, you know with that awful comedian, and no one else was free so I did it.'

'And she wouldn't put on lipstick for it, even though I like, begged her to,' said Cassie, earning a small laugh.

'Domestic violence, Al? Mikey here been knocking you around?' Callum batted at his friend. I remembered now how drink made him bear-like, swatting at you with clumsy affectionate hands. 'If he has, just say the word and I'll kick his arse for you.'

I saw that, across the table, Karen was trying to meet my eye, but I didn't want to remind Callum why I knew so much about that topic, especially not with the kids here, so I pasted on a smile. 'Ha, no. It seemed to go well anyway. Since then I've been getting back into features, opinion pieces mostly, lots of feminist stuff.' Cassie gave a quiet groan. She thought my new-found career was unutterably embarrassing.

'You want to watch it, Mikey, or she'll be doing a Lorena Bobbit on you,' said Callum. He caught Jodi's look. 'Only joking, Al. You've done brilliantly. Should get you in to give a talk to the office. We're swamped in sexual harassment cases, it's awful really.'

'What percentage of them are you?' I asked, to show I wasn't a humourless feminist, earning a laugh from Mike, and another – rare and precious – from Bill. I felt myself relax a little more. We were having a good time. It was all fine. 'Hey, do you guys realise it's coming up for twenty-five years since we all met? Scary or what? A quarter century.'

Jodi put a hand on Callum's arm. 'I almost forgot. Show them the picture I found clearing out. I was setting up the nursery and there was this whole shoebox full.'

'Oh yes.' Callum fished out the iPad he'd stowed under his seat. 'Look at this.'

He passed round the little tablet and I was looking at our faces, but from twenty-five years ago. It was the night we'd all met, in the bar of our college at Oxford. Mike and Callum had already made friends in that easy way boys do, whether they're four or forty. Both of them from private schools, living in the same corridor by virtue of their surnames *Morris* and *Mackintosh*. In the picture they were wearing Nikes and black jeans, Callum in a white polo shirt and Mike, trying to be a little cooler, in a Rolling Stones one. Callum still had the ruddy glow from his 'gap summer' in Greece.

'Bit more hair back then, Cal,' observed Karen, a tad bitchily. She passed it over to me to hold, returning to the cigarette she'd left burning on the edge of my expensive garden table. I wondered when she'd started smoking again.

Karen and I were in the photo too, our arms around each other's necks, drunken smiles on our fresh, badly made-up faces. We'd met earlier that day, standing in line in Boswell's department store with toasters in our arms, me reeling with relief that Mum and Dad had left early to beat the traffic and I could unpack my room alone. 1993. A lifetime ago.

'Who's that?' said Mike, peering over my shoulder and tapping the iPad – 'Fingers,' Callum grumbled. 'Oh.'

There was silence as we realised who else was in the shot, in the background, her white-blonde hair rippling down her back, laughing at someone out of frame. Martha Rasby. *Martha*. Her name seemed to sit in my mouth like a stone. All these years later and I still couldn't say it without wincing.

'She was so beautiful, wasn't she,' said Jodi. 'Such a shame.' No one else said anything.

'Time for bed, Benj,' I said, as his head dropped forward. It was dark in the garden now, and Mike had lit citronella candles using Bill's lighter, and the pool of light surrounded us, the shadows and rustles of the garden closing in. Just like that other night, so many years ago.

'Mu-um.' Despite his protests, he stood up willingly enough.

'I'll see him to bed and then I'll bring out coffee, if anyone wants.' I pushed myself to my feet, reluctantly, feeling the wine pull me down, like diving weights on my ankles.

Jodi shook her head. Her face was white in the dark. 'I might go up to bed too, if no one minds. This little one is kicking me like a football.'

'Want me to come, Jodes?'

I thought Callum said it too quickly. As if he knew the reply would be, as it was, 'Oh no, you stay. I'll be asleep in minutes anyway.'

'No coffee for me,' said Karen, whose legs were propped on Bill's chair, her bare feet brushing his thighs. 'I'm quite enjoying this drunken haze. Reminds me of uni.'

Mike agreed. 'Leave it, Al. Benji can put himself to bed, he's ten now.'

'I need to check he does his teeth.' Really, I wanted to make a start on clearing up. The mountain of dishes was daunting and I already knew I'd be hungover the next day.

Cassie stood too. 'I'm going up to bed too, Mum. Might watch a bit of Netflix.'

'What about you, Jakey?' I asked, trying to be kind. I knew how it was to be spotty and shy, to always feel left out.

'I'm going to my tent.'

Karen almost tutted. 'Love, you won't get any sleep. We're going to be here for hours yet.' Were we? It was nearly eleven.

'Why don't you chill in Mike's office for a bit?' I offered, knowing Cassie would roll her eyes at me saying *chill*. 'Until your mum needs the bed, anyway. If you don't mind, Karen?'

'Oh,' Karen said, her face lit in the cigarette glow. 'Well, of course not. Good idea, Ali.'

I followed Cassie in to the light of the kitchen, noticing Mike had left his jumper, his £200 Hugo Boss jumper, lying in a heap on the decking. I started to bend to pick it up, then stopped. It didn't matter if jumpers were on the ground or if bedtime shifted a bit. I had to start relaxing, letting more things slide. I couldn't work and keep the house perfect and the kids happy. I just couldn't.

Benji was climbing the stairs obediently and Cassie went to follow him. 'You OK, darling?' I called after her. I wondered why she didn't want to stay up with Jake.

Cassie's eyes skipped over mine. Her phone was grasped in her hand. 'Fine. Just didn't want to listen to more about the glory days of Oxford.' And she would likely not get to go now she hadn't made the stream. Perhaps she'd taken that harder than I realised.

'I know. You've been very tolerant, thank you. Goodnight, darling.'

She went up the stairs, saying nothing in response. Wearily I started stacking the dishes, rinsing the pots. Mike hated me putting them in the dishwasher, but then I didn't see him helping. I ran a cloth over the worktops and put away some of the half-empty bottles of wine that sat about – why didn't people finish one before opening another? – then took one of white and poured a splash into a clean glass. I loved these glasses. I'd found them in an antique shop – and I loved saying that as well, when people asked where they were from, felt it made me sound like someone with their life together – and adored the green glass stems and the way the old glass was full of small bubbles, turning everything to champagne. I sipped it slowly – too warm – looking out the window to where the four of them sat, wrapped in the candle glow, Karen and the guys, the edges of us dissolving in booze and darkness and nostalgia. Dangerous.

'Need a hand?' I jumped a little – Bill walked so softly I hadn't heard him come in.

'Oh! No, it's OK. I'll do the rest tomorrow.'

'Coming back out?' He ambled to the counter, lifted a bottle of red. 'OK if I . . . ?'

'Sure. You know, I might slip off to bed. It's boring, but I'm beat. Difficult work thing today. Anyway, it's starting to get cold.' There were one too many excuses in there, I knew.

Bill shifted, standing suddenly closer, so I could almost feel the hairs on my arm rise, his breath on my skin. 'We could stay in here. Have a drink in the living room? It's been ages since we talked.'

'I know.' I opened my mouth and shut it again. If I started to say some of the things I wanted to say to Bill, I might never stop.

'Ali, I . . .' I waited for him to finish the sentence, but he didn't, and the silence started to feel powerful, like another person in the room. He put out his free hand, and touched my upper arm, as if holding me back to tell me something, but I hadn't turned away, and he still didn't say anything.

I met his dark eyes, just for a second. *Bill.* Then I darted forward, wiping at some drops of red wine on the side. 'I – would you tell the others goodnight? If I come out I'll be another hour. And someone has to cook breakfast!' I dropped the cloth and went upstairs, telling myself it was the sensible choice. Go to bed, before anything went wrong.

I didn't know it, but it was already too late for that.

Afterwards, I could never remember what had woken me. A noise of some kind, or a feeling, deep down in my bones, that something had happened. Already I was dry-mouthed and hungover. The bedside clock, the one Mike had bought to wake him up with a fake sunrise, showed 3.30 a.m. I made him turn the display off when he set the alarm function, so that meant he hadn't come to bed yet. His pyjamas were still neatly folded under his pillow. I got out of bed, the old floorboards I was so proud of creaking under my bare feet, and went to fetch a glass of water.

The door to Benji's room was shut, and how strange it was to think that Bill was sleeping in there, just a wall away. Bill, not seen for so many years. Again, the twinge of annoyance that Mike had messed with my room plan, not listening as usual. I hoped Karen wouldn't be offended at being stuck over the garage. Cassie's door was ajar, and I could see in the slice of dark Benji's pale face on the camp bed pillow, fast asleep. The spare room door was open, the bed empty. No Jodi, no Callum.

The light was on in the kitchen, and the living room, and the hall. Either people were still up or they had no regard for our electricity bill. Jodi was in the kitchen in her pyjamas, holding the cafetière. I saw she'd emptied it straight into the sink, and the grounds sat in little brown clumps, like a swarm of ants. Didn't she know it would clog? 'Hope you don't mind? Callum's a bit worse for wear.'

'Where is he?'

She lifted the kettle, and I noticed how careful her gestures were, as if she was carrying a clutch of fresh eggs in her hands. 'Passed out on your sofa, I'm afraid. I found him there when I came down for water.'

I should have left her a carafe and glass. I usually did. I'd forgotten, what with Julie and everything. 'Maybe we should let him sleep, if he's out?'

I don't know what she would have replied, because that was the moment I heard the kitchen door – the groan and creak of it – and the sound of Karen's staggering footsteps. She had bare feet, and there was grass in her hair and pressed into her face, leaving small indentations in her skin. Her eyes were wide and a smear of blood was red across her cheek. And then, of course, she said what she said, and nothing was ever the same again. 'He raped me. He *raped* me.'

And Jodi, asking what I did not dare: 'Who, Karen? What do you mean?'

And Karen saying, 'Mike. It was Mike,' before she fell to her knees, utterly broken.

Bill

He was glad he'd come, on the whole. He hadn't been at all sure when biking down, marinating in sweat under his leathers. He hated this kind of town, with its boutique shops for the left-at-home wives, its unspoken snobberies. Even the countryside looked different. More compact somehow, rounded and soft and green. In Sweden, everything looked like it had been smashed into chunks, jagged, proud. He'd forgotten how squashed-up southern England was. It was strange too to speak English in the petrol station, hear the squawking Kent accent and even feel the familiar words in his mouth.

This wasn't somewhere he'd expected Ali to live. She'd always talked about Paris, New York, Berlin – not mid-Kent, with its commuter towns and overly pretty villages where a house would set you back over half a million. It was the kind of place Mike was always going to end up, and Ali had been dragged with him, pulled along like the tail of a comet. That was . . . disappointing. But not surprising. He told himself it was never going to end any other way.

Apart from all that though, the evening had been good. Callum's blokey banter was sometimes hard to adjust to, and where he led Mike followed, but it was good to see them all again and remember he'd had a life before Sweden, before Astrid. It was as if he was groping his way along, trying to find the Bill who'd turned up at Oxford aged eighteen, with two pairs of jeans, one pair of trainers, a tin of rolling tobacco and not much else. Bill, the name he'd chosen for himself, shelving the *Bilal* he'd grown up with on the coach journey down. He'd struggled to explain to his mother that he needed a new name for Oxford. That no one meant to be racist, not exactly; it was more that they'd grown up only seeing non-white faces cleaning their houses or serving in corner shops. Now his mother was dead, no one ever called him by his real name.

He was glad he'd come, yes, but all the same he'd felt the need for some time out after dinner. Smoking was very useful for that, an excuse to wander away when a conversation got too much. After he'd gone to see if Ali needed help – he was surprised at how anxious she'd been to have everything in order, a plate at each place and a bowl to sit on top of it, a tumbler and wine glass and napkin and cutlery; Ali who used to eat pasta and pesto out of a saucepan on the floor of the communal hall-way in college – he ambled down the garden. Part of him was kicking himself for the awkward moment in the kitchen. Stupid, to think they could go back to their old friendship, after so long. When he'd touched her arm, he'd seen the alarm in her eyes, and wanted to explain he hadn't meant – but he didn't know what he had or hadn't meant.

Outside on the decking, the night air was cool. The candles Mike had lit were out, and he and Callum sat in darkness, only the sounds of their voices showing anyone was there. Bill was pleased, though he couldn't have said why, that he liked Ali's house. It was a little shabby round the edges, the garden overgrown and full of flowers, foxgloves, night-scented stock, hyacinth, but in a way that seemed organic and not planned. He liked the way the trees formed an arch over the garden, and the cries of birds drifted down. Earlier, when showing them round it, all Ali could do was apologise for the pile of garden waste behind the shed, and it made him sad to think she couldn't enjoy this small paradise she lived in.

He wondered what Astrid was doing. Neither of them were on Facebook, which Astrid hated, but he could see the attraction of it now. Just to know where she was, who she was with. Have some small idea how she was spending her time.

Bill sighed. For years he'd been slightly baffled by the romantic dramas of his friends, while he and Astrid had moved along like swans swimming over a pond, cool and respectful. Now he felt the draw of all kinds of unSwedish behaviour. Hacking into her emails. Begging her to take him back. He knew it was over, they both did, but it was surprisingly hard to let go.

He remembered he'd left his phone in the saddlebag of the bike and he thought maybe he'd text her, or see if she'd texted him, or something. Even holding the piece of plastic in his hand would be some pathetic link to her. He slipped down the side of the garden, leaves brushing his face, past Jake's empty tent – the boy was so awkward and unhappy, Bill wished he knew him well enough to try and offer some words of wisdom – and ducked into the garage, which was bigger than his and Astrid's lakeside home in Sweden. Actually, it was just hers; she'd had it when Bill had met her, on a post-university bike ride through Scandinavia, three years older than him and a hundred per cent cooler.

The garage smelled of oil and woodchip from the stack of logs all along one wall. Karen, Bill knew, was staying in the office on the floor above; he could hear the sound of beeps drifting down. Jake must be playing a game of some kind. A two-storey garage: Ali and Mike had really bought into the post-Oxford cult of possessions. Ali had been funny about the room situation earlier, asking Mike why he'd put Karen there. 'I was saving it for Bill.'

'Bill can have Benji's room.'

'I know, but . . .' She'd seen him listening and smiled, in a fake shiny way that made his heart hurt. The old Ali had never smiled like that. He gathered she thought it more appropriate for him, a single man now, to sleep out here, rather than Karen on her own. Old-fashioned. Was that who Ali was now – or maybe who she'd always been? He could hardly claim to know her after all this time.

He found his phone: no messages. A feeling of desolation came over him, as if Astrid was moving further and further away with every hour that passed.

'So this is where you sneaked off to.' Karen was in the garage doorway, eyes glittering. She was very drunk, he thought.

'Not sneaking. Going to bed?'

'No way. Need a cardy. S'colder now.' But she didn't go upstairs. 'So. You're single now.'

'Guess so.'

'Do you miss her?' Karen was doing something odd with her feet, which were bare and dirty, balancing one off the opposite leg like a yoga pose she was too drunk to hold. He remembered how they'd been friends so many years ago, both into indie music in a college full of upper-class kids who only talked about rowing and drinking. He had no idea what her life was like now. A son of almost eighteen, the same age they'd been when they met.

'Astrid? Yeah, I miss her. We were together twenty years.'

'None of us thought it would last. We thought you'd be back from the frozen north in months. But it's taken all this time.' She sounded plaintive. 'We missed you, Billy Boy.'

'I missed you too.' He kept his voice light, in the hope of ending this conversation.

'Did you miss *me* specifically?'

'Of course. Shame it's too pricey to come back a lot.'

'Do you remember first year?' she said suddenly. 'Remember when we first met?'

'Er, I think so. That indie-soc meeting, yeah?'

'I couldn't believe it when you came in. I thought I'd already seen all the boys in our year and there you were.'

'Well, yes, I didn't really like the whole college bar scene.'

'Do you know what I thought?' Karen was leaning against the wall now, one leg up. Her dress was very low-cut. Bill suddenly realised what was happening.

'We should go back,' he began guiltily.

'I thought . . .' Karen's voice swooped up. 'I thought you were the hottest guy in our year. By miles.'

'That's very sweet of you. Long time ago, of course. I have a lot less hair now.'

'No, no.'

'Listen, Kar—' The moment stilled between them. She moved closer; her long hair brushed his face. Ali wore hers shorter now, a sensible Mum-cut. 'I might go to bed, actually.'

'Don't go to bed! Boring!'

'We don't drink much in Sweden. I'm out of the habit.'

'Oh. You'll leave me with boring old Callum and Mike, talking about boring work?'

Bill could have said he knew she didn't find Mike boring. But he wanted to be kind. Karen had been on her own for a long time, decades, and he'd only been alone for two months and it hurt like a knife in his ribs. 'Come on. I'll walk out with you.'

He extended his arm, meaning to shepherd her away, but she nuzzled into it. He could smell the booze on her breath, and the strength of her perfume. She must have doused herself in it. 'Oh Bill. You're always so nice. I wish you'd liked me like you liked Ali.'

'Don't be silly, I like you both equally.' His voice was neutral. Karen might have been drunk enough to share all her secrets, but he wasn't. Not yet, anyway. Instead, he went up to his bed in Benji's room, and stared at the glowing stars stuck to the ceiling, and thought of Astrid, and also of Ali in the next room, just metres away, and some time later he woke up to all hell breaking loose.

Chapter Six

I ran. When she said *Mike, it was Mike,* I ran straight out the door and through the grass in my short summer pyjamas and bare feet. I just had to find him, talk to him, and this would all be sorted out. What Karen said was insane. It couldn't. He wouldn't. I just had to find him. Afterwards, I'd have stinging welts all over my feet from the tiny sharp plants that lived in the lawn. I couldn't see Mike at first, it was so dark, the light from the kitchen spilling out but failing against the blackness of the countryside. People were starting to emerge – Jake must have still been in the room over the garage, and he was coming out now, hair sticking up like a grouchy badger, to see why I was shouting. I saw Cassie from the corner of my eye, near the side of the house. She was in her skimpy pyjamas with flip-flops and a long cardigan. I didn't understand why I was seeing that but I hadn't time to think because I had to find Mike. There was Bill, in a T-shirt and pyjama bottoms, coming down the stairs into the kitchen, and Jodi was standing on the decking in her pyjamas, still with the cafetière in one hand. Where was Mike? This was crazy. This was a nightmare.

I found him on the swing seat, the one where Cassie and Jake had sat earlier. He was out cold, his hair sticking up, a sloppy drunk expression on his sleeping face. I remember thinking it looked swollen, as if he was allergic to something. 'Mike.' It was all I could do not to shake him.

He came awake slowly, his face screwed up as if he was in pain. 'Oh God. Did I fall asleep?'

'What the hell's going on?'

He wiped his hands over his face. 'Christ, Ali, don't shout. My head.'

'Mike! Karen's saying that you . . . Someone's attacked Karen!'

And haven't I asked myself a hundred times since if I saw anything on his face? And I did. I know I did. A flicker of guilt. 'What?'

'She . . . she . . .'

'You bastard!' Jake was coming at him, across the lawn, and Bill was there, grabbing him by the elbows, murmuring something. 'What did you do to her? What did you do?' Jake kept saying it over and over.

Mike was gaping at us all – Jodi, Bill, me, Jake, Cassie lurking near the house still, pale and frozen. I could hear Karen in the kitchen, the high keening sound of her crying.

Bill said, 'I've called the police.' He was so calm.

I stared at him. I felt for a moment like he'd done it to hurt me, somehow. How could we have the police here? We could sort this out, surely. 'Why?' was what I said. 'No, Bill, this is just – this is ridiculous! It can't be!'

'I'm sorry, but she . . . she begged me to.' He sounded awkward. I saw the way he wasn't looking at Mike. I felt Bill's arm round my shoulders. 'Come on, Ali. We have to let the police sort this out. We just have to keep everyone where they are until the police come.'

◆   ◆   ◆

The police were so quick, I'd hardly had time to get my head around what was happening. I paced on the decking, in and out of the kitchen door, bewildered and shaking. It couldn't be true. She'd made a mistake. I'd tried to go to Karen, to help her or soothe or ask her what she meant, because she couldn't mean what it sounded like, but she'd pushed me away, stumbled from my touch. Her hands were trembling and her face was so white, as if all the blood had rushed out of her. Jake was in the kitchen with her, and Jodi was looking after her, and she'd shooed me away with a brisk, 'I think it's best if you stay outside, Ali.' In my own house! Mike was outside, still on the swing seat, head bowed, with Bill, who had also gently urged me away. Bill hadn't sat down but was standing awkwardly over him. It wasn't clear if he was guarding Mike or taking care of him. Callum, I guessed, was still passed out on the living room sofa. Cassie hovered on the decking, wrapped in her cardigan. I saw that her flip-flops had mulch on them, the kind of dirt and leaves you got in the woods just outside the back door. Where had she been? 'What happened?' she kept saying.

No one answered her. No one had the words. 'Mum. What *happened*?'

'Where were you?' I turned on her. 'Why were you outside?'

'I . . . I couldn't sleep. It was noisy. What's wrong with Karen?' It wasn't so long ago that she'd called her Auntie Karen.

Still I couldn't answer, and I suddenly felt cold all over, as if I was going to be sick. The words went over and over in my head. *It was Mike. He raped me.* My mind rejected them, because it couldn't be true. How could it be true? They were friends! We were all friends! But something had happened, I could see that from the marks on her neck, the way she shook and hugged her arms around herself. A mistake, then. She'd made a mistake. My mind would not take it in, the thing that Karen had said. For the first time in many years, I genuinely had no idea what I was supposed to do. Who should I go to? What was going on? It was Jodi who took charge again. She came to the door and put her arm around Cassie, who shrugged it off. 'Auntie Karen's not feeling very well, love. She says – well, she's saying someone hurt her. You should pop up to bed. It won't be very nice around here.'

'She's right.' My voice sounded raw, as if I'd been talking all night. I swallowed. 'Please Cass. Will you take Jake and go to your room?'

All I could think was to get them away from this, get the children out of here. Not that Jake was a child; he'd be eighteen soon. How could I even begin to tell Cassie what her father had been accused of? I couldn't, because it wasn't true. It would all be sorted out once the police came.

Although, of course, they'd never been much help to me and Mum, the times I'd called them back then.

Cassie's head turned as if she'd only just noticed Jake, who was crouched down beside Karen in the kitchen, whispering to her. 'Please Mum. Tell me what happened. Did he hurt you?' Karen didn't seem to see him. She was rocking, her hands clutching so hard at her elbows they were almost white.

There were feet on the stairs and I turned and – Oh, God, I'd forgotten Benji. In his Star Wars pyjamas, his rounded child's tummy poking out, he looked so innocent and sweet. 'What's happening, Mum? You were all shouting and you woke me.'

I wanted to move, to explain, to shield him from this even though I didn't know what it was, I didn't understand what was happening, but then I heard a noise outside, on the drive. A car on the gravel. The police.

'Come on, Benj,' said Cassie, seeming finally to get it. 'Let's go upstairs.'

The police were here. All I could think was, my God, we were all so drunk, and Cassie had been up to something, and we looked so guilty. All of us just looked guilty as hell. And I found myself remembering that night back in 1996, the night Martha Rasby died, and feeling that same mixture of fear and shame and terrible, crushing guilt.

They were very kind. I even knew the DC, who'd come to give a talk to the women at the refuge a few months ago. It was hard to say who was more embarrassed, him or me. They were good at handling the situation. I'd expected, I don't know – some kind of brutish denial that Karen could possibly have been attacked, here with her friends. Instead they took her away, efficient and serious. There was a sexual assault centre in Maidstone, I knew. I remembered writing something about the new centres, never imagining they'd fall within the sphere of my own life. They'd be doing tests and taking swabs and . . . my mind failed. It kept trying to grasp what had happened, and feeling it slip away. After a brief statement, I saw them lead her out, from where I still sat on the decking, and I tried to go with her. She was my best friend. Of course I had to go. 'Wait! She'll need someone with her.'

Karen's eyes grazed mine, frightened, wide. 'Not her!' Her voice was hoarse. I reeled back as if I'd been slapped.

Bill was there, quietly helpful, gathering his jacket. 'I'll go. If that's OK.'

She bit her lip, reaching out an arm for him. There was a murmured discussion among the officers, and it seemed to be agreed that Bill could go if he didn't discuss the case with Karen. He was a witness; we all were. I wondered what he'd said on the phone, if he'd repeated Karen's allegation. I watched, shivering, as they went down the drive – the lawn had been taped off, a crime scene – an officer holding Karen up like someone who'd been in a terrible accident. There was still a smear of blood on her thigh, red against the white of her skin. I felt the loss of Bill, and remembered it had always been that way, that his presence was a balm, making any situation bearable, calm, friendly.

That was a while ago. I'd lost my sense of time, but I knew it was light outside, so a few hours had passed since what happened. We were in the living room now, the DC and me, and I was shaking with cold and shock, thinking about wrapping myself in the blue wool throw on the back of the sofa, wondering if that might look bad. Like I was selfish, only thinking of myself. 'Will she be OK? Karen? What will happen now?'

He didn't answer. 'Tell me in your own words what happened, Mrs Morris.' How old was he? In his twenties, I was sure. When he blushed, his neck turned red. I couldn't remember his name, though he'd told me.

'Well, I went to bed, and then I woke up and came down for water, and then she – Karen – she came in and said . . . what she said. That he . . . But, God, he really couldn't have. He's not like that, not at all.'

He made a note on his little pad and for a moment I felt like tearing it away, seeing what he'd written about me. 'How long have you known Ms Rampling?'

'Oh, God, it's twenty-five years. We were just talking about it. Earlier. We're *friends*, you see. All of us.'

'And you were all at university, is that right?'

'Yes, the . . . the six of us.'

'And your children are also here.' He made it sound wrong somehow.

'Yes, Cassie, she's fifteen, Benji's ten. And Jake, he's Karen's son. He's eighteen. Almost.' I was trying to be as helpful as I could, in the hope of persuading him to believe me, that we were decent people. That Mike would never do anything like this.

He was still writing. 'And Jake's father . . . ?'

'We don't know who he is. She wouldn't ever say. I'm not sure she knows, you know. She was a bit wild back then, but . . .' I realised what I'd said. About my friend. Who had accused someone of rape.

Who had accused my husband of rape. 'Where is he?' I said, sounding wild myself. 'Where's Mike?'

'We've taken your husband to the station – he's been arrested.'

They'd be doing tests on him too. Scraping under his nails, combing his pubic hair, swabbing his cheek for DNA.

'You said you woke up.'

'I'm sorry?' I blinked.

'You'd gone to bed, but you woke up. Do you know why?'

'Oh . . . no. I just did. So I went for water. I usually take some to bed, but I forgot. Maybe it was Jodi who woke me.'

'That's . . . Mrs Mackintosh?'

'Yes. Well, she prefers her own name. Seiffert. She was making coffee. She's pregnant, you see, so she wakes up easily. She said Callum – her husband – was passed out on the sofa.'

'And your children were in bed?'

No, Cassie was out in the garden, her bare legs flashing, dirt from the woods on her feet. What was she doing there? 'Mine were. Jake – he was in my husband's office, I think. Over the garage.' Had Karen really left him there until after three? My head hurt, trying to process all this, keep track of who had been where.

'So when you went up to bed, your husband, Ms Rampling and Mr Mackintosh were in the garden still?'

'And Bill. Bill Anwar, our other friend.' I thought of the spliffs Bill had in his tin. The booze. Oh God. My throat felt as dry as the leaves in the bonfire pile behind the shed. 'But he must have gone to bed too, he came downstairs when she . . . I don't understand how this can have happened,' I tried. 'Karen and Mike . . . they've been friends for years. Maybe . . . I mean maybe someone got into the garden. Someone else.' My mind was rushing ahead. Was it possible, in the dark and drunk, not to realise which man was attacking you? 'He couldn't have done this. I swear. He's not that kind of person, truly he isn't.'

He didn't say anything at first, but then he said: 'I understand you're Chair of the local Women's Refuge, Mrs Morris?'

Meaning: of course you can be raped by a friend. In fact, you're more likely to be. I knew this. I'd thrown those stats like so many hand grenades. But Mike? Again I tried to grasp at it, like an acrobat flying through the sky, gripping empty air. There was just no way. I knew bad men, and he wasn't one. 'What will happen?' I said dully.

'Well, we'll run some tests, and we'll question Ms Rampling and your husband. If charges are going to be pressed, there will be a magistrates' hearing, probably on Monday or Tuesday.'

'Will he get bail?'

His face, which I'd formerly found so kind and open, was unreadable. 'That's not our decision, Mrs Morris.'

Did people get bail for something like this? I thought of the bruises round Karen's neck, the inky bloom of them. Mike? No, *never*. Mike had never raised a hand to anyone in his life, I was sure of that. He always joked that, being shorter, he had to get by on his wits, not his fists. Then I thought of Jake, running at Mike, the anger in him. 'Where's Jake?' I asked. 'Karen, Ms Rampling's son, I mean. He'll be so tired, I don't think he got any sleep last night. There's plenty of room, he doesn't have to stay in that stupid tent . . .'

'Mrs Morris,' he said. He had that combination of gentle and firm. I thought he'd go far, in the force, Detective whatever his name was. 'I think it's wise if Jake stays somewhere else tonight. We'll find him a place.'

It was in that moment I realised what had happened to us. I'd considered Jake and Karen as part of our family, but now the lines were drawn. It was them versus us. I thought of Karen's white, horrified face, and my heart squeezed. But *Mike*. No, just no.

His phone rang. With an apologetic glance at me, he answered. 'Right. Right. Right. I see, yes.' I waited, staring at the carpet in the living room. Someone had walked in grass, crushed and oozing, and it made me think of the stains on Karen's face, the leaves in her hair. As if her face had been pushed down into the lawn. He hung up. 'I'm afraid there's news from the examination. There's evidence of semen, as well as signs of force.'

I gasped. But semen didn't mean . . . it didn't have to mean . . . 'I need to speak to him. Mike. Please. I'm allowed to speak to him, aren't I?' I'd get him to look me right in the eyes and tell me it wasn't true, and maybe then this fear that was eating its way up my legs would calm, and I'd be able to help Karen, be there for her like a best friend should. Was it wrong of me to ask? Did it look like I was taking sides?

'You could take him some clothes to the station. It's possible you might be able to speak to him, if it wasn't about the case.' His face had shut down. I remembered meeting him before, how friendly he'd been, telling me about his mum and how he looked after her. Adam, that was his name, I remembered now. DC Adam Devine. An Irish name, though I guessed at least one of his parents was black. Unusual in this whitewashed, wealthy town. Now he was looking at me as if I was what I felt like – a criminal.

Chapter Seven

Mike looked like shit. He probably hadn't slept much beyond what he'd got passed out on that swing seat, which could only have been a few minutes. I couldn't get it straight in my head, him doing that to Karen then staggering over to the seat, sitting down cosily and falling asleep. It just couldn't be true. They had him in the interview room, wearing a sort of cheap grey tracksuit. I imagined they'd had to take his clothes to test them. I'd be allowed to speak to him for five minutes, the duty sergeant said. He made it sound like they were doing me a kindness, because of who and what I was, and I believed it. It was amazing to me how quickly they could commandeer your life. Make it so you couldn't leave, couldn't eat, couldn't go to the loo, couldn't see your wife without their say-so. It was the same station where I had been, just hours before, a respected member of the community. It gave me whiplash, the speed with which things had changed. How could this be happening?

I pushed open the door to the dingy, bare-floored room, and Mike raised his head. I saw how red his eyes were, the shadow of stubble on his chin. His face looked creased. We were too old to drink all night. Too old for any of this. My arms were full of the clothes I'd brought, soft button-less things, as if he was ill. They'd searched them for anything sharp, any laces. Anything he could hurt himself with.

I wondered where Karen was. What they were doing to her.

'Hey.' Mike could barely look at me.

'Are you OK?'

He shrugged. 'I've been charged.'

'Oh.' I knew that wasn't good. They didn't do that unless they thought there was a case. 'Did you – have you eaten?'

'They gave me food and stuff, a place to lie down . . . but I couldn't sleep. I mean, how could I? This is mad.'

A rush of relief under my ribs. He was denying it. He didn't do it, of course he didn't. 'What the hell happened?' I felt more able to ask that question now. I'd been told not to, but unless they had the room bugged, they wouldn't know. Was that even possible? I didn't know.

'I don't even know. We were drinking. Way too much, I know. I must have gone to the seat and fallen asleep. That's all I can remember. Bill had some weed – really strong stuff. I'm not used to it. I guess I blacked out a bit.'

'Blacked out or passed out?' Because those were very different things. Passed out, you couldn't do anything. Blacked out, you were still moving around, functioning. You just didn't remember.

'I . . .' He shrugged again. 'It's all a blur.'

'Oh.' I sat down, feeling how cold the plastic chair was. They must have had the air conditioning up high, which would have been fine during the hot day, but it was now seven on Sunday morning and my arms were goose-bumped. I hadn't thought to put anything on over the floral dress I'd pulled from the chair in our room before the police came. I could smell my unshowered body, exuding a sour alcoholic reek.

'Have you seen her?' Mike asked. I shook my head. No need to ask who he meant. 'I swear, Ali, I . . . I would never do something like that. Never in my life. Even when we were young. I never, never have and never would. Hurt a woman.' I felt a surge of relief, but then something clicked and Martha Rasby's face was in my mind. But no. That had nothing to do with this. Mike was gentle, considerate. He'd never hurt me, never slapped the kids even once.

'Why would she say it?' We were whispering, as if afraid they were listening. They might be listening. They might have the whole room wired, for all I knew. Would I get into trouble, talking to him about it? He'd been charged already. That meant they'd taken all our statements, Karen's and Mike's too, and concluded he'd done it.

'I've no idea. She was really pissed. We all were.'

'She had bruises, Mike. All round her neck. I saw them.' I thought of the blood sliding down Karen's thigh, that small drop, and I shuddered.

He frowned. 'She did?'

'Bad ones. Someone – it looked like someone choked her.'

He thought about it for a moment. 'Is it possible someone came into the garden? You know, it was dark, she was so drunk. Bill had gone to bed already. Where was Callum?'

'Passed out on the couch. He looked like he was out cold.'

'So maybe someone did come in. From the lane, you know. Or even through the woods. No security cameras that way.'

I thought about Cassie. Would she have seen something? And what was she doing out there? I took a deep breath. 'I . . . I know you'd never do a thing like this. But you need to tell me everything. Is there any reason you can think of that Karen would say it was you?'

Mike looked down at his hands. I saw there was a scratch on one. I also saw that he had something to say to me, and I ran cold all over. 'I . . . Please believe me, Al, I would never tell you this now, not like this. But I think it will come out. I think maybe they'll be able to . . . So I better. Oh Christ.'

I said nothing. Cold was trickling down me, all the hairs on my body raised from the air conditioning and sheer dread. For the second time that night I wanted to turn back time, run away from this moment, stop up my ears and close my eyes. *Don't say it, Mike.* I knew that, as soon as he said the words, our lives as they currently were would be over. But also that there was no choice. No choice at all. Because here we were in the police station and Karen was saying he'd raped her.

'Karen and me . . . but it was just once, I swear to you. I regretted it right away. That might be why. She might want to punish me or something, you know how she is about rejection, so . . .'

'You're saying you and Karen . . .' *Don't. Don't go there. Rewind.* 'You were having an *affair*?'

'Not an affair, Ali! Not that. Just one time, I swear. I don't know what I was thinking.'

I understood what he was telling me, even if my brain pushed it away. I understood it all the way up from my feet. 'You had sex? When?'

A long silence. I already knew.

'Yesterday? While I was out?'

'We hadn't seen each other for such a long time. I don't know why it happened. She just – came on to me, and it happened. I'm so sorry, Ali.'

'In our house? In our bed?'

'In the – in my office.'

Karen's hesitation when I'd suggested Jake go up there. Mike, wanting to shower before dinner, even though there wasn't time.

'With our children there? And Jake too?'

Nod. 'They were – they didn't know. I swear.'

'Oh my God.'

'I know. I know, Ali! I just . . . I couldn't help it. I swear, it was all her, she threw herself at me. I told her it could never happen again.' So that was why she arrived so early, why they were both so happy to see me off to my meeting. Everything fell into place so neatly. I reached out and clutched the cheap table, the plastic picked away to show the fake wood beneath.

'Why now? When you've been friends for, bloody hell, twenty-five years?'

He said nothing.

'Tell me, Mike. Why would you sleep with her now?'

His voice was low. 'You've changed.'

'Changed?'

'For years you were so . . . content. The kids, the house. You didn't need anything else. But lately it's like you're just so angry all the time. This feminism stuff. I guess I've felt like . . . you were angry at *me*.'

I gaped at him. The words coming out of his mouth made no sense to me.

'I know this is shit,' he said. 'I know it. But what she's saying, I could go to jail. We'd lose the house. I could be in there years – rape? That's a life sentence . . . But I didn't do it, Al. I don't know, she could have made those marks herself, to get back at me. Or maybe she made a mistake, maybe she's not well or, Christ, I don't know. Please, help me. I've fucked up but I'm not a criminal. Tell them I'd never do something like this. Please! Tell them – I don't know, tell them you saw me go to sleep or something, you looked out the window . . .'

I was trembling. The words were in my mouth before I knew it. 'This is just like Martha, isn't it.'

He recoiled. 'It's nothing like that. That was just – Christ, Ali!'

'You asked me to lie then, too.'

'It wasn't a lie!'

It was all so familiar. The gritty-eyed feeling of being up all night, dawn landing on us like a bucket of cold water. A woman – a girl, really – who hadn't made it through the night unscathed. Except by the time the sun came up that day, Martha Rasby was dead.

'Tell me this isn't the same.'

'What the hell are you saying, Ali? That was – some stranger who got in. I just – it was bad luck! Wrong place wrong time!'

'And this is a stranger too?'

'It has to be. What else could it be? Ali, please!'

The door was opening. Our time was up. I stood, as if in a daze. As I walked out the door he was shouting after me, 'Do it for the kids, if not for me! Do it for Cassie and Benj!'

1996

My back was burning. I could feel it starting, the tingle on my pale skin, and knew I should have brought sunblock. It was so expensive though, and with only days to the end of term, money was tight. I shifted, trying to find a patch of shade on the lawn of the quad. Beside me, Karen, who'd been face down on the grass in tiny shorts and a vest, reared up on one elbow. 'You're turning red, Al.'

'I know.'

'It'll clash with your dress.'

'I *know*. Lend me your shirt?'

Karen obliged, and I draped the checked shirt round my raw shoulders, smelling my friend's aroma of rolling tobacco and Charlie Silver. A flicker of excitement licked my skin at the thought of my dress. It was lilac silk, and when I moved round my room it rustled over my bare legs in a way that made me shiver. To pay for it I'd worked all Easter break in the Tesco near Mum and Dad's house, patiently putting up with the supervisor, who was seventeen and had a chip on his shoulder about anyone going to university, let alone Oxford. The sneers, the fact no one ever invited me to their post-shift drinks in Wetherspoons. The fact Mike had only written to me once all holiday, a postcard from France where he was with his parents who owned a 'little place' there. As if this was a perfectly normal thing. I'd written back, pretending I was studying hard for Finals instead of stacking cans of beans and lying awake listening to Dad shout at Mum over *Coronation Street*. Trying to forget that I'd not even been invited to France, not that I could afford the flight. Wondering if that meant anything. Hating everything about life in my home town, the school friends who already had babies, the boredom of it, the fact there was no bookshop, no theatre. The only thing that made it OK was knowing it was my last holiday there. Because after Finals I'd be living in London surely, with Mike.

A dart of panic scissored my stomach – I still had no idea what I was doing once university ended. Mike and Callum had law training contracts lined up, a houseshare in Clapham, and I'd been waiting to be asked to move in too, but it hadn't happened and I was too much of a coward to ask. Why hadn't he asked? Was he just assuming I'd come with him? I knew what Karen would say – *For God's sake, Ali, ask him. He owes you that much at least.* We'd been together, more or less, since the very first night of college, almost three years now. I should have been able to ask. But I was afraid. Something told me things were changing, our cosy college world about to end. This ball might be the last time we were all together.

I looked up in the haze of heat to see someone come across the lawn, a bottle in each hand and a stack of plastic cups under one arm. Bill, in his usual jeans and ragged shirt, sleeves pushed up, a rollie hanging from his mouth. I realised I'd sucked in my stomach.

'Thought we could get started on the Pimm's,' he said, flopping down beside us, and Karen sat up, clapping her hands.

'You're a genius.'

Jodi was always saying Bill and Karen should get together – neither of them ever dated anyone – but they didn't seem keen, and it was me he looked at now, holding out the first cup he'd poured of Pimm's and diet Tesco lemonade.

'Ali?'

I reached for it, and he smiled at me, and the night ahead spread out below my ribcage, with all the joy and excitement and longing I held inside me. It was going to be good. All my friends together. Mike. Bill.

Now I pushed myself to sit up, dizzy with heat and drink, because suddenly Mike was there too. Finally, having been gone all day, supposedly playing cricket, he was there. He and Callum looked drunk, weaving.

He focused on me. 'You're not dressed.'

'Neither are you.'

'But you'll be . . .' He twirled a hand at his head. 'Make-up and that. For hours.'

'Jodi started at dawn,' said Callum, swigging from the bottle of vodka he carried. It was as if he thought he was starring in a remake of *Brideshead Revisited*. 'And it's not even her final year.'

'You saying I need hours to make myself pretty?' I saw Bill look at me, caught the turn of his head at my tone, which had aimed for arch and come out shrill.

'Course not,' said Mike, but there was something uneasy running between the five of us and I didn't understand what, and for a moment I was angry at him, at the one postcard all Easter, at the distance he'd placed between us this term – sleeping in his own bed most nights, spending hours in the library – so I stood up, wobbling over against Bill. For a second I felt his hand catch me, steady me. The warmth of it, the strength of his wiry arm. I wanted to stay. I didn't want to go and get ready, leave this sunny lawn. I had the sense that, once I did, I was going to lose my grasp on something intangible. That everything would be over. College. My youth. And Bill. Which was stupid, because I'd always be friends with Bill.

'Well, you're right, I better get started on the de-trolling process. Kar? You coming?'

She looked at me over her sunglasses, inscrutable. Callum was already passing her a cigarette. For some reason, he never minded funding her habit.

'You go on,' she said after a moment.

I couldn't very well stay now, after I'd said I was going, but all the same I didn't want to, didn't want to leave Karen there in the sun with all three boys. For just a moment I lingered, unsure.

And that was when Jodi came trotting towards us, self-important, her hair twisted up in rollers under a ridiculous net cap.

'Ali,' she said, slightly out of breath, rushing to bring bad news, her favourite thing. 'I thought you should know. Your dad is here.'

Chapter Eight

Our house was full of photos. It was something I'd pushed for. Paid for developing, cut snapshots to size, picked up shabby frames in charity shops. Nagged Mike to put up nails. I didn't think a house was a home without pictures. And I realised, as I stood in my hallway, just back from the police station to a silent house – everyone in bed, probably – that Karen was in every one of them. At our wedding, standing behind me in a blue bridesmaid's dress. At graduation, in the tight group of the six of us, hugging, throwing mortar boards. At Cassie's christening, proud godmother. She'd turned up in jeans and stilettos to the church, which had scandalised Mike's mother. Karen was there every step of the way, standing over my shoulder. The worst thing was I wasn't even surprised by what Mike had told me. Shocked, shaking, sick to my core, but not surprised, not really. Maybe, on some level, I had always expected this.

'Mum?' Cassie stood on the staircase, in her winter pyjamas. Thicker and warmer than the ones she'd been wearing last night. It was so early. I hoped Benji was asleep. I hoped he knew nothing about this, but I would have to tell them both soon, try to explain what had happened. But not yet. I needed more time, just another hour even, before I had to shatter my children's worlds. 'What are you doing?'

I looked down and saw at my feet a pile of framed photos, the glass already cracked, Karen's smiling face in every one.

◆ ◆ ◆

I must have slept. I lay on the bed, face down in Mike's pillow, smelling his aftershave, and when I opened my eyes again the light was different. The clock – his clock – told me it was almost midday. I had two children and a houseful of guests and I'd been passed out on my bed for hours.

'Any better?' Jodi was standing in the doorway. She was dressed in a Breton top and jeans, her feet in Ugg boots, which were stained around the edges with grass. The hot weather had broken, and outside the air was uneasy and chill.

I struggled up. 'God, I'm sorry. You won't have had any breakfast.'

'We found some. Please, Ali, don't worry about us. We're going to take off in a minute, get out of your hair. Cal's just in the shower – he's got a wicked head on him.'

'But . . .' Would they be allowed to just leave? Suddenly I felt that if anyone left, if the weekend ended, we'd be stuck in this nightmare for ever.

'The police have taken our statements. Not that we could help very much, sadly.' She paused. 'I'm so sorry. I can't believe this is happening.'

My mouth felt parched and sour. 'Me neither. It can't be true. It must have been . . . Well, someone must have come into the garden. It was dark, she couldn't have seen.'

Jodi said nothing. She came and sat on the edge of the bed, her face set in sympathetic lines. We'd never been that close really, me and her. I knew so little about her, despite years of friendship – what her parents were like, if she had siblings. We wouldn't have taken a city break together or gone to see a show, just the two of us. Since university it had always been me and Karen, rolling our eyes sometimes behind Jodi's back, as she tagged along with Callum everywhere. I wondered how Karen was, if she was crouched in some sterile room somewhere while they poked and prodded her. If her eyes were like those of the women in the shelter – hunted. Haunted. I should be with her. But how could I, after what Mike had just told me?

'I don't know what to do,' I said. The air in the room felt heavy. I wanted to open a window. It felt too small with me and Jodi in there, and the absence of Mike, and Jodi's heavy belly pressing down.

'Just keep going. For Benji and Cassie. They have school tomorrow?'

'How could they go to school? People will know, won't they?'

'Maybe not. Has he actually been charged yet?'

'I think so, yes.' I looked at her. 'Jodi, what do I do?'

'He'll need a lawyer. I assume he had the duty one at the station?'

I didn't even know – I was so clueless. 'Will you . . .'

She twisted up her mouth. 'I can't, since I'm a witness. Anyway, I'm the size of a house. I can recommend someone though. In fact, I already made a few calls.'

I tried to think what I needed to do. Was there food in the house? Had the kitchen been cleared when I passed through? 'The kids?'

'Cassie's in bed. I gave Benji some breakfast. He . . . they were asking what happened, him and Cassie. I had to tell them. Some of it, at least.'

'Thank you.' My voice cracked on it. I had to go to them, talk to them. Be their mother. 'Did you see anything, Jodi? Anything at all?'

She reached down to rub a smudge off her boot. 'I was conked out, I'm afraid. I get so tired these days. Then I woke up and realised Cal wasn't in bed, found him sparko in the living room.'

'Do you think someone could have come into the garden?'

'Sure. That's always possible.'

It was either that or Karen had made it up. She'd done those things to herself, because Mike had rejected her. Suddenly I had to tell someone. And I could hardly talk to Karen, could I? 'He said . . . Mike says they slept together. Yesterday, while I was out.'

I waited for the shock. It didn't come.

'You knew?'

Jodi made a face. 'Not for sure. When we arrived they came out of his office together. They were sort of – strange. I thought she was just being flirty maybe. You know how she is.'

I did.

'Should I have told you, Ali?'

'I don't know. It's a big thing, if you don't know for sure.' Would I have wanted to hear it? Would I have believed it?

'Right. Right. And they're such good friends, it could have been nothing.' She shuddered. 'If it were me, I'd want to move out right away. Doing that here, in your house – urgh.'

How could I move out? This was my dream house. But already it felt tainted, tape fluttering around the edge of the lawn, dirty footprints tracked through the house, and the office – well. I wasn't sure I'd be able to go in there again. If it had been Jodi, no doubt she would already have booked a team of contract cleaners.

Mike. Karen. Mike and Karen. My brain was refusing to accept it. There was one upside though. Why would he have confessed to something so huge, if he wasn't telling the truth about the attack? 'Is there a way to prove it?' I asked pathetically. 'If people had sex, say, earlier on in the day, and then later she said he raped her?'

'It's her word against his. That's why so many rape allegations go nowhere – there's usually no evidence, if the people know each other, that it wasn't consensual.'

'So – they might not prosecute?'

'She did report it right away. And you saw what a state she was in. Plus the bruising. All of those things tend to be . . . taken into consideration. Aggravating factors, they call them.'

'She was drunk. Really, really drunk.' I could hear the words coming out of my mouth, but I didn't understand that it was me who was saying them. How could it be? I knew the correct way to talk about sexual assault and this wasn't it, plus it was *Karen*. But it was also Mike.

I felt torn in two, an ache running down the centre of my heart. 'I just mean . . . maybe she couldn't be sure.'

'I know. Honestly, Ali, it could go either way.'

'Did Bill see anything? Where was he?'

'Gone to bed, he said.' In Benji's room, which was at the back of the house, not overlooking the garden. Had he seen Cassie sneak out to the woods? And what had woken Jodi, why was she downstairs before me?

'Jake?'

She shook her head. 'I haven't seen him. The police took him somewhere – he was so angry.' She reached over and squeezed my leg and I felt a sob hiccup in my throat. 'Stay strong, Ali. There's a good chance this will all go away.'

But the affair. The knowledge of Mike and Karen together, in our house, with our kids there. How could that go away, even if it turned out he hadn't hurt her at all?

I looked up as there were footsteps in the hall and Cassie burst in, still in her heavy pyjamas, printed with little dogs, a total contrast from yesterday. 'Mum. What the hell is going on?'

Chapter Nine

Benji cried. He was still a little boy, after all. 'But I don't understand! Where's Dad?'

'He's at the police station, love. They're just asking him some questions, trying to find out what happened.'

'But why would Auntie Karen say he hurt her?'

'I . . . I don't know. Maybe she made a mistake.'

Cassie had her arms folded, staring at me across the kitchen. Callum and Jodi had packed up and gone, with murmured apologies and hands pressed to shoulders; his hair was still wet from the shower and his face ashen. We should all have been nursing nothing worse than skull-cracking hangovers, but look, Mike was under arrest, Karen was . . . I didn't know where, and Bill with her. The reunion had been intended to bring us together, and now we were broken, smashed like the pictures I'd thrown down in the hallway. Someone, probably Jodi, had cleared them up so well there wasn't a trace of glass, and I thought of my mother, how good she'd been at hiding evidence of thrown dishes, pictures, furniture.

'How could she make a mistake?' Cassie said, and I heard how cold her voice was.

'I don't know. But . . . she must have. When he's cleared, we'll sort this all out, I promise.'

'*When* he's cleared?' was all she said.

'Darling, you know Dad would never . . . this is all a big misunderstanding is all. He would never.'

Cassie's face was unreadable. I had no idea what she thought, whether she believed her father was a good man who'd never hurt anyone, or whether, as I'd always taught her, she believed that women rarely made false allegations. I didn't push it further. I was afraid to have that discussion.

'Did the police speak to you, darling?'

'They spoke to everyone.' Cassie had her phone clutched in her hand again, as if it was some vital piece of equipment keeping her alive. She was more careful of it than someone having an affair. *Affair*. It knifed me in the bottom of my lungs. I was dimly aware I still had not taken it in, either what had happened to Karen or what Mike had told me. I was just functioning and breathing and doing the necessary to keep myself going. Part of me was still positive it wasn't true, that he'd just said it in a moment of madness. That both of them were mad. The weed perhaps. Hallucinations. Was that possible?

'And?'

'They asked if anyone could have, like, got into the garden.'

I waited to hear her answer to this. She said nothing.

'Cass, I know you don't . . . I know you need your privacy. But you were out there. In the garden. Why were you?'

Nothing. Then she said, 'Mum, I don't think I'm supposed to tell you. Isn't it like, conferring about evidence or something?'

'Cassie, for God's sake . . .' I made myself stop, soften my tone. She was just upset, acting up. Benji's hot little hand was crushed in mine. 'If you know anything that could help your father, you need to tell me now. Could someone have come in? From the lane or . . . the woods?'

'I didn't see anyone.' Later, when Benji wasn't here, when I had sorted my thoughts into some kind of order, I would have to ask her what she was doing out there for long enough to know no one had come in.

'What about the front gate? If everyone was drunk, maybe nobody saw anything.'

'Jake was in the garage. He'd have heard someone coming in.' She touched her phone when she said his name, and I wondered had they been texting, if that was even allowed. How Jake was feeling, where he was. I should try to find out, see if he needed clothes or food. He was almost an adult, but that didn't mean he could look after himself. Cassie went on, 'Also, next door have that stupid camera.'

She was right. Our neighbours, a seventyish couple living in a six-bedroom house, were so paranoid about security they'd installed a camera that was trained on their front gate. If anyone came past down the lane, it would have shown up. The police would get the tape, surely.

Cassie had been scathing when we talked about getting a similar one. It seemed wise, living so close to the woods, and there'd been burglaries in town. *For God's sake, Mum. Why don't you put up a steel fence too, keep the poor people out?* Now I realised with a leaden weight in my stomach that the camera might be our downfall. Because if it showed no one else had come into the garden that night, where did that leave us? Either my husband was a rapist – but no, I couldn't even countenance it, of course he wasn't! – or my best friend was a liar. Both of them had already betrayed me. As I sat there, watching my son cry and my daughter turn away her cold, set face, I just didn't know what I believed. I was caught in the middle, unable to help anyone. I just had to hope a miracle would occur, some way to explain all this without losing either of them.

The lawyer Jodi had found was a young and perky solicitor called Anna McCrum. Northern Ireland, I thought, her voice forthright and loud. She wore a trench coat and black trousers cropped at the ankle, neat and composed on this Sunday afternoon. We should have been cleaning up the dinner party now. Settling down with the Sunday lunch Mike had promised to cook. Drinking red wine. Laughing ruefully at how hungover we were. Then waving our guests off, getting back to our lives, ready for work and school tomorrow. Now I didn't know what would happen. The mere act of ushering Anna into the living room, trying to find a cup and coffee and milk, almost finished me off, and I stood in front of the fridge for a full two minutes, staring blankly at the contents. Someone had put the leftovers away, neatly covered in cling film. Jodi, probably. Funny how I'd never seen the value of her before, her careful ways, her attention to detail, but she was the only one doing anything practical to help. It was the details that mattered when the entire world had fallen apart. Like was there any milk or clean cups and had someone loaded the dishwasher. I felt a wave of guilt that I'd never made more effort with her.

'It's Ali, yes?'

'That's right.' Everyone else had called me Mrs Morris, as if I was Mike's mother, someone old and fragile. Oh God – someone would have to tell his parents, ring them at their villa in France. I knew that I absolutely couldn't face it just now. 'Can you tell me what's happening?'

Anna folded her foot, neat in a ballet pump, over her leg. 'Right so. As you might know, they did find semen in Ms Rampling, consistent with sexual intercourse. They're trying to rush through the DNA testing on that I believe.'

'But he . . . he told me they'd had sex earlier that day. Consensual. So they might . . . find something from that.' My mind shied away from it. Was he saying they hadn't used a condom? That small extra betrayal sent a flare of rage through me, burning my oesophagus like acid. How could he. How could she?

I watched Anna's face to see if she was judging us, the mess of our lives, but she gave nothing away. 'Hmm. That does make it a bit complicated.'

'What about the bruising? They can match it to his hands or some-thing? I mean it wouldn't match, of course.'

'They can try, but that's not always conclusive. Now, Ali, we need to make sure we have all Mike's clothes from last night. He mentioned a jumper?'

I pictured it, bright red and glowing. The Hugo Boss one he'd left lying on the decking. 'He didn't have it when they took him in?' I remembered going up to him in the swing seat, noticing the gooseflesh on his arms. 'No, he wasn't wearing it, I remember now. He took it off. I don't know where it is.'

She tapped her pen against her notebook. It had owls on the cover, I noticed. A thing that a child might use to write their sums in. 'OK, well, we need to find that jumper. If any of his clothing's gone it'll seem dodgy. Now. They've made a decision to charge him, as you know, so that means it goes to the magistrates' court tomorrow.'

'Will he get bail?' I was realising how little I knew about this process.

'Most likely, yes. Even with the suggestion of violence it's rare not to.'

'So . . . he comes home?'

'Sure. Then you wait until the trial. Your husband is a lawyer?'

'Corporate, yes.'

'So, it's likely he wouldn't be allowed to work until cleared in the trial.'

'*What?*' I'd spoken too loudly.

She blinked. 'It's standard procedure, Ali. You can't practise law if you've a criminal record. Most companies would at least suspend an employee accused of something this serious, if not start disciplinary action.'

I thought of our bank accounts. I hadn't even looked at them for years now, too scared of the sums involved. Mike assured me it was all OK, we spent a lot but he made a lot too. He'd pay off the house move in a few months, and then his Christmas bonus would come. But now – the kids had school fees. I was barely earning. What would we do if he lost his job? Could they do that when he hadn't been convicted of anything? It occurred to me how this really was a case of her word against his. I'd never fully understood it before, for all my knowledge of rape. The same act between them could have been consensual or a crime, depending on the point of view. Was it possible he'd thought she consented a second time? But then again I thought of the grass stains on her face, the bruises round her neck. How could someone not know?

I realised Anna was looking at me expectantly. 'Your phone?'

It was ringing. I hadn't even noticed. By the time I'd fumbled it out, it was on voicemail. Giving the solicitor a tight polite smile, I keyed into it, hearing Vix's cool, confident voice. 'Ali, it's me. Trying to reach you. If you have time, can you swing by the office, please? I'll be there.'

Chapter Ten

Since when did Vix work Sundays? Sundays were for roasts and films and walks in the woods, not the office. Or maybe I was hopelessly out of touch and wrong to nag Mike when he checked his emails over the weekend or went up to London on Saturdays. Maybe this was expected now. I made a distracted note to bring it up in her next supervision.

I shouldn't have gone out. I should have been at home, tidying and smoothing and caring for the kids, trying to restore our home to itself, not a crime scene, not the place where all this happened. Where my husband had slept with my best friend. But I just had to get out, even for an hour, breathe some air that wasn't full of secrets and lies. I left Cassie looking after Benji and she seemed relieved, as if she too wanted me gone. Knowing, maybe, that we'd have to have a talk about her sneaking out, that I'd have to discipline her in some way. Usually I would have asked Mike to do it, since she was far less likely to fly off the handle with him. But he wasn't here. That was something to be dealt with later, when this crisis was averted. Because it had to be, surely. I still didn't believe it would go to trial. The magistrate would see it for what it was, ridiculous.

Benji had looked so miserable when I went, I asked him to look for Mike's jumper, as Anna had suggested. A project. He loved root-ing around in the garden, and this would give him something to do. I wondered, though, why the police hadn't found it when they searched the place. If someone had come into the garden, as I still hoped might be the case, could they have taken it with them? It didn't make sense. Probably it was in the house somewhere, carelessly tossed aside.

I put in the code for the office doors, concentrating hard. If you got it wrong three times the police were called automatically. We had to be careful. The office was empty, the air conditioning humming gently. Vix was not at her desk but in the lobby, on the sofa we'd had put in there to make it warm and welcoming. Two cups of coffee in cardboard holders were on the low table. I thought if I drank any more caffeine my heart might pump its way right out of my chest.

'Ali. Are you alright?' I saw from her face that she knew what was going on.

'How did you find out?' Naïvely, I'd thought we could contain this, that only the police and the six of us knew. Nine, including the kids.

She indicated her phone, which was also on the table. 'You haven't seen? It's already on Twitter.'

'What? How?'

She shrugged one shoulder. 'These things get out. And because of your . . . profile, it's attracting some attention.'

'I'd no idea people even knew who I was.' I sat down, remembering too late that the chairs were always a bit lower than you imagined. 'Oh God. It's a nightmare. I honestly don't know what to do.'

She smoothed her skirt over her knees, looking out at me from her little dark-rimmed glasses. 'This is . . .' She paused. 'Ali. I'm really sorry you're going through this. Obviously there's no way to hide that it's happened, or your position with us. But there's a chance to turn this situation into something positive.'

How the hell could anything about it be positive? 'It seems unlikely, given how things are at the moment,' I said, wobbly.

'No. Of course. I just meant from a PR point of view. You have a platform, Ali. You've spoken out on this issue and now it's affecting you. Whatever you do next sends a message, about how we treat victims of

rape. I'm afraid the MRAs are all over this one already.' She'd told me
this meant Men's Rights Activists. The kind of guys who didn't really
believe rape existed, except as a lie women told to persecute them.

'But I mean . . . he hasn't been convicted.'

'The allegation has been made, yes? He's been charged?'

'Yes, but . . .'

'Our policy as a charity is to believe any allegations that are made
in the first instance. So. If you're up to it, we can get you on the news
again tonight.'

I was bewildered. 'But – you want me to say every allegation is true,
straight up? I can't do that.'

'Of course not.' Vix was so calm. I couldn't imagine her ever being
rattled. 'But Ali, you know how hard it is for the woman in this type of
case. When it's acquaintance rape, and they've been drinking, as your
friend was?'

'She was hammered.' My voice sounded flat.

Vix flicked a black eyebrow at that, but said nothing. 'I know it's
difficult. I get that, I really do. All you have to do is say there's an
investigation and you fully cooperate with it, even though this is your
husband. That all victims should come forward, as your friend has,
and let the police do their job. They're trying to change. It's up to us to
support them.'

'But I don't . . . I mean, I don't . . .'

'Ali.' She set down her coffee and leaned forward confidentially. 'I
never disclosed this to you, but there's a reason I do this job. I was raped
at university. A friend of a friend spiked my drink, I think, and when I
woke up he was having sex with me.'

'Oh my God. Did you report him?'

She shook her head. 'I knew him. I'd been drinking – not enough
to pass out, but some. I tried to talk to a few friends but he was popular, and they didn't believe me. But then a few weeks later he did it to

another girl. I felt so guilty. If only I'd come forward, maybe he'd have been arrested and none of that would have happened.'

I could see where she was going with this, but followed to its conclusion it meant Mike was dangerous. That if we didn't deal with this now, my husband might attack someone else. And that was ludicrous. Mike was a good man. I had married a good man – I had been so very careful to.

She went on, 'If you could bring yourself to, you could just say that victims – I mean, alleged victims – should come forward. That's all. They aren't allowed to discuss any details anyway before the trial.'

For a moment, I considered it – clawing back control, being Ali Morris the Chair, the media personality, the campaigner – but then I was standing up, so quickly I spilled coffee on to my skirt. Images were flickering through my head like a crazed magic-lantern show. Mike, in that tracksuit in a dingy little room, the fear in his voice as he'd begged for my help. Karen in the kitchen, shaking, the blood running down her thigh. Karen. Mike. The two of them having sex in our house. But then there was Cassie, and Benji, crying for his dad. I knew what I had to do. I had to protect them, at all costs.

'I can't. He's my husband. I . . . I'm not going to say anything publicly at all.'

Vix stood up too. I saw her eyes harden. 'In that case, Ali, I'm afraid we have no choice but to ask you to stand down as Chair. The board are in agreement – we had a conference call earlier. I'll draft a statement saying you're out.'

Benji

Everything was horrible. Since the moment he'd woken up in the night, and seen all the adults standing about in the kitchen or outside, his mother shouting and Auntie Karen crying harder than he'd ever seen a grown-up cry, things were horrible. His dad was at the police station and no one would tell him why, just that Auntie Karen was saying he'd hurt her, and he didn't understand why everyone was fussing round Auntie Karen but no one seemed to notice Cassie had her black eye stuff smeared all over her face, like she'd been crying too. Hurt her how? he kept asking. How did Dad hurt Auntie Karen? But no one would tell him. Now his mother was gone too and it was just him and Cassie, and she'd locked herself in her room to tap at her phone, all she ever did these days. He knew she'd got up that night, gone out – he'd felt her stepping over him, trying to be quiet. He knew there were things she wasn't telling Mum. They were supposed to be having Sunday lunch right now but everything was wrong. He couldn't even go in his room because his things were all put away still for Bill to stay, his Minecraft bedspread replaced with the boring striped guest one.

He thought about the night before – waking up, hearing everyone shouting. He'd gone on to the landing, and the door to his room had been open. Bill wasn't in there, and Benji could hear his voice downstairs. Bill's bag, a sort of canvas one like an adventurer might have, was open on the floor, and Benji just couldn't resist. There might be anything in there. Guns. Fishing rods. Maps. Mum had made Bill sound a bit like Indiana Jones. So he'd gone in, just for a second. And that was when he'd seen the person.

Looking out the window of his room, into the woods (which sometimes scared him a bit, when he was alone at night, though he'd never have admitted it), he saw there was a man. Benji couldn't see who it was in the dark, but he was wearing a black jacket, like some kind of raincoat with a hood, and staring up at the house. It was only for a second, and then he disappeared into the trees. Benji didn't know if he should have told Mum, or if he'd get in trouble for being nosy in Bill's things. Probably it was someone walking their dog, stopping because they heard the sound of Auntie Karen crying.

Now, alone and bored and confused, Benji mooched into the garden. Maybe he could be the one to find the jumper Mum mentioned, and maybe that would help Dad. Though he didn't understand how. He'd seen the police crawling over the garden early that morning, in white suits like on TV. But maybe they didn't know all the places to look. It was so big in the new house's garden there were still even corners he didn't know, dark and overgrown. He poked around, looking under bushes and in the hedge. Nothing, though he did find a bird's nest with a clutch of blue eggs. He wished Dad was here to show.

The shed was locked up as always – only the gardener, Andrej, Benji's hero, ever went in there. Behind it was a pile of leaves and branches and grass and things. Usually Andrej made a big heap and burned them, but he hadn't come the week before. Benji saw something in among the greens and browns – a flash of red. He looked around – he wasn't meant to go behind there, he knew that – but there was no one to tell him not to, that it might be dirty or dangerous. No adults at all. He bent and pulled at it, and it came out, knocking over twigs and rubbish. It was Dad's jumper. How did it end up in the rubbish pile, all covered in bits of leaves and dirt? Benji hesitated. He remembered seeing a TV programme about detectives, where it said you shouldn't move evidence. He crawled back out, and went inside, up the stairs to Cassie's room. He'd left leaves and mud on the stairs, and Mum would be cross. He knocked. 'Cassie?'

She didn't answer for a while, and when she did her voice sounded like she had a cold. 'What?'

'You know Mum said to look for Dad's jumper?'

He heard her footsteps, then she pulled the door open. Her face was red and swollen. 'Don't be an idiot,' she said. 'If they find it, they'll use it to make Dad seem guilty.'

'They will?'

'Think about it. They'll say he hid it somewhere, even if he just, like, lost it.'

Benji didn't think the jumper could have got in the pile by mistake. After Cassie shut the door in his face, he went back across the garden and stared at it, beneath the twigs and branches and leaves waiting to be burned. Andrej came on Mondays, usually. That meant he would find it the next day. Was Cassie right – would Dad get in more trouble if it was hidden?

He wished there was someone to tell him what to do.

Chapter Eleven

Bitch

What a fucking hypocrite

Calls herself a feminist, don't see her commenting on her husband being a rapist

'It's not as bad as all that,' said Bill soothingly. He'd been there when I got back from the office, and without asking he'd made dinner from leftovers, and then washed up and fielded the kids while I sat numb, unable to do anything. I should have asked him how Karen was, I knew that, but my mouth felt stopped up. I was still reeling. In front of me, my phone spouted bile. Somehow, Mike's name had got on to Twitter, and the glee was hard to bear. I'd spoken out about rape, I'd scolded and berated, and now here I was, supposedly protecting my abusive husband. The urge to fight back, to shout that he'd never do a thing like that, that it must be a mistake, was almost overwhelming. I had just enough sense left to know that would only make things worse. I'd already had to call Mike's parents in France, because even they were on Facebook, then listen to their bewilderment, his mother's tears, all the while wanting to burst into some of my own. I wondered if my mother had heard. What she might say – *well, Alison, you've made your bed*. I wasn't going to call her.

Bill and I were now sitting at my kitchen table, glasses of whisky in front of us. I hadn't touched mine. It was so strange to have him there, to know that all I had to do was stretch out my hand and I could reach him, touch him, after all these years. I tightened my grip on my phone. The house didn't feel like my own. It had a discarded, dirty air, after all the strange feet that had tracked through it, the tears that had been shed. I realised I was sitting where Karen had when she stumbled in from the garden. I looked over towards the door; the drop of blood was still visible on the slate tiles. I wondered where that jumper of Mike's was – there was no sign of it around the decking, where I'd last seen it dropped. The last thing we needed was something else that made him look guilty. I'd cancelled Andrej for the next day, on the police's request, in case they wanted to search the garden again. Irrationally, I worried about who would cut the grass. I didn't know how to use the mower.

'Not bad? It's awful. The refuge firing me? It makes Mike look guilty as sin. And me, too, for standing by him. That's what all these people think. But Bill, what else can I do?' I honestly didn't see. An allegation had been made, not proven yet. Mike was my husband, father to my kids, the same person I'd lived with all these years. Except. He wasn't. He was the man who'd slept with Karen, in our house. A cold shiver ran through me, as if my body was rejecting what he'd told me. If he'd told me that, he must have told me the truth about everything. Right? Why else would he?

'It'll be OK,' Bill said again. But he couldn't know that.

I unlocked my phone and held it up to him. It was open on a Twitter search for my name. *Disloyal bitch. If my wife left me in the shit like that I'd be on to a divorce lawyer.* That was the men's side, wondering why I wasn't publicly supporting Mike. It wasn't only men, in fact. But worse, much more hurtful, was the feminist response. I'd thought that was my side, but now they were turning on me. Why hadn't I spoken out yet? *Why so silent, Ali?* 'They hate me. Both sides hate me.'

'Who cares what people think? You don't know them. I hate all this, this social media mob. We aren't meant to know what other people think in this level of detail.' Bill set down my phone at a slight distance and pushed the glass towards me. 'Drink. It'll help.'

I gulped down the burn of heather and smoke. 'What am I going to do?'

'Well, there's the hearing tomorrow. He'll get bail, most likely. Then he can come home.'

'But can he work? Will they fire him?'

'I don't know. It's not proven until the trial, so I don't see that they can fire him, no. They might suspend him, but they'd have to keep paying him at least.'

Bill was so comforting. I remembered bashing on his door late one night, in a panic over a Chaucer essay I hadn't finished. He told me to say I'd been ill, hand it in the following week, and then we'd sat up drinking and talking. I'd felt so grown-up. Bill was the only student I knew who had a bottle of whisky in his room, and even when I mixed it with Diet Coke he'd looked devastated, but said nothing.

'I've still been fired from the refuge.'

'Well, it's only voluntary, isn't it? Why not pull in your horns a bit – look after the kids, lay low? Wait till the trial.'

I set down my glass. 'Bill . . . you were in the garden last night. Did you see anything? Did anyone come in the gate?'

He shook his head slowly. 'I went to bed before . . . anything. But the police checked the tape from next door, didn't they?' Anna had already told me as much. Nothing had shown up.

'But . . . did you see anything else? From the upstairs windows, maybe?'

He paused. 'I looked out the landing window when I went to the loo. I guess it was . . . not long before it happened. I'd got back into bed and was half-asleep when . . . the shouting.' I understood. The landing window overlooked the garden.

'You're saying, what, you saw them in the garden? Last night?' My hands started to shake; I set the glass down. No, it couldn't be. I wanted to shout, *please don't say it.*

His face was screwed up. Bill hated this, other people's messy lives. 'I didn't know for sure, not at the time. But I think I . . . I saw him on top of her, Ali. It was dark, but I could see his clothes. But I thought . . . well, obviously I didn't think it wasn't consensual, or I'd have rushed out there. I keep thinking about it. I saw it happen and I just left her there.'

'You thought they were . . . together?' Having sex, right there in the middle of our lawn. It seemed unbelievable. I thought of myself, asleep in bed, oblivious, and I wanted to shake the clueless woman that I'd been just the day before.

He looked uncomfortable. 'I – they seemed quite flirty earlier on. I didn't want to interfere in whatever was going on. I've not seen you all in years, I couldn't just rock up and start – you know.'

Same thing Jodi had said. Did everyone know except me? I couldn't think about Karen, couldn't let myself feel sorry for her. It was horrible, as if she was clinging to a rope, begging for help, and I was sawing through it. 'You definitely saw him?'

'I think so.'

'Did you tell the police?'

He nodded. 'I'm sorry. I had to.'

'Mike told me they had sex earlier that day. While I was out.'

Bill looked like he'd rather be undergoing dental extraction than having this conversation. 'Maybe they did that too.'

The proof was there. Bill had seen them, and the semen was there, and no one else could have got into the garden. All that remained was Karen's word it had been against her will.

Suddenly, it was all too much, and the burn of the whisky rose in my throat and I got up, knocking the glass to the floor where it shattered, and I ran to the downstairs loo – the stupid candle I'd made Cassie buy still sitting there, with its reek of orange and spice – and then

I was on my knees and throwing up, shaking and retching. Some distant part of me registered, *That's interesting, I always thought that was a cliché.* Turns out that extreme shock really does make you puke. I cried, and retched, and cried some more. Pathetic.

When I'd cleaned myself up and gone back to the kitchen on shaky legs, Bill was sweeping up the broken glass. The kitchen stank of booze, not like my house at all. A frightening smell, one that took me back to places I didn't want to be. The smell of lives going wrong. My father stumbling in from the pub, the creeping dread of knowing it was going to be a bad night.

'Are you OK?'

I sat down heavily. 'I just don't know what to do. How can I . . . who am I meant to help? Which one?'

'I . . . Ali, I don't know if you can help either of them.' He looked wretched.

'You went with her. Was it bad?'

He said nothing for a moment. 'They were very kind. But . . . yes. It was bad. Ali, she's in bits.'

'Shit. Oh God, this is such a mess.'

Bill tipped the glass into the recycling bin. I almost said not to, you weren't supposed to put in broken pieces, but I stopped myself. So stupid, the things I worried about. As if any of it mattered now.

'I should go. I only came back to make sure you were OK.'

'You can't go!' The thought of him leaving too sent slimy trails of panic down my back. 'I mean, God, of course you can, but do you need to?'

'Not really. I was planning to just pootle about a bit. But Ali, are you sure you want . . .' He didn't finish that sentence. I think he was afraid to, and so was I. I thought of our strange moment in the kitchen the night before. Would it be too much to ask him to stay? I needed help. Not just with the kids but to stay sane, to talk it over, rake up the broken pieces.

I looked down at the table. 'I'd really appreciate it if you could stay the night. I might need someone to watch Benji or something, when we're at court or . . . would that be OK? I mean, as long as it's not inconvenient?' I heard the hitch of tears in my voice. 'Please, Bill. I just . . . need help.'

His eyes were fixed on his own whisky, the amber glow of it. 'Of course. Whatever you need, Ali.'

Chapter Twelve

'But why do I have to?'

My last nerve was snapping. 'Because, Benji, you're too young to be at court, and I'm not having you miss school. Get your uniform on.'

It was Monday morning and he was standing in front of me in his Star Wars pyjamas, hair sticking up, furious. 'But Cassie's going! It's not fair.'

I didn't know how to explain to him that I didn't think I could stop Cassie if I tried. She was starting to scare me, the way I felt the connection between us strain with every day. 'Cassie's older. Plus, her school's almost stopped for exams already.' I couldn't have him there. I didn't know what was going to be said about his dad. Or about me.

Cassie had insisted on going. She had been texting Jake, as I suspected, but he still wouldn't answer any of her messages, and she was frantic trying to contact him. 'He's never done this, Mum. He's not like other boys. He always answers.'

Cassie and Jake. I'd always wondered, of course, over the years. They were so close, those two. Would that spill over into kissing, touching? Karen and I had never said it, but it was something neither of us wanted. It was possible to be too close for love.

'Cass, did . . . when you were out in the garden that night, was that anything to do with Jake?'

He'd been in the garage, waiting for Karen to stop drinking and go to bed. Maybe Cassie was on her way to see him.

She just gave me a look. 'Mum. Jake and I are friends. Why can't you understand that?'

I'd thought Karen and Mike were just friends. And now look. 'But what were you doing out there? Please, darling. I need to know. Did you tell the police?'

She turned her back to me, brushing her long hair in the mirror. Her eyes met mine in the glass, hostile. 'You really want to get into this now?'

She had me there – we had to leave for court in a few minutes, and I still needed to get Benji ready. Bill was going to drop him off at school, using Mike's car. Already he was making things easier. 'I don't think you should be texting Jake, with everything that's going on. And you'll have to tell me sometime, Cassie.'

Her silence said: *Oh, will I?* And did I really want to know? We always think we want to know secrets, but what we forget is that they come with their own weights, heavy as millstones, and if you aren't careful this weight can crush you.

I'd been to Bishopsdean Magistrates' Court before several times, as an advocate for women who were finally prosecuting their abusive husbands. Today I hadn't known what to wear, in the end going for my funeral dress, black and sober but with a tailored waist that made me look slim. Cassie threw me a contemptuous glance as she hurled herself into the car, fastening her seatbelt. 'Why are you all dressed up? No one's going to be looking at you.'

I didn't answer that. I didn't even know why I was going. To support my husband – meaning I believed him, I stood by him? Or to bear witness for an abused woman, my best friend? My lying best friend.

My cheating husband. It was crazy to think I hadn't spoken to Karen since it happened. The police had said not to contact her, that it could be construed as harassment even. My fingers itched to message her. I didn't know what I'd say, though. *God Kar are you alright* or *Fucking hell Karen how could you*. Or both. Cassie herself was wearing jeans and a jacket. I was glad it was cooler now. I'd been on the verge of saying something to her about the skimpiness of her outfits, and then it really would all blow up.

Bill had stayed the night, moving to the spare room so Benji could have his back. He didn't come to court and I didn't ask him to. Two friends, facing each other across a courtroom. It was hard. I wished I didn't have to go myself, but I got into the car too and started following the morning traffic down into town.

We'd moved to Bishopsdean when Benji was on his way, after five years of raising Cassie in a flat in Stoke Newington. On rainy days she'd press her face to the window, woebegone, and when she finally got out it took all my strength to stop her darting into the road, twitching with excess energy. Mike was always at work then, coming home at midnight, one, two, three in the morning, or sometimes not at all. Karen asked me once – and that was yet another memory that now stuck in me like a barb – did I ever worry about him. *You know. All those women at the office.* But honestly, I never had. I knew he was too exhausted to even think about doing anything.

That was our life then. Desperately holding on to our work, the flat, Cassie. I'd been a journalist to start out with, subbing at an interiors magazine, but then it folded, and the one I went to afterwards, a cookery title, folded too after six months. The magazine industry was imploding. At least law was booming. But in order to fuel that, it took so much of Mike. Not just his time, but his mind and body and spirit, until he was worn to a nub of a person. One night he came home around eleven. Early for him. He sat at the table in his suit, his tie crooked, and put his head in his hands. 'I can't do this,' he said. 'We

can't do this.' I looked around at the kitchen table, where I'd been trying to send out freelance pitches in the middle of piles of laundry and
dishes and Cassie's school projects. The wall to her bedroom was so thin
we could hear her breathing in her sleep. And the rent on the flat kept
going up and up, despite its size and shabbiness.

'Do you ever think we should move?' Mike said, and I remember
the strange feeling of relief that had burst inside me.

When I told Karen, something went over her face. At that time
she lived fifteen minutes away, in a houseshare in Stamford Hill, where
she somehow kept Jake fed with her job in a health-food shop. I didn't
understand why she had never tried to retake her degree – too proud,
maybe. 'You're *leaving*? Then we won't be nearby.'

Then, I thought she'd just miss me, and maybe she was annoyed we
couldn't share babysitting any more. Now I wondered was it something
more – was she used to Mike being so close? Did she have feelings for
him – had she wanted him all these years? I'd felt guilty, leaving her and
Jake, a little boy I saw almost every day. But when we'd gone, and settled
into our first house in Bishopsdean, a three-bed terrace near the station
for Mike's commute, didn't I feel the relief again? Didn't I feel I could
somehow breathe? I'd thought it was London. But maybe it was her.

'Mum.' Cassie was staring at me like I was stupid. 'You've missed
the turn. You'll have to go round again.'

◆　◆　◆

We were late in the end, running for the courtroom after it took ten
minutes to find a parking space. Bishopsdean was crammed with four-
by-fours, yummy mummies off to coffee and baby yoga and the gym. I
used to be one of those. Once we moved here I gave up trying to find
any work in my ailing industry, and then I was busy with Benji, and
when I emerged two years later I was a non-working mother with two
children, just like the rest of Bishopsdean.

Cassie and I were walking to the courthouse at a swift pace, a sudden anxiety strung between us. 'What's going to happen?' She was breathless.

'He'll come home with us. They won't keep him in, not for this.' I'd been assured this was likely. So why did a gnawing in my stomach tell me it wouldn't be that easy?

'But what will happen then? Like, how do you talk to him? What do I say?'

'I don't know, darling. Just as normal. I—'

I felt Cassie strain beside me. 'Jake! Jake!'

Too late, I saw him too. He was skulking near the shrubs that surrounded the courthouse, stooping down. This young man I'd seen born, close as a cousin to my kids, and he was staring at us with naked hate. He was still wearing his black hoody and jeans. And my Cassie, my golden girl, was running towards him. 'Jake! Please!'

He was turning away from her. 'We shouldn't talk.'

'But we can still . . .'

'No. We can't.' He actually pushed her, his rough hand on her slender arm, and in that moment I wanted to hurt him. My godson, practically a nephew, and yet a spurt of rage boiled up in me.

Cassie stood watching him go, rubbing her arm in a kind of wonder, as he scuttled through the glass court door.

'Are you OK, darling? Did he hurt you?'

'He didn't want to talk to me.'

'He's just upset. This is very upsetting for everyone.'

'But me and him . . . I don't understand, Mum! I don't understand what's going on!'

I put my arm around her, and for once she let me. 'It's going to be OK. This will all get sorted out very soon.'

I wished I believed it.

◆ ◆ ◆

The court dazzled me. There was a glass panel in the roof and fractals of light fell on us as we took our seats. Karen and Jake were across from us. He held her hand tight in his, and both of them looked straight over our heads. I could feel Cassie quiver beside me, and I took her hand too. She held it for a moment, then dropped it. Anna McCrum was on the lawyers' bench. There too was DC Adam Devine, looking about twelve in his suit. Movement in the dock. It was Mike. It was my husband, but in that moment he looked like a stranger, pale-faced and old. He caught my eye, pleading, and I couldn't bear it. He looked terrified. Cassie stifled a sob.

'All rise!'

Everyone got to their feet, and so did I, stumbling.

It was time.

It was all over so quickly. It was confirmed that the case would be sent to the Crown Court. Anna made the application for bail and though I held my breath, it was granted. There was no horror or shock in the court. It seemed this was an everyday occurrence, and I supposed it was. Lives being shattered were par for the course in this place. Cassie turned to me, whispering shakily as we stood. 'He's coming home?'

'Yes. He'll meet us out front.' Though what I would say to him, I had no idea.

When we walked out, I saw the reporters. Not many of them, but a small cluster. At first I didn't understand why they were there – was someone famous on trial? – and then I got it. It was me. I was suddenly the news.

'Ali!' shouted one. 'Ali, can we have a statement?'

'Just keep walking.' I directed Cassie to the door. My heart was hammering. It goes against every instinct to ignore people calling your name, refuse to look them in the face. Mike was standing in the lobby, under the swirl of light. I couldn't see his face. The moment I'd worried about, confronting him, was swallowed up in fear. I had to get Cassie out of here.

'What's going on?' I heard him say.

'The press are on it. Because of – because of my profile. Come on. We're parked round the corner.'

He put his arm around Cassie, shielding her, and she shrugged him off. 'Dad, what's going on? What did you do?'

'Not now, darling, please. We'll talk at home.'

Together we got our daughter out through the crowd, who were all the while shouting my name. I was panting, sweating into my heavy dress. I heard Mike say, 'Jesus Christ,' and then the court officers were pushing people back, clearing a path for us.

'The car's on London Road. Get her there!' From the corner of my eye, I could see Karen and Jake standing on the road outside, by the bushes. She looked stooped, devastated, as if she'd aged ten years overnight. I wondered how they would travel home, if they'd have to get the Megabus again, or if they would stay in town. She spotted me, and I saw my name in her mouth. Calling out to me, maybe. Asking for help, or trying to explain herself. Part of me wanted to run to her, take her in my arms like she'd done for me so many times, get her away from all this. But I remembered what the police said about harassment. And what Mike had told me. Having sex in my house. And so I turned my back on her. I remember that very clearly. If I hadn't, if I'd kept my eye on her or even gone over and asked was she alright, ignored the official advice and just been her friend instead of the wife of the man she'd accused, then maybe what happened next would not have occurred. Maybe everything would be different now.

I was pushing my way along the road to the car, head down, focusing on Cassie and Mike beside me, when I heard the running footsteps. I turned, saw Jake flying at us. I'd never seen him run before. I heard

Karen shout something – I don't know what. I saw what Jake had in his hand.

Mike saw it too, and his instinct, as I think mine would have been, was to protect our child. He threw himself in front of Cassie, and so when Jake reached us, still running fast, sobs trapped in his throat, the knife he was holding went into Mike's side. I saw the flash of it in the morning sun. I saw the effort it took for Jake to push it in, through the layers of suit and shirt and skin and flesh. It was horrific, and I felt bile in my throat. The knife was sticking out of Mike, red blotting his shirt, and he fell down, putting one hand out to catch himself, then crumpling, as if all the strength had gone from his arm. His head hit the kerb. Jake was shouting, 'You bastard, you bastard, you hurt my mum, you hurt her . . .' Cassie was screaming, shielding her dad now, flailing at Jake with her bare hands. The knife was in Mike's side – and now I recognised it, the black rubber handle. It was my own, one of the Japanese set I kept wicked-sharp. Jake must have taken it from our kitchen.

All of this happened in a matter of seconds. Then there was a flash of reflective jacket, and the court officers were there, one holding Jake by the arms – he was sobbing, no resistance in him – and the other kneeling over Mike, on his radio for an ambulance. I remember there was blood on the tarmac and on Cassie's shirt. I remember that I turned, frozen and disbelieving, and I looked down the hill at Karen. But the sun was in my eyes, and I couldn't see her face.

1996

'What are you doing here?' I hissed. I'd hoped it was all some horrible misunderstanding, but no, there was my dad's old Ford Focus outside the lodge, and I could already see the irate porter marching out to tell him you couldn't park there.

Dad looked old and tired and my ears almost popped at the dissonance of seeing him there in his beige anorak, when just paces away, on the jewel-green lawn, my friends were drinking Pimm's and lolling in the sun. 'What? I've come to fetch you home.'

'It was tomorrow, Dad! Not today!'

Anger creased his brow. 'I've not got time tomorrow, I've an extra shift on.' He managed the bar in a working men's club, something that Callum and Mike always teased me about. *Does your dad have ferrets down his trousers, Al? Does he sup ale and eat gravy?* I smiled along but it wasn't funny. It was my life.

'But tonight's the ball! I can't come home now.' My mind was racing ahead. I hadn't packed my room up yet – it would take ages to peel all the posters down – maybe I could send him off with some of the bulkier stuff then get the coach back . . .

He turned off the engine and got out of the car. The porter had retreated after I waved him away apologetically. I stepped back as Dad reared up beside me, shock flashing through my head. He wouldn't . . . not here . . . surely. Then his hand was gripping my upper arm, hurting the sunburned skin. 'Stop this bloody nonsense. I've driven six bloody hours to pick you up, spoiled little bitch that you are, and you're giving me this about a ball? Grow up, Alison. You're back in the real world now. Real people have jobs, they don't swan about in ball dresses.'

I pulled away, noticing the marks of his hand on my arm. 'I'm not coming with you.' My voice was one I hated, the one that always came out of my mouth when I spoke to him. Pinched and scared. Not Ali the Oxford student. Ali the frightened little girl.

'You have to. Your mother needs you, she's not well.'

'Why, did you break her arm again?'

He didn't answer but I saw anger streak across his face and knew I was right, or close to it. And I knew what that would mean. A summer doing all the cooking and housework, a summer back in Tesco if I was lucky. I knew that, if I did go home, the town would suck me in, just as it had my mother. I would never leave.

'I'm not coming.' My voice was louder. I was on home turf. I did belong. He couldn't hurt me here, in front of the college lodge.

His voice went dangerously quiet, like the noise of air rushing out before a hurricane strikes. As a child, that was the most terrifying sound I could imagine. 'If you don't get your arse into this car, Alison, you can forget about coming home. Ever again. Support yourself, if you're such a big woman now.'

Fear gripped me. I was twenty-one, how could I support myself? I had nowhere to live and no job lined up, no way to even move my things out of Oxford. But I made myself raise my chin. 'Fine by me. Guess you'll be driving back alone.'

His slap took me by surprise, though it really shouldn't have. He'd been hitting me since I was five years old, and my mother for as long as I could remember. A small mewling sound escaped my mouth. As the sting spread out across my face and my eye watered and blurred, I remembered the way my mother used to take her slaps and punches. Hunching her shoulders, closing her eyes, accepting it as her due. As if staying very still and quiet would make him stop. As if she somehow deserved it. And I resolved: I would not be like that. I set my shoulders and made myself look at him, though my eye was swelling already. How would I cover that, for the ball? 'You're an embarrassment. Just fuck off, Dad. I don't need you any more.'

As I turned to go to my room, I saw Karen standing in the gateway to the lodge, watching the entire thing, her eyes wide with horror. And it was her I went to, and she pulled me into a fierce hug and whispered in my ear, 'You don't need him. He doesn't define you.' Then she shepherded me back to my room before anyone could see I was crying, helpless jagged sobs, and calmed me down with booze-spiked tea, held ice to my face and covered it with make-up, did my hair and helped me get dressed so that when she was finished, you couldn't tell what he'd done to me. You couldn't even see the cracks.

◆ ◆ ◆

Karen has always maintained Martha Rasby was on the lawn that day too. She must have been. Everyone was there, soaking up the heat and the last time we'd all be together. But as I got up to go, passing from the light into the dark, I have no memory of seeing her among the faces on the lawn, turned up to the sun like daisies.

Likewise, I do not remember seeing her at the ball at all, packed as it was, a whirl of silks like the ball at Twelve Oaks in *Gone with the Wind*. I suppose it was unseemly, the way we all jostled to be part of her story, a story that began sometime that night, or maybe months or even years before it, when she first arrived at college perhaps, with her smile and long netballer's limbs and her Nordic blonde hair that was almost white. Maybe girls like Martha are doomed from the moment they're born, or the day they grow breasts. She had even more glamour after it – tragic, doomed, beautiful. The press adored it. It had the quality of a locked-room mystery, even, though the college was quick to play that down. Although it was only our students at the ball, they insisted anyone could have climbed over a fence or wall or hedge. Anyone could have come across Martha alone in the Fellows' Garden, in her white silk dress – and who else would have dared to wear white? I had ketchup stains on my own precious ballgown within an hour. It did not have to be a member of our college, the upstanding young men who in a few short weeks would be in offices and suits, would be bankers and lawyers and brokers, set for life. It did not have to ruin anyone else's life, what happened to Martha. And how sad, to be so drunk that this kind of thing happened to you. To let it happen, like standing out in a lightning storm, as if no one else had control over what they did to you, not when you were so pretty you were like a walking wound.

Chapter Thirteen

Bill met us at the hospital, and I'd never been so relieved to see anyone in my life. It was hard to explain. When I caught sight of him in the waiting room, leaning forward in the seat in his leather jacket and jeans, his shaggy hair around his ears, I knew he would help me, as if I was eighteen again and going to him for advice with essays and tutors and things Mike had said to upset me.

He saw me. 'Christ, what happened?'

I ran to him, breathing in his smell of soap and leather. I forgot Cassie was there, I think. I sort of fell into him, clutching his arms. 'He *stabbed* him.'

'I know.' Gently, he detached himself and put his arm around my shoulders. 'Cassie, are you alright?'

She was white, her top still smeared with blood. 'It's – it's Dad's. It's not mine.'

'Have they brought him in?' My eyes were swivelling, looking for a doctor or anyone to ask. The ambulance had come so quickly, within minutes it seemed, and the paramedics said to follow them straight over. Everyone was so calm. It was amazing, really. Here was the worst moment of my life, terrible seconds crowding on top of each other until it seemed things could hardly get worse, and there they were in their reflective coats, the ambulance and court officers and the police, putting it all calmly back together just as fast as we kicked it to pieces.

'Let's go and see, shall we.' It occurred to me that Bill was one of those people. The ones who put things back together, who helped in a crisis. Who made meals and washed dishes and held hands. On top of all the other feelings, I was hit by a terrible regret that we'd lost each other, that I hadn't seen him in so long, not since Jodi and Callum's wedding, where even then he'd ignored me most of the night. My fault, like so much else. But I couldn't think about that now.

We made our way to the reception desk, which was crowded with people looking lost and confused. Legs propped on chairs and rags clutched to heads. A man in the corner was raving to himself, facing the wall. The receptionist, a middle-aged woman with thick blonde streaks in her hair, looked cross. 'You'll have to wait. You'll have to wait. Have a seat. Have a seat.' She said it over and over, till the words seemed to lose all meaning.

When we'd fought our way to the front, I said, 'Mike Morris?' Fully expecting to be told the same. But instead her gaze lifted from the computer screen. She picked up her phone and murmured into it. It sounded like *the wife's here*. And the trails of fear were back, like snails crawling down my skin.

I turned to Bill. 'Keep Cassie out here.' He nodded. Then there was someone at my elbow, a doctor in green scrubs, or maybe not a doctor, maybe a nurse. I didn't know how to tell.

'Mrs Morris? Can you come with me please?'

The hospital was full of activity, in that hushed controlled way. I tried to be comforted by it, by the soothing tone of the doctor or nurse's voice, the beep of machines and swish as we pushed through automatic doors. He was saying something: '. . . husband was quite badly injured . . .'

'Is he alright?' My voice was too loud but I couldn't seem to control it.

'He's stable for now. I'm afraid there was extensive damage to his liver where the knife went in. He also has a head trauma, from where he fell on the pavement.'

'Is he awake?'

'I'm afraid not. We'd try to keep him under in any case. He'll need a head CT but we're waiting for the neurologist to come in. Busy weekend, you know. We're a little backed up.'

I followed dully, waiting to be told where to go, where to sit. It was easier in a way, surrendering like this. I remembered it from being in hospital having the kids. The comfort of it, giving up all responsibility for yourself. Mike was being looked after, capable strangers putting their hands on his body, cutting off his expensive suit. But still I was afraid.

Behind the scenes was chaos. In three cubicles doctors were working fast, and I saw a child struggling and screaming on a bed, her arms livid with burns, and on another an emaciated young woman, machines beeping round her as doctors pressed on her chest. She looked no older than Cassie, but her legs were marked with sores and cankers. A drug addict, I told myself. Outside the realms of my life. Poor girl.

We approached the last cubicle, and I felt the doctor's hand on my arm, gentle, but stopping me. 'Wait here a moment, Mrs Morris.' He pushed aside the green curtains and I heard murmured voices. My stomach lurched. The swish of the rails was a terrible sound, somehow. He was back in a second, and I noticed he was careful not to let me see past him. 'We're just taking him to surgery, I'm afraid.'

'Already?'

'We need to get into his liver . . . there's a bleed we're concerned about.' How they couched it. A bleed. Concern. Panic seemed to be creeping up from the bottom of my lungs, so that I could only breathe into the top of them, as if concrete blocks sat on my chest.

He directed me calmly back to Reception, but then he turned and I saw him dash – sprint, really – to where Mike was. I saw his face change. And I remained standing where I was, unnoticed, as seconds later a whole team rushed out of the cubicle pushing a bed with Mike on it. Someone was holding an IV bag. Someone was on the cart with him, pumping at his chest. And I could see they all were spattered in blood.

Mike's blood, all over the scrubs of the nurse running beside him, calling out codes and numbers, and the person on his chest, and the one with the IV. Mike himself I could barely see. He seemed shrunken, grey, his face settled with the awful stillness of stone. As I watched they swept him away, down the corridor and into the bowels of the hospital. I heard a loud sob, and turned to see Cassie standing behind me, watching her father wheeled away, unconscious.

Chapter Fourteen

Bill took Cassie home. He said he'd get Benji from school, and feed him too: 'Though I don't know what I can make. Does he like soused herring?' I was so grateful. I was already trying to imagine in my head how I could thank him, and failing. Karen would normally have done these things. It was her who'd come when I was having Benji, when my father finally died and I had to spend a week at my mother's, when Mike broke his ankle running and I was back and forth to hospital for three days. I wondered where she was and what she was doing. I imagined her in a flat maybe, with the kind of scuffed and bland furniture you found in cheap hotels. We'd helped women get into them from time to time. Now it was someone I knew going through this. I still couldn't take it in. Karen accusing Mike. Jake stabbing Mike. I remembered the little boy who'd throw his arms round me. *I love you, Auntie Ali.* The way he'd sat at the table and cried, so quietly, when I told him we were moving away. It was never really the same after that. I saw him running at us, the knife flashing, Cassie in his path. My head was twisted, full of blood and lies and screams. I told myself I just had to get through this. Mike just had to survive, and then we'd sort it all out.

One breath at a time.

DC Devine turned up at some point, still in his suit. He looked neat and fresh, whereas I could smell my own body, sweaty and terrified, a smear of blood on my arm that I hadn't washed off. I should have told

Cassie to take her shirt off and soak it. He sat down beside me in the waiting room. 'Have you eaten anything today?'

I shook my head. 'I'm not hungry.'

'You should drink at least. Let me get you something. Tea?'

'Thank you. Black, please.'

He came with something in a small plastic cup, tasting metallic and flat. I drank it anyway. I was dehydrated, I knew, but it seemed wrong to drink and eat while Mike was somewhere in this place, being cut open.

'Did you catch him?' I asked. 'Jake, I mean.'

'We have him in custody, yes.'

'He'd brought the knife with him. I saw him hiding it before the trial, I think. In the bushes. I think it's from our house.'

'I saw the whole thing myself, Mrs Morris. I was watching from the court steps.'

'Right, so . . . what will he be charged with? He stole the knife. That's premeditated, right? That means he planned it.' It chilled me to think of it. When had he taken it? After everything happened – or before?

Adam said nothing. He just watched me, his eyes almost sleepy. 'Are you close to Jake Rampling, Mrs Morris?'

'I was. Karen and I used to share childcare when the kids were small. But lately he's – well, you've met him. He's a teenager.' That made me think of something else. 'Would he be tried as an adult? He's almost eighteen, you know. Do you have to be eighteen for that?'

'Usually. The court can use its discretion, in certain cases.'

Like for murder? Was that what this was, an attempted murder? Jake, little Jake, trying to stab my husband? Again, the image of Cassie flashed behind my eyes, frozen as he ran towards her with the knife. The glint of it in the light, the moment I realised what it was and saw Mike hurl himself in front of her. Karen, further up the road, watching as her son did this. Had she called out? Tried to stop him? I didn't know.

'Will he be released? What if he comes here, tries again?' How vulnerable Mike was, unconscious on a bed.

He was just watching me, and I began to feel strangely ashamed. 'Mrs Morris. It's been a very difficult time. All this, so close to home . . . can I make a suggestion? Try not to think about what's going on with Jake. Focus on your family, your husband. He got bail, as you know. We have to press on with preparing for trial, despite this . . . setback.'

'He's unconscious!' I spoke too loudly again. 'They're cutting into him right now.'

'I know. But the prognosis is good with this kind of injury. The liver can regenerate.'

He spoke so calmly I had to turn my face away. As if it was a good thing, that Mike would probably recover, so they could put him on trial for rape. The thought of Karen crystallised in me again, hard and sharp like I'd swallowed a piece of glass.

'What will happen now?' It was my overriding need. To know what would happen. To plan, and make lists, and be ready. I hadn't been ready for any of the last few days and I was still scrabbling, trying to find the bottom with my feet.

'We'll let him recover. Meanwhile, the CPS will be working on the case. The defence can obviously apply to postpone the trial if he's still in here.'

'And Jake?'

He stood up. 'I can't talk to you about Jake, Mrs Morris. We'll need to get statements from you, and your daughter. We have him in custody, I can tell you that.'

That should have been plenty, enough to keep him somewhere safe and away from Mike, at least until we could sort this all out, find out what on earth he'd been thinking. So why did I feel this fear still, this terrible slippery fear that the thing was not over? That the events set in motion on Saturday night were like a Greek tragedy, and would continue to unfurl until everything was destroyed?

'It was like I didn't know him,' I said. 'Like he – like he wanted to kill us all.' Jake was like family. I'd practically brought him up, and now he'd tried to kill my husband. And Adam was there looking at me with his steady kind gaze, as if it saw all the way through me. 'He's not safe. I mean, he's not, is he? You saw. Mike's in danger if he's free. And my daughter, even. I think he might have tried to . . .' I swallowed hard, struggling to put it all into words, how a boy I had loved was suddenly an object of terror to me. How I knew I had to, as Mike had done, throw myself between him and Cassie. Just keep him away from my family, until we could sort all this out. If we ever could. 'He needs help. He can't be out in the world, hurting people. Right?'

He just nodded. 'Try to get some rest. You'll be no use to anyone if you collapse.'

◆ ◆ ◆

I waited in the hospital for hours, bloodied and exhausted, until eventually they told me Mike was out of surgery. Alive, at least, but he wouldn't wake up for ages. There was no point in me being there. I drove home through the town, realising I had no idea what time it was. Late, probably. The streets were empty, that worn-out feeling of delayed shock that comes after a long, hot weekend. Everyone else would have gone to work today, Callum, Jodi back in their offices, where things made sense. The rest of us, me and Mike and Karen and Jake, our lives were stopped short. I wondered if Benji had been OK at school. Would people know? Would he be bullied for it? Our house looked used and discarded, police tape still fluttering over the gate and the lawn trodden in strange footprints. I imagined the neighbours knew all about it. They wouldn't be happy – there was an Alveston Lane Neighbourhood Watch association, just for the four houses on this road. I parked up and walked over the grass, and it felt cold and slimy somehow. The table in the garden hadn't been cleared because the police had been searching the lawn, so I scooped up armfuls of crockery and glasses. There was a wine glass marked with Karen's dark pink lipstick, a little heart of colour smeared on to it. Everything was swimming in rain and dirt, and there were smears of food on the table. I couldn't carry it all but I had to. I was staggering back over the lawn when Bill came out. He was wearing jeans and a heavy jumper and flip-flops.

'Ali, I'll do that.'

I was almost panting. 'It's all dirty. It's so dirty.'

'Well, we'll clean it up. Cassie and I have made a start.' I saw her slim shape through the window, white and insubstantial. 'Benji has homework,' Bill said. 'We just got a pizza. I hope that's OK.'

'Of course.' I told myself it didn't matter if the kids ate badly for one night.

'How's Mike?'

'He's . . . stable, at least. They wouldn't really tell me much more. He's not awake.' He was taking the plates from me, his hands big and capable. 'Thank God you're here, Bill. I don't know what I'd do otherwise.' I followed him back inside, noticing that the kitchen was clean, the dishwasher rumbling, the counters wiped down. He'd folded the dishcloth on the counter, neat, but different to what Mike would do, which was hang it over the cupboard handle. 'Thank you for this. I think coming back to an untidy place would have finished me off.'

'You remember Leyton Road?'

I smiled reflexively. 'They practically had to condemn it after we moved out. We were disgusting. Except for you.' It was Bill who'd kept that kitchen and bathroom tidy in our shared house during second year, the only one who'd actually learned that you had to clean up after yourself as an adult. The rest of us filled it with burnt pans and ashtrays and pants drying to a crisp on radiators. 'Is Cassie OK?' She had flitted out of the room as I came in, as if driven away by my presence.

He was stacking the plates from the garden by the sink. 'She's very quiet. In shock, maybe. There were a few phone calls – I think her school friends, though they sounded more confident than most adults I know. She wouldn't take them. Not answering her mobile either.'

'They all are at that school. I didn't want her going there, but . . . well, Mike thought the comp wasn't good enough. It had terrible results.' I sat down at the table, enjoying how scrubbed and clean it was. Even the floor had been washed. I looked but the blood spot was still there, a small indelible stain. 'Don't you wish we'd had that kind of confidence? God, I was such a little mouse at Oxford. I wasted all those opportunities.'

'You wouldn't have been you if you'd been confident. Not that kind of confident, anyway.' He paused for a moment, rinsing plates. 'I saw you on TV, you know. I streamed it.'

'Oh.'

'You were brilliant. You took him apart, but not like you were angry or irrational or any of those things people say about feminists. Like you were his mum telling him off or something.'

'That's how I tried to imagine it. What I'd do if Benji comes home in a few years' time and starts with this sexist crap they all seem to pick up. Where do they get it from?'

'The internet, I imagine. It wasn't like that for me growing up in Leeds. I only got what my mum told me. You remember her?'

'Of course. Amazing woman.' Bill's mother had raised him alone after his father died, despite barely speaking the language.

'Yeah. She liked you.'

I was remembering that Bill's mother had died a few years ago. I hadn't gone to the funeral. We were barely in touch then, which had been the case for the past twenty or so years, until he sent that email to us all a few months back, saying he was coming home, he and Astrid were over, and I'd had my bright idea. A reunion. Twenty-five years. If only I'd known. I should have gone to the funeral anyway. 'I'm sorry, Bill. It must have been hard.'

'Well, she was all I had, really. I knew I'd lose her sometime. But when she went it was — like I didn't really know where to put myself in the world. I had a rough time after it. Astrid had to look after me.'

I was surprised by the pang of something that struck me. Something like jealousy, or more likely sadness at the friendship we could have had all these years. Had I not made the choices that I did. 'Have you spoken to her?'

He shrugged again. 'We're over. She wasn't expecting me back or anything. I was sort of planning to drift. There's . . . well, there's no one waiting for me.'

'So . . . you could stay for a bit? I mean only if you can. I know it's a lot to ask.'

It seemed to me that it was a long time before he answered. 'I'll stay.'

Bill was making me a sandwich. There was plenty of food left over from the weekend, he assured me. I should go and have a bath and relax. I doubted that would be possible, but a certain feeling of peace did engulf me as I sank into the hot perfumed water. I loved this bathroom, with its old cracked tub and antique sink. Another reason I'd begged Mike to buy the place, despite the dodgy wiring and leaky roof. I'd kept the original eau de nil tiles, scrubbing them up and filling in any cracks, and arranged white towels in piles, a wicker laundry basket, photos in white frames. Of course, going for that interiors-mag feel was deeply pointless when you had a teenage girl spilling make-up everywhere and a little boy walking in mud and grass, but I tried. I always tried, that was the point. Right now, there were blades of grass smudged on the floor under the sink, and I wondered would the house ever feel truly clean again.

I sank deeper into the water, feeling my back muscles soften. I tried to take stock. Mike in hospital, stable after his surgery, but unconscious. His liver held together with stitches and hope. And when he recovered, if he recovered, then a trial, and maybe prison.

But he wouldn't go to prison. He wasn't guilty. I still couldn't believe he'd ever hurt a woman. He was a liar, yes, and a cheat, and I hadn't known any of those things about him, but he wasn't violent. I knew the signs of that and he'd shown none. Hadn't I looked for it, all the way back at university? I wasn't stupid. I knew that if you came from a home where violence was normal, it felt comforting to seek it out again, though of course you wouldn't realise you were doing that. You'd think you'd chosen a man who was loving, and passionate, and intense, until the day you said the wrong thing or made the tea the wrong way and he'd throw the cup right in your face. That was not Mike, despite the lies. Sure, he got stressed at work, and yelled now and then, but everyone did that. If anything, he was more patient with the kids than I was. I'd lost count of how many screaming rows between Cassie and me had been defused by Mike, with a few well-chosen words. And there must be lots of trials that ended with acquittals. That was the whole point, surely.

There was a knock at the door. Soft, inconspicuous, unlike the way Mike roused me from the bath when he couldn't find his running shoes or thermos or Fitbit.

'Ali?' said Bill.

'Yeah?' I was naked on the other side of the door. He must know that. It felt wrong, somehow. Too intimate, him there and me in here, in the silky water. I could hear him breathing, and I flashed back suddenly to the kitchen, the night of the party. We hadn't talked about it – if it had even been a thing. There was a pause.

'Um . . . sorry to disturb you but I think you should know . . . Karen's here.'

Jake

'Oi. Posh boy.'

He didn't look round. Already his hands were trembling, his breath catching in his lungs. *Don't be scared. Just stop it. Stop it.*

'What you in for then?' A kid – he looked about fourteen – was calling to him across the rec room. Jake had been sitting in it on an uncomfortable plastic seat for – oh, he couldn't remember. Hours. Days. Over and over, every time he closed his eyes or couldn't manage to hold the thought back like a door in the wind, he saw it. Mike going down. The way he'd held up his hands, the way he'd jumped in front of Cassie, like Jake was going to hurt her. The way Mike's face had changed, from thinking *Oh it's Jake, Jake won't hurt me* to *Shit he's going to*. And then the look when the knife had gone in. The terror. No one had ever been afraid of Jake before, and the power was terrifying in itself. He'd made that happen to Mike, Mike who he'd first known as part of Uncle-Mike-and-Auntie-Ali, then Cassie's dad – and Jake had no dad of his own – but also as the man who came round sometimes without Cassie or Auntie Ali, and when he went away his mother cried. Jake was not supposed to tell when he came round, but one time he forgot and then his mum and Mike went quiet, and Auntie Ali looked between them, and his mum quickly said something about having to go, and it was all fine, but Jake knew he'd made a big mistake. He was seven, but he knew this was something he was meant to lie about. Even to Cassie, his best friend. Not long after that, Ali and Mike and Cassie and the bump in Ali's tummy moved away, and Jake knew it was all his fault. His mother cried even more then, in the kitchen when Jake was supposed to be sleeping on the other side of the thin wall. Back then, he'd sworn not to trust the Morrises again, not ever. They pretended you were family, but then didn't mean it. They didn't mean anything.

Something hit him on the face and he flinched. A bit of paper, soggy with spit.

'I said, what you in for?'

He cleared his throat. 'Stabbed someone.'

The kid whistled. He was skinny, his arms like broom handles, and he had freckles all over his white face. 'No shit?'

'Yeah.'

'Who'd ya stab, fella?'

Jake shrugged. 'This guy. He hurt my mum.'

The boy was nodding. 'You stood up for her. Good on ya.'

'He hurt her . . .' Jake cleared his throat. He wasn't going to cry in here. No way. No matter what. 'He hurt her bad.' It was a joke, this kid calling him posh boy. When the only holidays he and his mum ever had were on the Morrises' charity. When his trainers were from Tesco. His bloody mum, making him not one thing or the other. Going to Oxford but failing, so she couldn't even get a proper job. Giving him a posh-ish accent but no dad and no money. Landing him here, because you had to defend your mum when someone hurt her, no matter who he was. She'd been so drunk. So drunk and so stupid, like a twenty-year-old, a girl half her age. If a girl at his school acted like that they'd call her a slut. But it was his mum. And look what had happened.

If only he hadn't gone to the garage, left her drunk with the men. Laughing, shouting almost, remembering their oh-so-fun time at Oxford. His phone had lit up with a text from Cassie as he climbed the stairs to Mike's stupid office. *This one time, at Oxford, we stayed up past eleven o'clock!*

He'd smiled and texted back. *LOL. So you gonna do it or what?*

She replied with a shrugging emoji.

Mate, don't, he'd texted back. *You'll regret it, honest.*

Cassie was a terrible liar. She always had been, even when they were little and her mum was on the warpath asking who'd eaten all the bourbons. So when she said she was going to bed, Jake knew exactly what she meant. He went into Mike's 'den'. His mum's wheelie case was on the floor, her clothes spilling out of it, and the cover on the sofa bed already messed up. When they'd arrived, his mum had said something about wanting to change and sent him up to Cassie's room, but then she'd taken ages, almost an hour.

He could see the light in Cassie's window as he sent another message. *Are u going to c him?*

She didn't reply for a while but he knew she would. In the mean-time he concentrated on what a twat Mike was, with his boring DVDs and his drinks cabinet shaped like a jukebox and the red leather arm-chair, like a gentleman's study. When he was little his mum had pushed him to spend time with Mike – *boys' day out!* – thinking he needed a male role model or something like that, but Jake had made it clear he didn't like football or golf or any other stupid male bonding activities, so it had stopped.

None of your business. Cassie had texted back, after a while.

Don't do it.

Cassie sent back an angry-faced emoji and Jake knew she'd do it anyway, sneak out to see that guy, and he'd pressure her, and she'd give in, and then he'd throw her away like a bit of tissue he'd wanked into. Anger swelled into him and he got up, walking round the room. The urge to smash something was strong. What if he broke one of Mike's DVDs and put it back in the case? He was willing to bet they were never watched and that Mike spent all his time up here clicking through internet porn instead.

Nothing after that. Cassie was ignoring him, going ahead with her stupid plan, and his mother was outside on the lawn laughing too loudly, and he was alone. He'd kicked the side of Mike's desk to relieve some feelings, but after that he'd sat down on the sofa bed and kind of got into one of Mike's lame DVDs – *The Hangover!* FFS – and so he hadn't realised things had gone quiet in the garden. Hadn't known his mum was being attacked, until she started screaming, then Ali was running out shouting *Mike, Mike.* She was almost worse than Mike. So patronising, with her birthday presents and little questions. *How are you, Jake? How's the uni search going, Jakey? Got a girlfriend, Jakey?* She was so fake, they both were. He didn't know why his mum was still friends with them. Callum and Jodi were even worse, always competing over who could cook the fanciest dinner or go on the most expensive holiday. This new guy, Bill, he was alright, but the rest could go suck it.

'Rampling?' Back in the here and now, one of the guards was calling him. They weren't too bad. In fact it wasn't too bad at all in here, there were video games and TVs and you could wear your own clothes.

'You're in for it now,' said his new friend, whatever his name was. 'Don't tell 'em nothing, y'hear?'

He stood up. The guard beckoned. 'Your mother's here.'

He hoped his new-found mate hadn't heard that, but the kid was engrossed in Mario Kart. No violent games allowed. Jake was led out through door after door, clanging shut behind him until he stood in the visitors' room, and there was his mum, the bruises on her neck standing out against the white of her skin. The anger rose up in him again, at Mike, at Ali, at his mum. All of them.

'What do you want?' He hated her, for letting this happen, and he also loved her, so much he'd put his hand through the glass of the window if she needed him to.

'Sweetheart.' She swallowed, and he saw her throat move underneath the bruises. 'There's something I have to tell you.'

Chapter Fifteen

I was leaving big damp footprints on the grey landing carpet, hastily tying the silk robe Mike had bought me for Christmas. 'She's here? In the house?'

'Should I not have let her in? It's raining.'

It occurred to me again how ridiculous this whole thing was. How could I ask Bill to lock our friend outside in the rain? 'Of course. It's fine.' A lurch of fear went through me. The last time she'd been in my house, look what had happened. Everything smashed and broken.

He followed me down and melted into the kitchen. 'I'm here if you need me. Should I bring tea or something?'

'No. No, it's fine.' I didn't want to be reminded of the hundreds, thousands of times Karen and I had drunk tea together, all the way through from university to this house. She even had her own mug, a lumpy one Cassie had made in nursery school and insisted belonged to 'Auntie Karen'. I paused with my hand on the living room door. I wasn't sure I could do this. But I had to.

Karen was sitting in semi-darkness, and it took me a moment to spot her in the living room on the grey marl sofa. I'd been so pleased when the room was finished, adding the final touches of duck-egg blue cushions and throws and ornaments. Just looking into it usually gave me a feeling of happiness, of peace. Not tonight. I fumbled for a lamp and she appeared to me. She looked terrible. Hair unbrushed – and I hadn't realised how much grey there was in it – face crumpled, dressed in a baggy grey sweatshirt. Her hands were rammed between her thighs. 'I . . . Ali.'

I sat down opposite her on the matching sofa, laying my own hands on my legs, pulling the dressing gown over me. 'Are you alright?' My voice sounded stiff.

'I . . . not really.' She struggled with the answer. 'I – Ali, I never meant for this to happen.'

'Which bit?' How cold I was. 'Karen, Christ – I don't even know what to say. What's going on? Should you even be here?' I was pretty sure we weren't meant to be talking.

She looked down at her feet, which were in Converse, leaving tracks of mud on the carpet. 'Probably not. But I had to. I didn't make it up.' Her voice was small. 'It really happened, Ali. Look at my – look at me.' She pulled her collar aside so I could see the bruises on her neck, thumb prints clear as ink. 'I know you don't want to believe it. I didn't want to either. That's why I think I – I think I froze at first, I was so shocked, and then it was. Too late.'

'But you'd had sex with him hours before. Literally hours.' My voice was hard and brittle. 'Hadn't you?'

Karen paled even more. 'He told you that?'

'Yeah, he told me that's why you came early, so you could fuck him while I was away.' I didn't recognise myself speaking. 'Christ, why? After all this time? Why now?'

Karen paused. 'He said it was only one time?'

There is a certain feeling when the worst happens, and the bottom falls out of your world, and you somehow pick yourself up from that and stabilise, adjust. There is another feeling when you suddenly find out this is not the worst, not by a long way. 'Wh-what?' I could hardly push the words out of my mouth. 'It wasn't?' My mind scrolled back through the years. University? When Jake was born, and Karen used to stay with us a lot, desperate to get away from her houseshare? When Cassie was born? Weddings, christenings, parties. All of them suddenly covered in a greasy film.

She said, in a flat voice: 'I slept with Mike the first night I met him.'

'But that was . . .' That stupid photo Callum had. 'That was the night he met *me*!' All this time I'd treasured the memory. Oh yes, Mike and I met on the first night of university, inseparable ever since. The next day we'd gone for a walk over Magdalen Bridge in the cold October sunshine, both of us in blue and yellow college scarves, talking about all the nothings of our lives the way you do when you're eighteen, and after that we were just a thing. Ali and Mike. We had our ups and downs, sure, but somehow we kept going, as all our peers hooked up and broke up and moved systematically between each other's beds. But that first night, after I'd gone to bed, still a virgin and the worse for wear on four peach schnapps and lime, Mike and Karen had. Done that. I shook my head in disbelief, as if trying to clear water from my eyes. 'I don't believe you.'

'It's true, Ali. I mean, God, way more off than on, but it's been years now. If he said it was just once, he was lying.'

I gripped the edge of the sofa. 'When I was having Benj. When I had to stay in hospital that week.' Karen had come down, helping to look after Cassie, then just five.

She just nodded.

'When my dad died?' Mike had been so sweet to me then, rubbing my back as I cried myself to sleep for ten nights in a row, holding the fort at home while I went north to help my mother clear out the house.

'Yes. Ali – you realise it hurts my case. If we had a previous . . . relationship. I'm telling you so you know I'm not lying that he hurt me.'

'But you lied all those other times!'

She looked at her feet. 'I didn't lie. I just . . . never told you. Jesus, Ali, what would I have said? I love you. You're my best friend. But him and me – it's like some drug you can't quit. When I saw him on Saturday . . .'

'I don't believe you! You're lying!'

'Why would I lie?'

'I don't know!' To hurt me, I was thinking. To take everything I had and crush it. 'Why would he do – what you're saying, if it was going on for years? It doesn't make sense.'

She paused. 'We'd ended it. That day.'

'He said *he* ended it.' Or rather, he'd said she'd come on to him, moment of weakness, never again etc. And how easily I'd believed him.

Karen stared at the ground. 'Ali, I don't know. Clearly, he lies sometimes. And anyway, just because we – I still didn't want it later on. He still forced me. That's still – Ali, I shouldn't have to tell you this. You know what rape is.'

I bit down hard on my lip. 'How did you know it was him? You were drunk. All of you were so drunk. And it was dark out there.'

'I . . . Ali, for God's sake. Who else was there? No one got into the garden. The police already checked.'

'There was Callum. There was . . . Bill . . .' And there was the problem. If it had to be someone, then it had to be either my husband or these friends of ours.

'Cal had passed out, you know that. He was hammered, and we'd smoked all that weed. And Bill had gone to bed ages before, and – I think I'd know the difference in six foot four and five foot nine, Al.' Her usual tone had crept through, even in all this. Karen the wise and cool, showing me the ropes. Teaching me about real life. 'Anyway, I *know* him. His jumper. His smell . . . I know him, Ali. Even if I was drunk. I'd have thought you, of all people, would know that shouldn't matter.'

'Maybe he didn't know. Maybe he thought you'd say yes – if you had so many times before.' I was clutching at straws now and I knew it. I'd lost this fight, lost it comprehensively, and now I was throwing punches, trying to hurt her maybe. As if she hadn't been hurt enough. I'd seen that, hadn't I, the bruises? She hadn't made it up? But he couldn't have. He *couldn't* have. I was looking for a way for this all to fit, for Mike not to be a rapist and Karen not a liar. Maybe that didn't exist.

She pulled on her collar again. 'He knew. And even if he hadn't, I was way too drunk to consent. Again, Ali, I know you're not thinking straight, but hear what you're saying. You. I was drunk and maybe I wanted it because we slept together before? Come on.'

'You're saying you slept together for years! Twenty-five years, behind my back!' It burst out of me. 'What the hell?' Did I even believe her? Mike had said just one time.

'I know.' She looked at the floor again. 'I should say sorry, I know that. And I am sorry for hurting you. God, I'd never want to hurt you, not ever. You're . . . But there was just this thing, between us, this terrible dark thing that I couldn't stop. We'd try but it . . . it always came back. Sooner or later. From the moment we met, that's how it was, and I watched him with you all these years, and I didn't say anything because I loved you too.'

'Not enough not to sleep with my husband.' I was crying now, tears falling on to my already damp robe, and Karen was screwing up her face, wiping the back of her hand over her eyes.

'I know. I know. There's nothing I can say. But none of that means this didn't happen. Believe me, I wish it hadn't.' Her voice broke. 'I don't feel safe anywhere. Not in bed, not in an interview room. I can't sleep or eat or even lie down and I . . . I don't know if I ever will again. He took that.'

'What do you want?' I said desperately. 'Why did you come here? I'm sorry that you're hurt, truly I am, and I wish I could help, but how can I? What am I supposed to do?'

'I came for Jake.'

Then, I understood what she wanted from me. 'I can't . . . even if . . . Karen, it's not up to us. The police actually saw it happen. He'll get done for assault.'

'They're saying attempted murder. You know how long you get for that? A life sentence, could be. He's only seventeen, Ali, but they could try him as an adult. You could – you could say that's not what you want. Say he's not like this, not normally. He's a good boy, he's not dangerous. Or that it was an accident, he didn't mean to hurt Mike. He just slipped.'

I hesitated. 'But Karen, you know that's not true. You were worried yourself. Remember?' A few years ago, she'd taken Jake to a psychiatrist, concerned about the amount of time he spent in his room, his lack of friends, his sullen manner.

She recoiled. 'That's not fair! It's a totally different thing. He's never been violent.'

'Karen, I saw him stab Mike! Right in front of me! He's still unconscious! And Cassie was there too, and she could have been hurt, she . . . I'm sorry this has happened, God knows I am. I wish none of it was true and we could just reset to Saturday morning. But we can't. I can't lie to the police. And if Jake gets out, he might try to hurt Mike again. He needs help, Karen. Let him get it.'

She just looked at me. I looked back. And I felt the years of our friendship, the foundations of it under me, crumble away to nothing. She spoke so quietly at first I could hardly hear her. 'I did it for you.'

'What?'

'Martha. I helped you.'

I opened my mouth to say it wasn't the same at all, that had nothing to do with this, and I realised I was echoing Mike.

'That night, Ali – he was with me. But not the whole time.'

I stood up. 'You need to go.'

Karen nodded. She stood too.

Bill was hovering in the kitchen, and Karen turned back to give me a look on her way out. I saw in a flash how it must appear to her. Him with the tea towel over his shoulder, the rumble of the dishwasher, the smell of pizza. Me in my dressing gown, naked and still soapy underneath. The domesticity of it all. As if Bill, the one who'd gone with her to the assault centre, the worst moment of her life, had chosen sides. Had chosen me. Karen said nothing as she left, but she didn't need to. There were no words left.

Chapter Sixteen

'Will he wake up?' Benji's voice quavered as he watched his dad. Mike was grey and still, a terrible looseness in his face that told me he wasn't simply asleep. Benji was in his school uniform, shirt creased with a smear of bright green marker on the collar. His face needed a scrub. Cassie, on the other hand, looked like she'd touched up her make-up before coming to the hospital. She hadn't been back to school yet – she'd begged me to let her stay off, and I couldn't find it in me to force her. Her face was like a doll's, smooth with foundation, and her hair wafted hairspray as she moved. It was the next day. Time unspooling away from the night it happened, already Tuesday afternoon. I wanted to gather up these broken, fractured days, and run back and dump them in a heap, start again from Saturday. Not go to the meeting with Vix and Julie. Not let everyone get so drunk. Not go to bed when I did.

'He'll wake up,' I said, though I wasn't at all sure. The doctors were being cagey with me, comforting but vague. 'He hit his head, so he just needs to rest it for a while.'

'Jake did it.' Benji's lip was trembling too. 'Why did he do it?'

I looked at Cassie; she turned away. I said, 'Because. He was very angry and upset, and he lashed out. I'm sure he didn't mean to hurt Daddy.'

'He meant to.' Cassie's voice was low and hard. 'He looked right at me and he did it.' Benji bit his lip. His eyes were full of tears, glassy and about to fall. 'Dad threw himself in front of me,' she told him. 'He was really brave.'

'Jake wouldn't have hurt you, darling.'

She looked at me. 'He hurt Dad. Did you ever think he'd do that?'

I thought of Jake, the sweet shy boy who'd come to my house every day after school until he was seven and we moved away. Crying on the day we left, the tears sliding down his nose and landing on the Jammy Dodger I'd given him to try and sweeten the blow. He hadn't touched it, as if it was a point of principle. Even though I told myself we had to do what was best for our family, I'd found it hard to shake the feeling I'd abandoned Jake. Abandoned Karen. That we'd left a part of the family behind us.

At least it must have stopped after that. The affair. Not an affair, he'd pleaded. Just the one time. And Karen saying no, it had infiltrated every moment I'd known both of them. Most of my life. Who was lying? The truth of this was for me a double-edged sword. Either the affair was real, in which case he'd lied to me, or she was making it up to hurt me. But why would she damage her own case like this? And if it was real, why would he rape her? I knew intellectually this was not how rape worked, but all the same I couldn't get my head to accept it.

I looked at Mike, his slack face with the tube pushing his lips out. Grotesque. He would have hated this. There were so many things I would have asked him. What really happened? I wanted dates, times, details. I wanted to go back to every photo, every memory, and have him tell me which ones I needed to burn and slash. Which ones were spoiled forever by what they'd done. Really, I wanted him to tell me it wasn't true. Karen was a liar. None of this was real.

I thought of what Karen had said the night before. Martha. Bringing it up after all these years. The memories gave me a sick feeling in the pit of my stomach. What did she mean, saying that?

I looked at the clock on the wall. Already five. I had to get the kids home, feed them, soothe them somehow, keep them on the rails. Cassie had her exams. Benji had SATs and football try-outs and God knows what else. It seemed never-ending, the hoops they had to jump through. And another worry was nagging at me – I had to speak to their schools and Mike's firm. If he got suspended, what did that mean for his salary? The money I brought in barely covered food for the month.

'Come on, guys, we should go.'

'We can't leave Dad here by himself!' Benji's voice was thick with tears.

'He doesn't know we're here, sweetheart.'

'You don't know that. I saw a programme where people were in comas and they could hear voices and they knew you were there and everything.'

I put my hand on his head, the springy soft hair that was so hard to brush. 'Maybe he can, darling, you're right. But he'd want us to go home and have dinner and do homework. You know he would.'

'Mrs Morris. Hello Cassie, Benji.' It was DC Adam Devine, sounding genial and relaxed. Benji brightened to see him; he thought being a policeman was cool, like in *Kindergarten Cop*. Catching the bad guys, keeping us safe. But who was the bad guy in this case? Benji's father?

Adam met my eyes and a chill went through me – what now? Could there be anything else he had to tell me? Surely we were at rock bottom now? 'Cass, will you take Benj to the snack bar?'

'Can I get cake?' said Benji. Cassie scowled. She felt her brother was getting too fat.

'Of course, baby.' I fumbled a tenner into Cassie's hand, pleading with my eyes. *Please. Don't judge me. Cut me some slack.*

DC Devine watched them go, then looked at me.

'What is it?' My voice was trapped in my throat, fluttering like the birds that sometimes got into our chimney.

'We should sit down.' He guided me to a rack of chairs at the end of the corridor, upholstered in pale green pleather. I wondered how much bad news had been delivered between these walls. I did as he asked, adopting the same straight-backed ready-for-a-job-interview stance I'd taken while speaking to Karen last night.

'What is it?'

'Jake Rampling's bail hearing is tomorrow.'

'Will they keep him in?'

He screwed up his face. 'It depends. If they think he poses a danger, they might.'

'And if they let him out, and he comes here? If he tries to hurt Mike again?' It was unthinkable, Jake in jail, but if the alternative was him coming here and stabbing my children's father, it had to be done. 'So you came to tell me – what, he might get out?'

'There's something else you should know. Something that might affect the case.'

I waited. I had learned, already, to wait for the blows, bracing myself.

'Ms Rampling is claiming . . . she's stated that Jake is your husband's son. That Mike is his father.'

Karen

The police had helped her find a small flat to stay in while Jake was in custody. A living room with a strip of kitchen and cupboard of a bathroom, a small bedroom. Nicer than many flats she'd lived in when she first had Jake. She wondered where he was now, what kind of cell he was sleeping in. Even though it hurt her like an ache below her heart, to imagine him in there, she also knew she couldn't bear to have him here. Pitying. Picturing her like that, helpless and hurt and bleeding. She hated it.

Karen lay down carefully on the borrowed bed, the sheets that bit more shabby and worn than you'd get in a hotel. Wondering about the other people who'd passed through here, the victims and witnesses, the scared and the fleeing. The act of lying down, of being horizontal, itself brought flashbacks, and she left the light on so it burned behind her eyes, and, realising it was inevitable, allowed the memories of the night before to return to her.

In her head it was like a film, except one she was in, one she was reliving, but which she could do nothing to change or stop. It was that night – the night that had changed her. She was so drunk. Forty-three years old, a son almost off to college, and she was swaying like a student during freshers' week, fuzzy round the edges, words sticking in her mouth. The grass was cool under her bare feet – she'd felt sexy earlier, bohemian, in her short dress with her smooth legs. At least she had that, even if she'd messed up her degree and career and never made anything of herself. At least she still looked young, alongside Jodi, like an inflated white pudding, and Ali so prim in her sack-like dress and her sunglasses like an Alice band on her hair. Ali had always been like this – lower-middle-class respectability to the core, a make-up-thin layer of college rebellion on top. Shots in night clubs. Blushing, her blouse undone, on bop night. And he loved her, he went back to her every time, but still he couldn't leave Karen alone.

Mike. Like her shadow, like an old illness she thought she'd recovered from that crept back into her bones, so that every time Karen thought she'd moved on there he was. Carl the electrician, a decent simple man; Jim the university lecturer with the ex-wife and two blonde daughters. OK, neither perfect, but both a chance for her to have a life, a husband of her own at these get-togethers instead of waiting for scraps from Ali's table. Like a messed-up harem, but Ali didn't even know she was in one. Rearranging the plates while under their feet roared a vast fault line. How could Karen do this, sleep with her best friend's husband? It was like being two people at once. She loved Ali, she'd go after anyone who hurt her. But she'd also slept with Ali's husband, over and over, time and time again as the years went by. She'd try to stop, get on with her life – she'd even moved to Birmingham to try and end it – and then Ali would say *we really must all get together*, and Karen would walk into a room and see him and it would all start again.

She and Mike knew the dark core of each other. Even though he'd said that afternoon it was over – *I can't do this any more, it's not fair to Ali* – even though Karen felt the blow like a slow-leaking wound she'd been walking around on all night, covering her pain with bright, flirty laughter, even with all that, part of her knew it likely wasn't over this time either. She had lied to Ali about that, she wasn't sure why. Trying to salvage some pride, maybe. They'd been here before, after all – all the way through university on and off, sneaking to his room when she was meant to be in the library; surely the reason she'd failed her Finals. A tense drink in a Wetherspoons near London Bridge when he'd moved out here, a tearful alleyway shag before Karen went to Birmingham. The elastic lines between them pinging back each time. Then the guilty meetings in London, the afternoons in the pub when he was supposed to be working, the Megabus down, Mike putting his wedding ring on the bedside table of the hotel room you could rent for the afternoon. She hated the fact he planned ahead like that. She wanted it to always be overwhelming, something primal between them. Because how else could she justify sleeping with her best friend's husband?

She couldn't. She'd always known that. But still, the thing that was between them, it did not go away, it did not die, it just kept getting hungrier and hungrier, and sometimes the sheer power of it, of knowing she would do anything for it, hit her like a wave. It was wrong. But sometimes that didn't matter.

She'd forgotten why she was in the garden. It was dark, the lights switched off in the kitchen. Out here in the virtual countryside, the sky got very black. She was alone. Callum and Mike had wandered off in search of the loo, another drink, who knew what. She sat down hard on the patio table, bruising her coccyx. A few tears gathered in her eyes, self-pitying. Turned down by Bill – stupid, throwing herself at him like that – and dumped by Mike, all in one day. Forty-three, and her son almost grown, and nothing left to show for twenty and more years of waiting for Mike. The way he'd waited till they'd slept together before saying it. *Listen, Karen . . .* Putting his arm around Ali only minutes later, like nothing had happened. He hadn't even showered since her body had been all over him; Ali wouldn't let him.

She cried a little, in a loud animal way, through her mouth. The garden was so dark, full of rustles and sighs. She heard a noise then. Someone else stumbling on the lawn, and she was sure it must be him, and the relief made her sag and weep. He was back. It was OK. Her eyes were blurred and swollen, and it was so dark, and all she could see was the hand, the sleeve in the red jumper. She smelled his aftershave – she'd bought a bottle of it once just to remind her of him, though it was more than her budget for the week. She gave it to Carl but he didn't wear aftershave, thought it was girly. And it wasn't the same on his pale smooth skin. Not Mike. Not enough. Just . . . not him. But here he was now, and part of her might have thought, *Thank God, I was right.* Part of her might have been pleased he'd come back so soon, that he couldn't do without her.

Next thing she knew her head was twisted and she was down on the grass on her front. A rough game – not their thing really. And his breath was in her ear, heavy and wet, and she felt her skirt forced up and the world shift, like when you close one eye and open another. And since then, since Mike had forced himself into her, and she'd heard herself give out a noise of fear and pain like the ones she'd made having Jake, since she realised his hand was around her throat and *he wasn't stopping, he wasn't going to stop*, and that thing was happening to her, the thing all women are afraid of since the moment they first grow breasts, since then, nothing had shifted back again.

Chapter Seventeen

'Say something, darling.'

Cassie was staring at her feet. They were dirty and dry, I noticed, the red nail polish chipped. I should take her for a pedicure. We were in the living room, and Bill had taken Benji to the kitchen. I could hear them discussing fractions, a surreal note of domesticity. It was all the same, except for it was the wrong man. Except for Mike would never be home this early. Seven o'clock being early in his world.

'So Dad shagged her.' Her voice was flat. I couldn't bring myself to censor the swearing. In my own head I'd been swearing ever since I found out.

'You see, sweetheart, we were all friends at university, and I think they were very close, and it just . . . I supposed it spilled over from time to time.' That wild look in Karen's eyes when she talked about it, as if she saw something I could only dream of. As if I'd always been left behind.

'He shagged her for years. Jake's eighteen nearly. I bet Dad shagged her at uni too. From then to now. It's *years*, Mum.'

'I don't know if it was the whole time or . . .' She silenced me with a glare. Why was I defending them? I didn't know. 'Obviously it's a nasty shock, darling, but I don't think Daddy knew that Jake . . .'

'How could he not know? He shags her, she has a baby, there's no other dad hanging around. Jesus Christ, Mum! How could any of you not know?'

Because we hadn't wanted to. 'I'm sorry.'

'Don't you be sorry. You did nothing, Mum. He's the one who shagged her then neglected his kid. Jake's life's been ruined. He never knew his dad, he had no one, they're always broke and Karen's off with different men . . . How do you think he feels?'

'Jake is a troubled boy, darling. He always has been. You only have to look at what he did to Daddy . . .'

'Of course he's troubled! Christ, he's my – what, he's my *brother*, and I grew up here and he lives in that shithole with no money, and all his life he thinks his dad just didn't want to know him. Of course he's messed up! And it's all Dad's fault.'

'He didn't know,' I said weakly.

'What, like he didn't know he was raping her?'

I didn't know who she was, this angry, whip-smart girl in front of me, with chipped nail polish and freckles on tanned skin. I couldn't recognise her as my flesh, though I knew I'd given birth to her. Could I blame Mike for not seeing what was under his nose all this time?

'Cass, I know you're upset. Everyone's upset. What we have to do now is help Daddy.'

'How?'

I took a deep breath. 'What Karen said – that it's been going on for a long time, for years – it could help Daddy's case. Show that maybe it wasn't – what she says it was. So if you did realise that you remembered something about that night—'

She stared at me for a long time. My own eyes looking back at me, accusing. 'You're crazy. You want me to lie?'

'No! I just need to know what you saw. What you were doing that night.' I took a deep breath, steeled myself for her anger. 'Was someone else there, in the woods? Were you meeting Aaron?' I'd always tried to give Cassie her privacy, remembering how it was when I was that age. *I heard you were down the town with a boy. I won't have my daughter acting like a slut.* The slaps that would follow if I talked back, explained it was just a schoolmate, or someone I'd spoken to only once. But I had to make her tell me what she'd been doing.

Cassie was quiet for a long time. When she spoke, her voice was surprisingly calm. 'Mum, I told you. I didn't see anything. No one got into the garden. I was just . . . I couldn't sleep.'

'You didn't see Dad, or Karen, or . . .'

'I didn't see anything! I can't lie, if that's what you're saying.'

'Darling, no, not lie, it's just that we do need to show that it isn't true, that she's making it up, and . . .'

'Mum. Don't you realise? I hate Dad. I hope he goes to prison. If I were Jake I'd have tried to stab him too. So how dare you ask me. How *dare* you.'

'You have to open them sometime,' said Bill, gently. I regarded the pile of envelopes on the table. Some had come in the last few days, and some I'd found in Mike's briefcase, which was still in our room. I told myself it was OK to go through it, when he was still unconscious. Bills, letters, flyers from legal firms. I found the last particularly insulting. It meant everyone knew what we'd become, a family who needed a defence.

It was the following morning. Benji had gone off to school, clean and neatly dressed and fed, thanks to Bill. Cassie was upstairs in her room still. I had to make her go back to school this week. I was trying to pretend things were normal, and that meant doing normal things. Like opening the post.

I reminded myself the bills couldn't be that bad. Mike had only been off work for a few days. That would be covered by sick leave, surely. I picked up a thick cream envelope with the crest of Cassie's school on it. It was addressed to Mr and Mrs Michael Morris, because in their world it was 1937. I wondered why it was in Mike's briefcase, why he hadn't left it for me to open. The words swam in front of my eyes. Numbers, figures.

'I can't make head nor tail of this, can you? It's a bill?'

Bill took it from me. 'It says the fees were last paid in January. Months ago.'

I snatched it back. 'What? That can't be right. I'm calling them.'

I seized the phone and punched in the number, my hands shaking with anger. All the money we'd poured into that school and this was what happened. A stupid mix-up. Maybe Mike's account was suspended since he was in hospital. But how would the bank even know that? I thought of all the bills that were on autopay, everything down to the Netflix account. As if I needed that right now. 'Yes, hello? It's Ali Morris here. I've just had your letter.'

The school secretary was twenty-five but efficient as a cog gear. 'Good morning, Mrs Morris. It's the bursar you'd need to speak to if it's about fees.'

'Have you any idea what we're going through? My husband is in hospital, in a coma.'

'Yes, I'm very sorry to hear that.' Her voice was so cool. I was trying to think of her name. Alicia? Yes, that was it. 'But unfortunately we can't make special exceptions for . . .'

'Cassie has her exams. Does she really need this extra pressure?'

'It's just, Mrs Morris, the fees have been overdue for some time. We did write to you several times.'

What? It seemed to be happening over and over, that I would reach for a certainty I knew to be true, only to find it melted away. I'd seen nothing from the school, and Mike had never mentioned this. 'I – we never got those letters.' My mind was stumbling over it. Some mix-up at the bank? Or they had our old address still? But this one had come to the house. And Mike had, for some reason, picked it up and hidden it in his briefcase.

'Perhaps your husband . . .'

Rage swelled in me. She'd no idea what it meant to even have a husband, slog away side by side for twenty years, and then find out he'd been sleeping with your best friend on the side. 'Look, this is ridiculous. We've been paying you a fortune for years now, and you're causing an issue over a few missed bills?' Surely just some mistake. We were never late. Why would we be, when we had such a comfortable safeguard?

'You really need to speak to the bursar.'

'Put me through then.'

'He's at a conference today, I'm afraid. But there is usually a policy of barring pupils from exams if the fees aren't paid and . . .'

I slammed the phone down on her. 'Little *bitch*.' Bill was watching me in his calm way, saying nothing. 'Fine, fine, I know it's not her fault, but really. You'd think they could have a little understanding.'

Bill was sifting through the envelopes, which he'd been opening with his large hands. 'There's a lot of bills here. Too many for only a week. Do you think . . . ?'

'What?'

'I'm sorry to pry, Ali, but were you having money problems? Because a lot of these have been outstanding for a while. Look, is this Benji's school? That's overdue too.'

'I don't understand.' I looked down at the paper, spreading out and covering the table. 'I don't get it. There was plenty coming in. Thousands every month.'

Bill had been going through our bank statements, I saw, and I blushed for a moment, thinking of all the stupid purchases that would show up. Ocado delivery. Vast amounts spent at Joules, and on my weekly facial, and our last holiday. 'There seems to be a few big amounts going out,' he said, screwing up his eyes. 'Here, you see? And there. It's every month.'

I squinted at it, the columns of numbers swimming in front of my eyes. 'What's that?'

'I don't know. Looks like an account number.'

I got my phone and typed it into Google. Nothing. 'No. I don't know what it is.'

'Did Mike have any investments, things like that?'

'Not that I know of.' And I realised, thinking about it, it was quite possible I wouldn't know. I sorted the kids and the house, and he did this. Our money. The ground under our feet. I'd been stupid. I'd taken all that for granted, when in reality I had no idea whether it was solid or not, and here we were running about on top of it. 'Is there a way to find out who the account belongs to?'

'I'm sure there is. I can look into it.'

'Are you sure?'

He shrugged. 'I've got nothing to do at the moment. Let me help you. Please. I'd like to.'

It was the same thing he'd told me all those years ago, and I hadn't listened then, and look where it had got me. But sometimes it takes a long time to learn our lessons.

Chapter Eighteen

'What were you doing with the money?' I bent over Mike's face, still blank and slack. Around him the machines beeped and the leg compression socks pumped, trying to keep him from getting thrombosis. I counted the needles going into him – five in total. That seemed a lot. And there I was with so many questions, faced with this wall of silence. He wasn't awake. I knew he couldn't hear me, despite what I let Benji believe. I knew he wasn't there at all.

So these were the facts. Mike and Karen had been having an affair for twenty-five years. As long as I'd known him – in fact, if what she said was true, she'd slept with him first. Jake was Mike's son, or so she said. That meant they'd been having sex in 1999, for definite. I remembered a Millennium party, everyone very drunk, Karen and Mike disappearing. It sank into my stomach, another stone in the well. More facts: Jake's bail hearing was currently underway, and soon I would hear if he was being let out, perhaps to come after Mike and finish him off. Mike and Karen had slept together on the Saturday of our party, and later that night, Karen had accused him of raping her in the garden. And our bank accounts told me another fact – we were broke. I was waiting on a call from Mike's boss to tell me what was happening with his salary, but it was clear a lot of money had been going out somewhere, leaking like water from a dam. Where to? Did Mike in fact know Jake was his son, and was he paying for him all this time? Was the money going to Karen? Was I the only one who knew nothing?

'Wake up,' I hissed in his ear. He smelled different. Of antiseptic, and stale breath. His face didn't even flutter. He wasn't there. I didn't know where he was.

The phone in my bag buzzed and I snatched it up before the nurse could look disapproving. I took it to the corridor, trying to clear my throat. 'Hello, Ali Morris.' Was this the news about Jake?

A man's voice, measured and harried. 'Hello, this is Arthur Ravenscroft speaking.'

Mike's boss, returning the call I'd made earlier. 'Yes, hello. We met, at the Christmas do last year?'

'Of course.' He'd no idea who I was. 'We're terribly sorry to hear about Michael's accident.'

'It wasn't an accident, sadly. He was attacked.' By his own son. I wondered how much people knew. 'Mr Ravenscroft, there are some . . . discrepancies in our accounts, and I wanted to check what the position was with Mike – with my husband's salary.'

His tone changed. 'Ah. Yes. If it were just a case of sick leave, then we'd pay that for a month, then statutory thereafter, but I'm afraid we have a strict policy for employees who are accused of a crime. They're immediately suspended and we reserve the right to terminate their employment.'

My mouth was so dry I couldn't speak for a moment. 'But what if they're acquitted? If it's a false accusation.'

'There's compensation available, I believe.'

'But . . . we don't know how long it will take to come to trial. He's not even conscious.'

'I know, Mrs Morris. But the firm can't be associated with a crime of this nature. Our client base is somewhat . . . conservative. And we signed up to a zero-tolerance charter on sexual harassment. We have to distance ourselves.'

'So what – what do we do for money?' My voice was too loud, I knew. A nurse stuck her head out of a cubicle, frowning. It was undignified, but I was starting to panic. This couldn't be happening.

'I would hope that with our generous bonus scheme, Mike had savings. Or of course if the case were to collapse . . . I'm sorry, Mrs Morris. This is the policy and we're perfectly within our rights. We could have fired him already. Now, I must go. I do hope he recovers soon.'

The line went dead. So there was my answer. If I wanted to keep my home for my children's sake, I had to get Mike's case dropped, and fast.

It felt as if my whole life was bound up in Karen's, the way bindweed coiled around the plants in my garden, a loving choke, pulling them down. Karen and my husband. Karen and my daughter. Karen and my husband's son. I paced back and forward by Mike's hospital bed, unable to sit down, my pulse jumping in my veins. I found I was making a list in my head. That guy from college, what was his name? Mark Simons. Karen leading him on, in her flimsy cowgirl costume, dancing close, then running away and hiding. I remembered her leaning against my shoulder, a smell of sweet alcohol on her breath. *Oh God, he's after me now.* Poor Mark, blundering about dressed like Luke Skywalker. Of course he thought she was interested. She did it all the time, flirted enough to get their interest, then dropped them. That was all she wanted, the interest, and she took it from them like she was strip-mining, gave nothing back. Had she done it to make Mike jealous?

Other things. Karen travelling down to London with a young Jake, asking for an under-25 discount and saying he was her little brother. That holiday in Crete, a different story every night for the pink-faced boys we got talking to, on her insistence. *We're nurses. We're sisters. We're trainee zoo keepers. I do the snakes, she does the alligators.* Lies, lies. They came as easily to Karen as smiling. Karen necking the wine from the bottle, her legs bare, her skirt showing her pants. Karen flirting, touching Bill with her chipped pink toes. Leaning over the table, laughing so her shoulders shook, her cleavage wobbling. It wasn't even that funny, whatever it was.

We think we understand love – that it's simple, like a warm bath. That it's inherently a good thing, positive, a sign that we are decent people. *I love my kids*, say angry women on TV, as if they expect a pat on the back for obeying biology. I had known these facts for a long time – that I loved Cassie, and Benji. I loved Mike. And I loved Karen, like a sister, the way I hadn't been able to love my own family. But what we don't understand is that love can turn on a dime. We don't know how easy it is to feel it flip over to a dark side, cold and dead, like the moon spinning on its axis. I looked down at the list I'd made, scrawled in blue ink on the back of Mike's hospital notes. *Lies. Booze. Shagging around.* There was so much I could add to that one. The married man – the other married man – she was carrying on with for two years, the one who shagged her in his office after hours, leaning on the window in the boardroom looking over Canary Wharf. God. Was that *Mike*? Would she do that to me, tell me stories of my own husband, just to watch me try to be OK with the cheating? I was so uncool compared to her. Yes, I believed she would do that. I believed anything of Karen, now.

I stared down at the list, noting where the pen had scored right through the paper, realising how unhinged it made me seem. Would I really do this? What was the alternative? The alternative was waiting until I saw her in court, and grabbing her by the ratty ends of her hair, and swinging her head against the glass walls of the building until I heard a crack, and the glass was smeared with red. I had to destroy Karen, one way or the other. And I didn't kid myself. The only reason

I wasn't doing it that way was this: Benji and Cassie didn't need both parents going to jail.

A text shook my phone in my pocket. I took it out – a message from Adam Devine. Jake had been denied bail and was being remanded in youth custody. Finally, something going my way. I thought how very far we had travelled, when my way was this.

Chapter Nineteen

'Still no baby then?'

Jodi didn't smile or laugh as she opened the door to me. She looked exhausted, a round ball of a person, lumbering on swollen feet. I remembered that feeling, and part of me felt guilty for imposing when she was so close to the birth. But another part needed to know what they knew. I needed to be with people who were there that night. It was Jodi who'd seen Karen stagger in at the same time I did, her hair and eyes wild and blood running down her thigh. Who'd found out at the same terrible moment I did. I had to find out what they'd seen, and hopefully, get something I could use in my plan. I was sure she'd rather not host me for dinner at such short notice, on a Wednesday night, but I'd essentially invited myself around all the same. Manners, social etiquette – just another thing that was out the window.

I hadn't spoken to Jodi, bar a few texts, since they'd left on Sunday. Only three days ago! It felt like years, to the point I was surprised she was still pregnant, likely would be for another few weeks yet. I followed her into the house, which despite her advanced pregnancy was clean and smelled of a wood-smoke scented candle. Not a single cup or glass or book sat out of place. I noted the mosaic floor tiles, the polished wooden stairs with no backs. All beautiful, all stylish, but a death trap for a baby. I saw no signs of preparation as she led me through to the kitchen, no half-assembled cots or discarded cardboard packaging. It was hard to believe there'd be a squalling infant here soon, invading this tranquil, design-magazine home.

'Sit down, Ali.' It felt like an order, so I perched awkwardly on one of the stools by their breakfast bar. 'Would you like some wine?'

Wine reminded me of that night, the sour taste in my mouth. 'I'm fine, thanks.'

She just nodded. 'I made cassoulet, hope that's OK.'

'Oh, you shouldn't have gone to any tr—'

'It's no trouble. They sent me home from work anyway. So, how are you? I'm sorry I've not been in touch. Work's crazy, for both of us.'

'Not good.' I filled her in on the past week, surprising myself at the litany of horrors. Mike on trial, then Mike fighting for his life. The blood on Cassie's top. Jake in a youth prison. The missing money. Then, the thing that Karen had told me, about their long affair. I said it tentatively, hoping she would rush in and deny it, tell me how absurd it was, that Mike could never do that for so long. Instead, she squeezed a tea towel and didn't meet my gaze. 'You knew?'

'Not for sure. At uni I sometimes wondered – they would fight so much, and flirt. But you know, we were always so drunk, all of us.' That was kind of her, but in fact Jodi rarely got drunk. She was always in control. 'Then recently Cal told me he suspected something. You know they go out for their stupid boys' lunches. He saw something on Mike's phone. From her.'

'Oh.' Was that proof? They were friends, it could have been nothing. I felt myself still desperately trying to believe, despite all the evidence. Stupid of me. 'And – Jake? She's saying he's Mike's.'

Again, no surprise. 'I suppose it makes sense. There wasn't anyone else on the scene.'

I opened my mouth, wanting to ask had she always known or suspected that Mike was Jake's father, and if so why she hadn't told me, but I hadn't the words. A noise at the door made Jodi swing her head; her jaw tightened. 'Cal's home.'

He came in with fanfare, slamming the door, slinging his jacket off on to a chair, kissing my cheek with a wet smack. I thought I smelled whisky on his breath. 'Al, sweetheart, how you holding up?' He rubbed my shoulder, and I was grateful for the contact.

'Oh, not so good.' I couldn't face outlining it all for him again. Jodi had turned back to her Aga. 'What about you guys? Exciting times, huh?' I faked enthusiasm as best I could. 'How do you feel about being a dad? Scary?'

'Oh, Jod has a handle on all that.'

'You're a pretty big part of it too, Cal.'

'Am I?' He moved into the kitchen, nosing for food like a truffle pig.

'Leave it,' Jodi scolded.

I had the feeling this meetup was sliding away from me somehow. I took a deep breath. 'There was a reason I wanted to talk to you guys. Karen came to see me the other night.' Her name felt like glass in my mouth. 'She mentioned something about Martha Rasby.'

Jodi was so slow these days. She turned in space like a gyroscope, a frown gently spreading over her face. 'Martha? Why on earth . . . ?'

'What did she say that for?' Cal scooped an olive into his mouth, chewing the black flesh.

'I don't know. I guess because – what happened back then. When we had to talk to the police.' I was choosing my words carefully, for myself more than anything else. I had to think about that night, the one more than twenty years ago, in very certain terms. Why I'd done it. I had to keep it clear in my head.

'You mean like a threat?' Cal frowned. 'What did she even have to do with it?'

'She . . . backed me up. About what I told them. Where Mike was that night.' He was with her, maybe, when I'd lost him for those few hours, the ones I'd lied about. *Not all the time*, she'd said the other night. What did that mean?

Cal was picking at a sliver of olive in his teeth. 'What can she say after all these years? Mikey was just in the wrong place at the wrong time. You helped him out, that's all. I mean, Jesus, it was over twenty years ago!'

'I bet Martha's parents don't see it that way,' said Jodi, stacking plates. 'They never found who did it, did they?'

'No.' But that wasn't my fault. I'd just helped Mike avoid becoming a statistic. In the wrong place. No alibi. Last seen with her. Had I in reality helped cover up his cheating?

'Sounds like Karen's distraught,' said Jodi. 'I guess what happened, it brought back memories of all that. You remember?'

I remembered. I didn't want to think about that pale hand, the white silk in the dirt. I turned instead to another worry. 'Cal – did Mike ever talk to you about money?' The two of them had stayed close since uni, meeting for lunch in town at least once a month. I'd felt jealous and cut off so many times, isolated in my country paradise. As if real life was going on somewhere without me.

Cal tore a hunk of pitta bread from the platter Jodi had set out, Parma ham draped artfully over olives, cheese, dips. She did everything so well. I thought of my abandoned, shattered party. The wine glasses filling up with rain. 'Hmm. I don't know. Something wrong?'

I told them about the money missing from the account, noticing the quick worried glance between them. My stomach fell. Maybe I was in worse trouble than I knew.

'And you've no idea where it went?' said Jodi, peering into her Le Creuset pot.

'No. They're saying the kids' school fees haven't been paid. I don't know what I'm going to do.'

Another silence, in which I felt them communicating, as Mike and I had been able to do, through some kind of couple's telepathy. The space between, the webbed bands that held us together. Maybe cut now, for ever. I could not trust a thing Mike had said.

'What about his parents?' Callum sat down at the table, dripping hummus from another hunk of bread. Jodi tutted, wiped it away with a whisk of a cloth.

'Mike's? They maxed themselves out with their house in France.' They'd made some bad investments, taken in by pyramid schemes. Needless to say, my mother had nothing. Mum. I knew I had to call her, sometime, but I was putting it off, thinking one day at a time. Not today. I'd spare myself that.

I wondered if they thought I was angling to borrow money, and maybe I was. But I wasn't sure they even had any. This house would have cost at least a million, and if Jodi was about to give up work . . .

'I'll figure it out,' I said, taking my burden back. 'It's just, God, I can't believe all of this. Have you spoken to her?'

Jodi jumped slightly, catching her hand on the hot pot as she sprinkled in herbs, and then there was a fuss of running water and taps. Callum just sat, folding bread and putting it methodically into his mouth.

Eventually Jodi said, 'She called a few times. Ali, I didn't know what to do. I mean – it's such a mess.'

I knew it was. Was I asking them to choose me and Mike over Karen? Karen and Jodi had never been close. I didn't know what I wanted to happen. It was like trying to bail out a sinking boat with just my hands.

'I know,' I said. 'It's so awful. I can't understand it, really. I wish I knew what happened.'

Jodi flicked water from her hands, then pressed them dry on a clean tea towel. The meal was on the table now, the pot steaming, the bread warmed, only slightly mangled by Cal's hungry hands. An exhaustion hung over the table, and I realised I shouldn't have come. These two were about to face the battle of their lives, and they didn't need to take on my problems too.

'I think it's best if we stay out of it,' Jodi said, with an air of finality. 'I hope you understand. We're so sorry for what you're going through, but we can't talk about what happened that night. We told the police what we remembered.'

She was right. However much I wanted to pull and pick over the details of that night, it wasn't going to change. Karen and Mike had sex on the lawn. The question was whether it had been consensual. *Maybe he thought it was*, my mind offered up. How sickeningly easy it was to find these excuses. What I had to do now was find a way to pay these bills, let Cassie do her exams, let Benji stay in his home. Do my best to speak for Mike, when he couldn't speak for himself.

'Before I forget,' I said, seating myself, knowing that as soon as I'd eaten I would leave, and be on my own through this. 'The pictures?' I'd texted her about them earlier.

Jodi hesitated. 'Ali—'

'Please. I just need to – look at them again. In the light of what I know.' Jodi and Callum exchanged another glance over my head, then she opened a drawer and passed me a shoebox full of photos, shiny and sharp. Us, back then. Three years of college photos, which Jodi had dutifully snapped at every important function, and got developed, and at one point pinned to the cork noticeboard in her room. Some of them still had little holes in, I could see. Maybe, in this bundle, there would be something I could show to the police to say – what? Karen was a liar? Mike was a good man? I didn't even know.

I put it into my bag, and sat to eat the too-hot meal, even though it burned my mouth. Not long after, I left. Jodi stayed in the kitchen washing the dishes, while Callum walked me to the door, wrapping me up in a hug, and mumbling in a fug of wine how sorry he was. But I didn't want pity, so I pulled myself away and went home.

1996

This is what I do remember.

We gathered on the lawn half an hour before the ball, to take photos of 'the group'. Karen was at one end, still in sunglasses though the
sun was dipping, a fag hanging from her mouth. She wore black silk,
with a red rose in her hair, like a Mafia widow. She was angular, beautiful, pale despite the sun. I was squashed between Mike and Callum,
my face pink. The curled hairstyle didn't suit me, made my face look
piggy. But I was happy, because the boys were hugging me, both of
them already dishevelled and pie-eyed. Jodi was on the other side of
Callum, and Bill between Karen and her. Awkward in the group hug,
holding himself away from us. Afterwards, I'd try to tell where his eyes
were looking, to see if he was staring at me, but I couldn't. Mike was
looking at Karen but she glanced away, at the camera maybe.

I realised years later that Martha Rasby was in the corner of the picture, snapped forever in her white dress and flaxen braids. I wondered if the
police back then had scoured our pictures for clues. I remember we were
asked to hand in our negatives after the ball. Before smartphones, we only
had the pictures that came out, and I was a lousy photographer, always
somehow trapping or spoiling the film. Jodi took the best ones – the boys
rarely bothered, and Karen was too busy living, as she put it.

I remember there was champagne on the lawn, or more likely spar-
kling wine, and I remember Mike looked at me and the make-up Karen
had put on me and blinked. 'You're very dressed-up.'

I took that as a compliment, but maybe it wasn't. The drink had
emboldened me enough to play drunker, slip my hand through his arm,
and he didn't drop it, because he was well-brought-up, at least in these
things. 'Can't believe uni's over, can you? I can't believe we won't be all
together after this.'

'We'll see each other all the time,' he said. 'Clapham is like a mini-
Oxford. And I'm moving in with Cal.'

'Can't get away from me, mate.' Callum clapped him on the shoulder.

'I don't know where I'll be,' I said pointedly. Mike didn't answer and I felt the anger grow in me. I was their friend too. Why shouldn't I move in with them? Why shouldn't he ask me, when we'd been together since first year? 'And Bill will be gone. Touring the world.'

'Shagging those Scandi chicks,' said Callum. 'Well jel. They'll all look like Rasby.' I remembered that comment in the aftermath, but of course it was not unusual, because all the boys thought Martha the most fit in our year, the most desirable, especially as her older boyfriend, Christian, who was French, commanded all her attention. I think they'd have been scared if they'd been able to have her. 'Not that she's available.'

'She is now,' Jodi said, bursting with the pride of knowing gossip we didn't. 'He's ditched her. Didn't want to move here after all, and she has that internship at *Vogue*, so . . .'

Callum whistled. 'Rasby available. And here I am shackled down.' Jodi swatted at him and he put his arm around her.

Was that the moment? Did I see a flicker on Mike's face, a flame of interest at this news about the most beautiful girl in our college? It was easy in hindsight to remember the wrong thing. But the events that followed made me think that maybe, just maybe, the thing that would happen later on that night had already started, right there on the lawn.

Chapter Twenty

The girl in the pictures was skinny, anxious, her make-up badly applied, her clothes a poor approximation of what had been trendy in the nineties. The girl was me, though I felt like an entirely different person now.

I'd come back late from Callum and Jodi's, the train dotted with weary, late-night commuters. The same train Mike used to get back. I'd spent the next day going through the bills again, looking for answers, and cleaning the house, even though I knew it was futile, trying to feel like it was mine again. I still hadn't been into the garage, and wasn't sure I ever would. Now it was Thursday evening, and I was on the floor of the living room, which no longer gave me joy, only reminding me of that meeting with Karen. Of being interviewed by DC Devine. Of Callum, passed out on the sofa. My lower back was complaining at the odd angle, and I was surrounded by old albums from our university days, as well as the photos I'd taken from Jodi and Callum's. The slip covers of the albums had come loose and the pictures spilled out, curled at the edges. Our young faces, me and Mike. Karen. What I was doing was looking for clues. Scanning these old, shiny pictures, some of which still bore the marks of tape and BluTack from when they'd been stuck on my college walls. Looking for Martha. We hadn't been friends, but it was a small college. There she was in the corner of that shot of me and Karen in our subfusc, arms tight around each other, finishing Finals. Another shot of her at a bop, dressed as a witch, but looking beautiful instead of sweaty and drunk, like I did in this picture of me and Mike. Somewhere in the background was Karen, snogging a boy in the year above. I groped for his name. Connor? I wondered how it had worked between Mike and Karen. Did he mind when she got off with so many other guys? Was it to make him jealous? How, when I'd been with one or both of them so much of the time, had they even managed it? I was thinking of nights I'd spent in the library, terrified I'd fail my exams, dreading the phone calls home, when Dad would bark questions at me. How much work had I done. Was I spending his money on drink. Was I sure I'd pass, because I'd better make damn sure I did. The way Mike withdrew in our last term. Always studying, or so he said. Karen, failing her degree.

'What are you doing?' Cassie was haunting the doorway. I noticed how pale she was, the line of her collarbone jutting over the collar of her pyjamas. In the folds of flannel, she looked like the child she still was. I felt guilt roil in my stomach. In my head, the interminable to-do list was out of control. Find some money. Get Mike's case thrown out. Visit him in hospital. Look after Benji, get him fed and to school. And Martha – I didn't even know why it felt important to look at these pictures. Maybe because of Karen's veiled words – *I did it for you* – the fear they'd sent prickling up my neck. The need to get ahead of whatever she was planning. With all these things to do, Cassie, who'd always been so independent, had slipped to the bottom. I was sure she hadn't told me the truth about that night, but I couldn't think how to get it out of her.

'I'm just – looking at old photos.'

'Why?' I could hear the frustration in her voice. 'Mum, dwelling on it won't help. I know you think you all had this amazing time in Oxford, all like, I don't know, that stupid TV show about the posh people, but I bet it wasn't as good as you remember. People change, you know? You don't always remember things right.'

I was floored for a moment – how could she know this, when she wasn't even sixteen? 'I know. I'm just . . .' *Looking for a sign your dad had nothing to do with a girl's murder.* 'I'm just sad, is all. That this happened.'

'I bet Karen's sadder.' Her voice was so cold. She'd turned entirely against her father in such a short space of time, when they'd always been so close.

'Cassie, it's not as simple as that.'

'How is it not? Dad lied, for years and years. She says he did it. Why do you believe him, not her?'

'Did you want me for something?' I heard the snap in my voice, the tone that so often came out when Cassie pushed my buttons. The way my own mother had so often spoken to me.

She twisted her hands together. I couldn't read her face; hadn't been able to for years now. 'No. When's dinner?'

'I don't know, I think Bill's making something.' I felt ashamed saying that. I'd let him take over, cushion the sharp edges of domesticity, which he was so good at.

'I'm not really hungry anyway.' Anxiety. She was too thin.

'Cass, you have to eat. We have to carry on. And you have to go to school tomorrow, OK? You need to face it sometime.'

'Why, so we can pretend it's all normal? Mum, I just found out my best friend is my brother. Dad shagged Auntie Karen for years, and if he ever wakes up he might go to jail. Nothing is normal.'

She was right. As she swept away, making no noise in the thick socks she wore, I found that my hands were trembling holding the photos, and the shiny surfaces wobbled as a few tears dripped on to them. I looked down at an old picture of me and Bill – was it strange, the way we held each other so tightly back then, my head pressed against his chest? – then looked up to see the real one standing in the doorway, older, balder.

'Is Cassie alright?' he said.

'I don't know. I guess the kids at school know what's happening.' I could only imagine what Aaron's snobby mother, Magda, would have to say about it. She already disapproved of Cassie for not being in the Oxbridge stream. 'Any luck with that account?' If I could find out where all our money had gone, maybe I'd be able to get it back.

'No. It's strange – the sort code doesn't match any of the UK banks, or at least not that I can see. I'll keep looking.'

'Thanks.' What the hell had Mike been up to?

Bill came into the room, bringing with him a waft of chorizo and soap. 'Why do you have these out?'

I said nothing for a moment. Then: 'Martha.'

He frowned. 'Why?'

'Karen said something. About how she'd – helped me out with it.' Bill just looked at me, as he had all those years ago, and I felt the old familiar shame ooze through my veins, the excuses come to my tongue. Mike was my boyfriend. What else could I do? He just needed my help. 'Please. I know what you think about it. I need to get it straight in my head. Can you help me remember what happened that night?'

Chapter Twenty-One

'You couldn't find him,' Bill said. We were in the kitchen, and his eyes were turned away from me as he stirred the pasta sauce. 'It was a few hours into the ball and you couldn't find Mike. I remember you were upset.'

'I was pretty drunk.' I'd been drifting quite happily around the ball, chatting to people, for several hours, until all of a sudden I realised I had lost both Mike and Karen. Karen was much drunker than me, downing shots with the rugby team, a glitter in her eye that I'd come to worry about. It was late, around three maybe, and the fuzzy lamplit joy of the night was suddenly starting to seem muddied. I began to notice the puddles of beer on the floor, the dirty footprints trodden through it, the grass and ketchup stains on people's ballgowns and shirts, their piggy, tired eyes. 'I don't know where Mike was. Maybe with Karen.'

'I'd just been with Karen. She was – upset. Crying.' Bill's tone hid something. I couldn't tell what. So, as she'd said, Mike had not been with her all night.

'Did you see her? Martha?'

'Sure. She was so beautiful that night, remember?'

I did. I could picture her on the lawn in her white silk dress, with her fair hair gleaming. We all knew her relationship was over, but she seemed undaunted, brighter than ever. And the boys did not fail to notice that.

'Mike always said he found her pretty drunk, and took her into the Fellows' Garden to sober up. He left her there.' That's what Mike had gasped in my ear a few hours later. *I left her there, Ali, honest. I was just looking out for her. But if people saw me with her – Ali, shit, this could be the end of everything.* And of course I'd believed him. I knew Mike wasn't the perfect boyfriend – at that point I might even have believed he'd cheat on me, but not that he would have hurt anyone. 'What you said to me that day . . .' The memory made my skin tingle, and I forced myself to look at Bill, but he was still turned away, stirring. I watched the shift of his shoulder blades. How thin he still was, when the rest of us were padded by middle age already. Suddenly, I wanted to put my hand on his back, along the lines of his ribs. My eye was caught by the block of knives, which had one missing, of course – it was impounded in the police station somewhere, covered with Mike's blood.

Bill shrugged. 'It was a long time ago, Ali. I'm sure you had your reasons.'

'I was trying to help him.'

'I know.' Again, the words in the silence. What if I was wrong? What if Karen was not the first woman he'd hurt? But I couldn't believe that. Mike and the kids and this house were all I had. I had to fight for them, until someone could come to me with clear and undeniable proof and say, *Look, Ali, your husband is a bad man. You thought you had chosen so well, but surprise, you did exactly what anyone would have guessed you'd do.*

'Do you remember anything else from that night?'

Bill hesitated, and I knew he was thinking of the same thing as me. What he'd almost said to me, on the lawn, as dawn broke. His hand in mine. For a moment, I thought he was going to say it. Instead, he said: 'Nothing useful. Come on, we should eat. The kids will be hungry.'

◆   ◆   ◆

The next morning, at the police station, Adam Devine moved through the pictures with gentle hands. I had a feeling he'd have liked to be wearing gloves. 'I'm not sure I understand, Mrs Morris.'

'I just wanted to show you. What she's like. Karen. She's been with so many guys – married men, even.' It wasn't coming out right. I tried again. 'I know that it's not – that it shouldn't be a factor. I just want to show that she does this kind of thing. She lies. She's been lying to me the entire time I've known her.' So had Mike, of course.

'Mrs Morris – this would be a matter for Mike's barrister, when you have one. It's not our decision to prosecute, it's the CPS's. And they felt able to proceed.'

'But if they knew this – if they knew Mike and Karen had an affair for years, wouldn't that make a difference?' Again that cool look of his. I could feel the judgement behind it. 'Look, I know what you must think of me. I know she's my friend. But he's my husband, and I don't, I just don't believe he could do this, and I can't stand back and let him go to prison. We have kids.' Kids who'd be kicked out of their school, and possibly their house, if this didn't end soon. 'Could they drop the charges? Does that happen sometimes? If they decide she lied about it?'

'Sometimes. OK, why don't you give me a statement anyway about the pictures, and we'll take it into consideration.' His large, sure hands gathered the pictures in, and I felt as if I'd handed him our younger selves on a plate, Karen and Mike and me. Back before any of this had happened.

Cassie

She felt them as soon as she walked through the school gates. The eyes. In school, you were nothing if you didn't have eyes on you. You weren't really alive unless people saw you. Your new shoes, the streaks in your hair. That you'd lost two pounds on the 5:2 diet, throwing away the sandwiches your mum packed like you were five. She'd been seen before, of course – not too smart for her own good, pretty, rich-ish. Dating the rugby captain. It had been nice, to walk down the corridors and see people nod to her. Even sixth formers. *Morning, Cassie. Hey Cass.*

This was not like that.

Cassie's mum used to say how lucky she was. How it was being unpopular at her northern school, too bright and awkward and nerdy for anyone to like her, not willing to smoke behind the bike sheds or go too far with boys. How she realised much later it was a blessing, to be invisible at that age. But Cassie had always ignored that part, and understood instead how lucky she was to be seen. But today something was wrong. She heard the whispers almost at the edge of her hearing as she walked in. Not loud enough for words but still: something. A tiny gust of a laugh, or was it just the wind? She tried to smile at Sarah, off the hockey team, and Sarah turned away, fiddling with her phone. She was a long way off. Maybe she hadn't seen. But suddenly Cassie was finding it very hard to walk across the school yard. It had felt just last week like her catwalk, like she couldn't wait to cross it so people could see how she'd done her hair and make-up, how she made the navy school uniform look like couture. Now her legs felt heavy and she stared at the ground, at the crushed remains of a packet of crisps someone had trampled on. She only knew she had to get inside, quick, away from the eyes.

Inside, the hall seemed impossibly loud and echoing. Voices bouncing off the high glass windows. Even teachers seemed to frown at her. Another laugh skittering at the edge. Cassie knew these kids but suddenly she didn't. Their faces had changed, shut down. She saw Amira, her straight black hair shiny and swinging. She bumbled towards her. What was going on? She wanted to look down to check her skirt wasn't tucked into her pants or she hadn't started her period and bled right through, but to look down would make it real and worse, much much worse. You had to keep your head up high. Everyone knew that. Amira would tell her. She almost ran. 'Hey, what . . .'

Amira's gaze clicked up to her, down to her phone. Up to her. 'I thought you wouldn't come in.'

Her heart failed. 'Why? What do you . . .' Because of her dad, obviously, but Cassie knew she had to style it out. It was possible everyone didn't know yet, and even if they did, it might not be true. He might get acquitted. She knew some of the boys would buy that, the idea that women lied, made things up to ruin their lives. 'Course I'm in. We've got exams. I'm so bricking it, are you?'

Amira wrinkled her pretty nose. 'Cass, like, don't take this the wrong way but . . . maybe you should go home?'

'I can't go home!' Just then, Cassie saw him, and her hands started to shake. He hadn't messaged her all week, despite the ridiculous number of texts she'd sent him. Part of her knew that was a bad sign, that everything she'd been warned about was happening, but all the same she couldn't accept it. She ran towards him. 'Aaron. Wait! Wait!'

People were staring. She shouldn't have shouted. You never did anything to stand out like that, not shout, not run, not cry, not get brilliant marks, not get bad marks. She slowed down, hanging her head. Her face was getting red, she could tell. But Aaron had stopped. He was waiting for her, his blazer slung over his schoolbag and his sleeves rolled up. At the sight of him, his powerful rugby-playing body, the fair hair flopping over his face, all her skin seemed to flare. 'Why didn't you text?' she hissed.

He just stood there, scuffing his shoes on the ground. 'Dunno.'

'I've been having a really shit time.' She felt the tears in her voice and tried to swallow them down. 'I really needed to talk to you.'

'Cass . . . Mum saw the news. About your dad. Everyone saw it.'

'We don't know what happened yet, OK. Maybe she – maybe she lied or something.'

'Thought you said girls didn't lie about that.'

She had said that, parroting her mother's views, though she'd never have admitted it. 'This is different. She – I don't know. She's in love with my dad or something. She's trying to ruin our lives.' She heard the words coming out of her mouth, even though she'd said the opposite to her mother. Even though she didn't believe this, not really. She didn't know what she believed.

He looked over his shoulder, to where his mates were waiting, hanging around in that half-moon formation they always took up. Bros, who had each other's backs. 'Mum doesn't want me seeing you. I've got my exams.'

'I've got my exams too!'

'Yeah, well.' Meaning, he was smarter than her. Meaning, who cared about her stupid exam results.

'I thought you loved me.' She knew it was a movie line even as she said it, and hated herself.

Another shrug. 'I'm just really stressed right now, Cass. I don't need this. I'm under a lot of pressure.'

He was under pressure? 'My dad nearly died.' Her voice was thick now, like she had a cold. 'You didn't even come to visit.' When his granddad was dying, she'd taken flowers, grapes. Trying to be a nice girlfriend. That was what her mum would do, when someone was ill.

'Get a grip. How can I visit him? He's a *rapist*, Cass. I have to go.'

'Wait. Is this about – what happened?' Her voice shook. 'At the weekend?'

Aaron's face changed. 'It never happened. OK? Get that straight in your head.' Then he sloped off, arching himself away from her, and as he reached his mates she heard the laughter bubble up and she stared at her feet, biting the inside of her mouth until she could be sure she wasn't going to cry. That was who she was now. The rapist's daughter. She would never forgive her dad.

Someone was coming over. Miss Hall, the deputy head, in her black suit, her tired eyes. Striding past the kids, who scattered and broke up like mercury. Was she in trouble?

'Cassie.'

'I . . . I haven't done anything.'

In the background, Amira rolled her eyes. Cassie saw that, registered it. Amira had never done that before, not to her. They rolled their eyes at other people.

Miss Hall said, 'Cassie, I think you should come with me.'

Sitting in the nurse's office, with its crinkly exam couch and smell of plasters and lollies, waiting for her mother to pick her up, Cassie found herself reliving it. That night, and all the different things that had happened. Things that her mother didn't even know about.

'He sounds like a total prick.' That was what Jake had said, when she'd finished telling him about Aaron.

'He's top of all his classes. Oxbridge stream.'

'Oxbridge stream,' mimicked Jake. 'Since when does that make someone not a tosser? Look at this lot.' He and Cassie were back in the swing seat, with the bottle of wine Cassie had pilfered while her parents were busy fussing over their guests. *Would anyone like an amuse-bouche? Or even some crisps? Dinner's a little held up, sorry.* Cassie's mum was so anxious all the time. For someone who didn't really work, she seemed mega stressed. Who cared what time dinner was at? It wasn't even dark yet. The grown-ups, six of them, were sitting round the wooden picnic table. On one bench were Callum and Jodi, like a massive marshmallow. On the other were her parents, her mum looking round her anxiously every few minutes, at the kitchen, or at Cassie, or the living room where Benji was playing Xbox. Bill, who was a cool guy, was sitting on a chair at one end and Karen was at the other. She'd dragged over a stool and her legs were propped on it. She'd changed since earlier. Instead of jeans she had on a black jersey dress, a bit like something Cassie might wear. On one of her legs there was a bruise that looked fresh.

'So this what's-his-name . . .'

'Aaron.'

'Whatevs. Have you done it yet?'

Cassie said nothing for a minute. 'Not really. Nearly.'

'But not?'

'He wants to.'

'And you?'

She shrugged. 'I'm old enough. Everyone else has.'

'That's not a good reason.'

'You can talk, you big old virgin.'

Jake drank some of the wine, making a face. 'Well, I don't want to just shag the first girl who'll do it. I'm not an animal. I want someone I can talk to, so it won't be awkward and shit and a mess. Someone older would be better. That Swedish woman Bill lives with . . .'

'She's like fifty! Gross! Anyway, they broke up.'

'Shame. She was cool; I remember from the wedding they came to.'

Cassie picked at something on her ankle. An ingrown hair. 'I should do it. Get it over with. It's not really fair, we've been going out for months.'

Jake had looked so angry then. 'Fuck's sake, Cass. Do you never listen to anything your mum says? If you do it and you don't want to it's rape.'

'It's not rape! For God's sake.'

'It is, if you don't want it. So make sure you want it. Anyway, I bet it would be rubbish.'

'Because you know so much.'

'I read stuff. Blogs. Books. I'm educating myself ready to meet a hot older student. Maybe a tutor, who knows.'

'Gross,' she said, but she'd made her voice cold and distant, like her mother when she was pissed off with Dad. Jake nudged her with his foot.

'Hey, Cass. I mean it. You're awesome. You deserve someone who isn't a prick, and I don't care if he's going to bloody Oxbridge. Fuck's sake. That's not even a thing. OK?'

'OK,' she said, still distant. 'Maybe you're right, Virgin Man.'

Bloody Jake. He'd ruined it for her, the tentative feeling of excitement she'd held in her stomach all through the boring-ass dinner. They might think they were so old and smart, but she was going to have sex that night. She had a boy, a cute and successful boy, who was going to wait for her in the woods and they were going to do it. But then Jake had started with his *Don't do it, he's forcing you*, and it was nearly all ruined.

Cassie was able to sneak downstairs with no trouble. She'd heard her mother go to bed ages before, pissed probably. Benji was fast asleep and so was the annoying pregnant Jodi. The door to Benji's room, where Bill was sleeping, was also shut. She peeked out the hall window: her dad and Karen and the rest were out in the garden still, even though it was pitch black. She saw the white flash of her dad's T-shirt. The only light came from the tips of cigarettes that she thought probably weren't cigarettes. They were passing it round in a circle. Dad too. She stored that one away to counter his next lecture about her drinking. She eased open the back door, which creaked from lack of use, and went out the garden gate. It was the reason her mum had bought the place, the fact it backed on to the woods. It also meant it was easy for Aaron to get out from his house a mile away, cycle through the woods and meet her.

'Hey.' He was there already. All in black, the hood of his raincoat pulled up even though it was the driest and most scorching night of the year.

'Hi.' She was whispering. The woods weren't scary woods – the main road was only like twenty metres away – but it was different at night. Sounds were different. And there were rustlings. 'The aged boozers are still up so we have to be careful.'

He pulled on her leg, making her sit down beside him under a tree. Then his mouth was on hers, crushing it.

'It's all dirty.' Plus there might be fox poop. Aaron made a noise of annoyance and took off his coat, spreading it on the ground. It felt cold and rubbery under her bare legs. Without saying anything else, he started to take off her top.

'I don't know . . .'

'For fuck's sake. What's the matter?'

'Someone might come.'

'It's three in the fucking morning.' His hands were on her thighs, moving under the waistband of her pyjama shorts. She wondered what she was doing – out of her house, in the woods, in something so flimsy? He was now pulling her shorts right down, and she let him, knowing it would be easier, unable to explain why she didn't want to. Was he forcing her? No. She was just letting him, even though she didn't want it. That was different.

Aaron was quickly unzipping his jeans, his breathing getting faster and faster, and then she was lying back. She could smell him. Sometimes she literally couldn't cope with it, his aftershave, his hair gel. It sent her crazy. Aaron, the most popular guy in school, was her boyfriend. Was that even true? She knew lots of girls would give anything to be in her position, about to have sex with him.

'Wait.'

'What?' he snapped.

'I don't know if I . . . I'm not ready.'

Aaron sat up. It was dark, but she could see he was cross. 'You said you were!'

'I know, but I – maybe I'm not.'

'For Christ's sake, Cassie. It's been months now.'

'I'm sorry.' She wanted to cry. But Jake's voice was in her head, say-ing don't do it if you're not sure, you can't take it back. She was trying to get her shorts back on. Her bum was numb and cold. 'I can't.'

'You can't just say yes then say no!'

Cassie started trying to explain, trying to channel her mother, tell him that of course she could, that was how consent worked, but the words wouldn't come. 'I have to go.' She scrambled up. 'I . . . I'm sorry.' She liked going, actually. Leaving while he still wanted her. She hated it when she could feel he wanted her to leave so he could play Call of Duty or watch Netflix. But this, to leave him like this, it was a big risk. Was she making a mistake?

His voice had gone low and cruel. 'Walk away from me like this, you'll regret it.'

'Look, I just can't right now, OK? Not tonight. I'm sorry.'

As she left him, he was standing on the wood path, only his pale face visible in the dark. And then she went back into the garden, squeez-ing round the side of the house, and everything was different, for ever. Now Jake was in prison, and her dad was in hospital and would maybe go to jail too if he ever woke up. And Aaron had finished with her. The rush of fear was so huge she couldn't breathe for a moment. No. It wasn't true. She'd held on to him for six months, longer than anyone thought. It would all be sorted out. Just as soon as she could prove her dad was innocent.

How long had Aaron been in the woods before Karen started screaming? It had taken her a while to creep round the side of the house, pushing through the bushes that grew against the fence, afraid of spiders. Plus, she had been crying a bit, upset by what had happened. When had the screaming first started? She wasn't sure. It was all so jumbled up.

The door to the nurse's office opened, and on the other side she saw not her mother but Bill. And even though she'd only really known him for a few days, and even though it was weird he was hanging round their house when her dad was gone, a strange sort of calm came over her, like the same feeling she got when she was little and came home on a cold day to the fire lit and cartoons on and snacks ready on a plate. Her mother the way she used to be.

'Hey, it's OK,' said Bill, as Cassie burst into tears.

Chapter Twenty-Two

'Is she OK?'

Cassie had been in her room when I got back from the police station, and was there again now, saying nothing in answer to my questions. Benji had fallen asleep, tired after the school week. Bill had gone to pick them up, made dinner, and was now washing up. Was this man too good to be true?

'Hard to say. Maybe she shouldn't go back to school for now.'

'But her exams! Oh, why can't something go right for once?'

Bill looked at me. 'Where were you today?'

A dart of shame went through me. I knew what Bill would think of me if he found out I'd gone to the police station and sold Karen down the river. But I had to. I couldn't see any other choice. 'Just at the hospital. Thank you for getting her. Thanks for everything you've done this past week. I couldn't have coped without you.'

He bowed his head. 'Ali – I think maybe I should leave tomorrow.'

'What? Why?' Panic opened into my veins. He couldn't.

He paused, looking away from me at the sink. 'I think you know why, Ali. It's just – too hard, after all these years.'

I watched the back of his neck, the taut brown skin, and I thought of Bill walking me home that night I'd drunk too many vodka Red Bulls in the King's Arms. Putting me to bed. I'd woken at six, twitchy and furious, to find my bin placed thoughtfully by my bed with a glass of water. Bill, catching a trout off the back of a punt. Bill, folding the tea towel on the counter. Before the worst happened, and the wave hit, and left us all stranded on this alien shore. But there was still Bill, unmoving as a lighthouse. When I was young – when I'd spent most time with him – I used to think a lot about how things happened. How you went from hours sitting on a boy's bed, talking at right angles, both of you offering up band names and countries you'd been to, collected like Scout badges. Waiting for one of you to make the move, like a grown-up game of Blink. How sweet that feeling was, that delay. I'd had it with Bill, I remembered, many times. Gathering bands I thought he'd think were cool. Nirvana. Pearl Jam. Once, his hand on my foot, stroking gently. Sometimes falling asleep together, but nothing more. He was gay, maybe, we speculated, not knowing where to put a teenage boy who didn't mark you like his territory. I could have pushed it but I never did. Afraid maybe. That I'd lose what I had with Mike, gossamer-thin as it was. I'd lose my moral high ground too, that sense I'd waited for him so patiently. Or maybe afraid of losing what I had with Bill, the vague delicious sense that he *saw* me. That I was wanted, to feel I could matter to him a lot, if only I leaned over.

Now I was old, and I'd forgotten how to play these games. When things happened between Mike and me it was as scripted as steps in a dance. Saturday mornings after the gym, or 'mum and dad' time on Friday nights. Something we'd said to the kids, now a semi-joke. Mike had said it in front of Cassie once, meaning it as a special wink-wink message to me, only to see her gag. She was ten. We'd both been surprised she understood.

'Bill.' I rarely said his name, and it felt so formal. I put my hands on the table as if to steady myself. So expensive. Mike had forbidden any spills or hot food on it. How stupid was that – a table that was no use as a table. 'I don't know what I'd have done without you. This past while. You've been . . .'

He shrugged off the compliment. 'I was happy to. But – I can't stay.'

'But you've always been there for me.' It was a cliché, and both of us knew it wasn't true. Not since the end of uni – that summer ball. Not since I'd chosen Mike. 'Except once,' I said, judging the tone carefully. 'You didn't come to my wedding. Why didn't you come to my wedding?'

He could have said: the money, the distance, work. He paused, as if judging it too. 'You know why.'

Something flooded through me. Joy, relief, a wild fear. I'd opened it, that locked box. I'd pushed things over the line. 'I . . . I think I might.' I stood up from the table. There was only a few feet between us, and already I could feel it drawing me in, whatever it was between us that had never gone away. An energy, a magnetism. How had I lived without this for so many years? 'And . . . after all this time?'

He looked at the water, the pot he was scrubbing. 'I loved Astrid. But, well – these things don't just go away, no.'

He'd handed it back to me, the box. The court. I could have said: I wish I'd picked differently, but we'd never acknowledged that I had picked at all. I didn't want to hurt his pride. 'I'm glad,' I said. 'I'm glad it didn't go away.'

I knew that, as soon as he looked at me, it would happen. I kept my gaze steady, and then, finally, his eyes met mine. Twenty years and more between us since we'd sat on our beds and drunk red wine from mugs. 'I missed you,' I said. Still he didn't move. Twenty years is a very long time to suppress something. I'd have to go to him, I realised. 'Will you . . .' I held out my arms. 'I need a hug, please?'

He hesitated, but it would have taken a colder man than Bill to say no to that. And he turned, and slowly put his arms round me. His hands were damp. I breathed him in, smoke and soap. He was so tall. My mouth fitted into this collarbone, and suddenly I'd found a pulse there, and I felt a shudder go through him.

'Ali. Are you . . .' So many reasons to stop. Mike. Astrid. Karen. Cassie, Benji. But now I was in his arms, my mouth on his skin, I understood that some things are right in themselves. And I knew he had to stay, that he couldn't go away again. I fell into him, offering my mouth like a sacrifice, and thank God, thank God, after twenty-five years of turning away, Bill took it.

◆ ◆ ◆

When I woke up the next day, the world was different.

Throughout the night, he'd said several things to me.

'Is it because of him?' Meaning: are you doing this to get back at Mike, Mike who screwed your best friend for years behind your back.

No, I said, into his mouth. No, no, no. And it was true. I wasn't.

'Ali,' he said, as if meeting me for the first time. As if seeing me. Being naked with him felt familiar – even in the bed I shared with Mike, even with Benji and Cassie in their rooms nearby – as if we could finally say the things we hadn't said for years. I'd forgotten how delicious that was, to talk of your past together with a lover. When you first saw each other. When you first realised. He said, 'Do you remember, it was in the bar, and you had this T-shirt on with some cartoon on it . . .'

'She-Ra.'

'Yeah. And you looked around you like you were lost, and it was all, I don't know, wonderful to you . . .'

'It was. I grew up in Hull, remember . . .'

'And I saw you come in. Right across the room I saw you.'

'You remember that?'

'Yeah. I remember everything.'

Other memories. 'After the summer ball . . . you remember that?'

'Of course.' He turned over in bed, propping himself on an elbow so he could look at me. His chest was firm and muscled, where Mike had gone soft. I marvelled at the differences. Bill so tall his feet dangled over the edge of the bed. The different smell of him in the sheets. My hands shaping themselves around his shoulders, his ribs, his hip bones.

I remembered that night. Me and Bill running through the gardens, me barefoot in my taffeta silk, the skirts billowing. Dawn breaking on our bleary-eyed faces. No sign of Mike or Karen. 'Did you want something to happen, that night?'

His long fingers traced patterns on my stomach. 'I never thought it could. You and Mike. But I saw him with Karen, earlier, at the ball.'

I sighed. 'I'm so stupid.'

'No. You trusted them. Should I have told you?'

'I don't know. I might not have listened.'

'What will you do?' It was a wider question, I knew. The light was lifting in the bedroom, the grey of a summer dawn. It was a long time since I'd stayed up all night and it made me feel exhausted, and young, and reckless.

'I have no idea. I just have to look after the kids right now.'

He flipped on his back, and I rested my head on his chest as if we'd been doing this for years. I could hear the thud of his heart beneath me. 'It must be nice in a way. To know what you're supposed to do. Your first priority. I've no idea what to do with myself now. I'm a forty-three-year-old man with no wife, no home, no job.'

My heart quickened on the word *wife*. This was Bill. Single at last, and me – was I single too? I couldn't think about that.

Chapter Twenty-Three

'I'm so sorry.'

I thought of how often I'd heard that phrase in the last week. Police, doctors, lawyers. They were sorry, but professionally so. They saw this all the time, lives ruined, screeching off their pathways and mangled to bits against walls. It didn't really matter to them, not really, if Mike never woke up or if he did wake up and went to jail for something he hadn't done. They would still go home and sleep at night.

This doctor was the young female one, with a piercing through her upper ear that I'd seen Cassie admiring. Short, scrubbed nails. Practical hands. How I envied her, watching her bustle around. The certainty of knowing you had skills, you could save someone. Pushing aside much older people to insert needles and tubes and read machines and pump life back into patients through their chests. Why hadn't I steered Cassie to the sciences? Why had I let her drag along the bottom in school, spending more time on her eyeliner than her work?

'Mrs Morris?'

'Yes. Sorry.' I did not want Child Doctor to think badly of me. 'You were saying?'

'His liver isn't doing so well. You understand what this means?'

I would have snapped back that I had a degree, I went to Oxford, except I really didn't understand. The words were going into my ears but my brain was rejecting them. 'He's not getting better?'

'Not as fast as we'd like. The liver can regenerate when it suffers trauma, but the damage was extensive. If there's no improvement in the next few days, we'll have to put him on the transplant list for a donor organ.'

Waiting for someone else's life to crash, in other words. A shudder ran through me, thinking of those accidents and deaths still to come.

'I think it would be wise to push ahead with matching tissue types within the family, also. It's possible to donate a small section of liver, which can then grow to full size in the other person. You yourself are unlikely to match, and your son is – ten, yes? So too young. But your daughter might be a candidate, if she matched. She's sixteen?'

'Fifteen.' She'd be sixteen in a matter of weeks – young for her school year – and that was another thing I had to think about. How could I give her a birthday with all this going on?

The doctor was frowning. 'It's young. But if you consented, and she was willing, that might work.'

Cut into Cassie, and take out her flesh? Her golden unmarked skin, sliced open? I started to shake. 'What would that mean?' My voice sounded echoey. It was like when you're really drunk, you hear yourself talking but you don't really understand that those words are coming from you.

'It's not to be taken lightly. It can be quite debilitating. And the scarring and so on.' I felt like she was running through a checklist of things to say to the family. 'Why don't you discuss it with her, anyway. If not, we'll have to wait for an anonymous donor.'

I didn't know what to say. How could I ask Cassie to do this, cut up her body, take bits out of it, for God's sake? Did Mike even deserve it? I nodded mechanically, and the doctor gave me her tired, automatic smile, and went out. I'd promised I would talk to Cassie, but of course I didn't have to. I was her mother, and she was underage. I could just not give consent. I could just not tell her the tissue matching was an option.

Mike was there, but not there. I felt I was alone in the room, even though he lay there, his chest rising and falling, his cheeks yellow-tinged. His face was growing greyer by the day. His skin was dry, shrivelled, washed by efficient hands with astringent hospital soap from a squirty jar. He would have hated that, with his moisturisers and toners. I brushed the hair from his face. Despite myself, despite knowing he'd cheated on me multiple times, and in my own home too, I felt guilty. I was as bad as him now. I'd taken Bill into our bed.

And yet I didn't feel bad. I felt as if, finally, I'd done the right thing. How patient Bill was. What a stupid, naïve girl I'd been, dangling myself in front of him like that, darting back to Mike if things ever went too far. It served me right that Bill had been swept up by a beautiful, assured older woman. But it all could have gone so differently that night of the ball, and maybe it would have, if Martha Rasby hadn't died.

'What happened that night?' I muttered to Mike, once again. 'Did you really leave her safe in the garden?' It didn't sound right, as I said it out loud. If he was so concerned about helping the poor drunk girl, why not stay with her, see she was safe? Why take her to a secluded spot then just leave her? *Oh Mike. Just wake up, will you, so I can ask you these questions?* Under his dry grey eyelids, his eyes moved. I wondered what he was dreaming.

Mike was in a coma. Maybe he had no idea that, as soon as he woke up, he was going on trial for rape. He'd no idea I knew about the extent of his affair with Karen. Or that Jake was his son. Had he really not known, never suspected? I thought of the money going out of our accounts, the neat regular sum every month. Almost like child support. Had he been paying Karen off all this time? My mind told me it was impossible, unthinkable, but I knew that nothing was impossible any more. I wondered what he'd say, if he knew the choice was between him and Cassie, if he'd want her to donate part of her liver or if he'd rather take his chances on the transplant list. I wondered, once again, how we ever ended up here.

'Mrs Morris?' It was DC Devine again, with a light tread.

I jumped. 'Oh, hello. There's no change, I'm afraid.'

'I know.' He looked at me, his kind features rearranging themselves into formal, anxious lines. 'I'm afraid I have some bad news.'

1996

Here's what I know. Although it's hard to recall the details over so many years, this is the truth as far as I can remember, as opposed to what I have sometimes imagined late at night, lying awake beside a sleeping Mike.

Martha was 'on it' that night, was what I heard muttered by Victoria Adams in the loos several hours into the ball, and I was flattered she was even speaking to me, Victoria who kept her own horse stabled just outside of town. 'Jesus, she's really on it,' was what she said, flicking at her long blonde hair in the mirror. 'I should take her home.'

I could tell she wanted me to talk her out of it. 'She'll be OK. Everyone's a bit pissed. She won't want to go.' I lowered my voice and jerked my head to the door. 'Karen never goes home when I try to make her.' She rolled her eyes at me and I thought how strange it was, me and her in cahoots as the sensible friends, and Karen and Martha – Martha! – the unstable pissheads. In truth, I had lost track of Karen some time ago, and had been drifting in a pleasant haze from quad to quad, room to room, conversation to conversation. It seemed as if finally everyone wanted to talk to me, ask how I'd be spending the summer, get me in their photo. Compliment my dress.

'Looking hot,' said Stephen Magill, his bow tie askew. I flushed. I felt hot. I felt sexy and popular. I just wished Mike could see me. On and on I drifted, the night air cool and perfumed on my skin. It didn't feel like England, or the quad we crossed daily with our books tucked into our arms, or the coffee room we sprawled in watching *Neighbours* at lunchtime. Instead it was transformed into a Moroccan tent, clinking with beads and coloured lights. I paused to pick up a glass of something minty and sweet and boozy. This had been so worth the money. My father was wrong.

I didn't want to think about my father, how he'd raise his eyebrows at the drunken students snogging on the lawn, the whoops from the dance floor, the melted ice turned dirty by passing feet in heels. Alison Carter's £100 wrap abandoned on the grass, a fag burn in it. He'd think we were wasteful, spoiled, extravagant. But what else were we meant to be when they'd brought us here and told us the whole world was spread out under our feet, just ready to be walked on? I wished I'd realised this sooner. There was nothing wrong in being elitist. We *were* the elite, and I'd let my insecurity keep me down for three years. I'd let Mike keep me down. I wasn't going to do it any more. Stephen Magill had said I was hot tonight, I was bloody well going to go and enjoy myself. There had to be more to my university experience than Mike, even if it was at the very last minute.

Suddenly, he was there. Standing in line at a gin stall. He saw me, and his eyes flicked away, and that told me everything. Still, I went to him. I didn't have enough self-possession to walk away. 'Where've you been?' My voice was louder than I meant. 'I was looking for you.'

'Jesus, Ali, we're not joined at the hip.'

'Who's that for?' I pointed at the gin and tonic some poor first year was pouring, her hands red with cold. 'Your date?'

I was joking, because Mike was supposed to be my boyfriend, but he frowned, and I saw that, suddenly, precariously, all bets were off. 'What's going on, Mike? This was meant to be our night.' I felt tears prick at my eyes and the whole expensive night was threatening to go south.

Mike shrugged, irritated. 'I just want some space. We've been stuck together for three years. This is my last night to hang with people. I just – stop nagging, OK?'

At that point, I could have cried or made a scene, sent some sympathetic girl to find Karen. But I managed to turn and walk away from him, and I've always been proud of that. Finding a little dignity, even with the sting of my father's slap still on my skin.

I walked over the lawn, which usually we weren't supposed to do, my heels catching in the grass. Impatiently I kicked them off, hooking them in one hand and letting my toes sink into the grass in relief. This was life. Screw Mike, he didn't matter. I was barefoot on an Oxford quad, my hair tumbling down, silk around my legs, a drink melting in my hand, and a man in a tuxedo crossing the lawn to me. Bill. I saw right away it was Bill, from the height, from the hang of the old-fashioned tux that looked so cool on him. He was here. And I knew that, despite what he'd said, Mike was watching me across the lawn. I was tired of it, I realised. I was twenty-one and uni was over. In the real world I would have no more hold over Mike than anyone.

I walked to Bill, whose tuxedo had been his grandfather's. It looked cool – hipster before such things were invented, the trousers loose in the hips and the shirt ruffled. And for the first time since I'd known him, I didn't look back at Mike. And that was why I didn't know exactly where he was when Martha Rasby died.

Chapter Twenty-Four

It's funny how simple things, when you overthink them, turn into impossible tasks. I was sitting holding our landline phone, and I'd been in the same position for twenty minutes now and still not dialled the number. It wasn't that I'd forgotten it. How could I, when it was the first one I'd ever memorised. It was just so hard to pick up the phone and call.

What were my choices? Mike was facing not only a rape charge, but also possibly one for the murder of Martha Rasby in June 1996. Adam Devine had explained it all to me, that not only were the CPS not dropping the rape charge, but that they were also going to reopen Martha's case in the light of new evidence. No one had ever been caught for her killing. We'd all told ourselves it was some rando who got into the grounds, found her alone. Even though there was security, and brick walls topped with broken glass, to keep the poor people off our lush lawns.

What new evidence, I had asked him, but he wouldn't tell me. It didn't matter; I knew. Karen had delivered on her threat. She wanted Mike in prison, no matter what, so she'd told them the truth about that night. Maybe they even knew what I'd done, that I'd lied back then. Was that a crime too? I wished so much I could remember every moment of the ball, sift through my vague drunk recollections, pick out the right image to tell me what really happened. The wilted carnation in Bill's buttonhole. The dawn sun glinting on a discarded champagne bottle. The gleam of Martha's white silk dress, disappearing into the Fellows' Garden, a man in a tux holding her up. Mike. Only imagined, since I never actually saw them together. And where was Karen? How had my best friend abandoned me so thoroughly for our last night at uni? Where was Callum, where was Jodi? All of us pieces on a chessboard, moving around the college that night. I wished I knew.

I could have tried Mike's parents, asked them for money. But I knew they didn't have much, had managed to sink it into property or lose it in dodgy investment schemes. I should call them anyway, explain how he was, but I couldn't face their twittering confusion, the fact they were clearly alarmed at the prospect of travelling back from France. I'd wait until I had more news. If he got worse, of course, they'd have to come back anyway. To say goodbye.

There was no choice. Mike was not being released from hospital any day soon, or the charges dropped, and that meant we had no money. And that meant desperate measures were called for. I steeled myself, as if jumping into freezing water. It rang once, twice, three times. She'd answer of course, she never went anywhere these days.

A click. A wavery, hostile voice. 'Hello?' Even with caller ID, she didn't know my number, I called so seldom.

I swallowed. 'Mum, it's me.'

Growing up, I hated my father. It was something Callum and I had in common, that we'd been able to bond over despite our differences. His dad was tyrannical, cold, demanding. And mine was – angry. Violent. I remember the feeling of shame when they came to visit me that first term at uni, appearing in their navy Focus with the dent from where Mum ran it into a bollard at Sainsbury's. Dad yelling at me because it was hard to park in central Oxford. Mum's floral suit from the eighties, too tight. I'd hustled them away as fast as I could. My parents could not afford to take me somewhere like Gee's or the Old Parsonage, so we went to Pizza Express. Dad examining the menu over his little bifocals. 'Bloody rip-off for a bit of bread and tomato.'

Mum trying to remember the names of my friends, ones I'd thrown out casually in my rare phone calls this year. 'And how's Kate?'

'Karen.' I lifted a dough ball, smelled the garlic off it. Put it back down. Dad had already spilled tomato sauce on his anorak. I felt it rise up in me, anger, frustration, sadness – I didn't know them any more, I barely recognised them – and I monosyllabled my way through the dinner, Dad querying every item on the bill.

'And what was this? And this?' So embarrassing. I sank down in my seat, hoping no one else from college was there.

When I'd left them – they were driving back that night so as not to pay for a hotel – I ran all the way to college. Down the high street, where freezing fog was already gathering. I'd already learned to love Oxford like this, silent and blurred, the spires looming out of the mist. I picked up my pace on the cobbles of Radcliffe Square, the low heels I'd put on for dinner catching on the stones. The Radcliffe Camera, so proudly round, and I had a ticket that let me in behind those windows, still lit at 9 p.m., late-night studiers bent over books. I was in this world. I could go in there if I wanted, take down some rare book, stare out at the misty streets. I ran past the spooky empty walls of All Souls – like Willy Wonka's factory, you never saw anyone going in or coming out – and down Holywell Street towards home. In the wicket gate, punching in the code to Mike's staircase. My face was red and flushed and my heart beat high in my chest. I was part of this world. I belonged. And I deserved to have this boy, the one who kissed me in the quad and in Queen's Lane under the gargoyles, then blanked me in the bar, the one who turned up at my door sweaty and drunk from rugby nights out, crashed out beside me smelling of curry. We were together, and yet not. He'd never called me his girlfriend. He'd never touched me beyond those kisses. Maybe because he knew I was a virgin, and frightened. But I was sick of being that. Maybe I'd take up smoking like Karen, wear more black, hang out outside the English faculty being louche and talking about postmodernism. I could do it. I belonged here just as much as they did.

I banged hard on Mike's door. The corridor always smelled like hot bleach, the products the scouts – what we called our cleaners – used on the bathrooms, and the too-high heating. Doubts tried to prick at me – what if he had another girl in there? – but I shook them off. This was what I deserved.

He opened it in his pyjama bottoms, a Nirvana T-shirt on top, and from behind in the dark room I saw the blue glow of a TV and heard recorded gunfire. He was watching something – and how mad it seemed to me that he had his own TV in his room! 'Oh, hi,' he said, surprised.

'Can I come in?'

He blinked, as if seeing me properly. 'Are you pissed?'

'No. I was out with my parents.' I wished I could explain to him how I felt, that I realised now I had to shrug all that off, BHS and road atlases and querying the bill. 'I think you should let me come in.' I was trying to be coquettish. I wished I was drunk, in fact. It would have been easier.

He stood back slightly and I went in, throwing myself on his bed. 'Would you like some tea?' he said politely. This was going well. If he hadn't wanted me there I knew he wouldn't have opened the door to me. Said he had an essay or something.

'Anything stronger?' I said. I propped myself up on my elbows like a model, then realised I had my shoes on. And tights. I'd have to pop out to the loo and take them off. My dress rode up around my thighs.

Mike poured us rum into mugs – his had Star Wars on; mine had He-Man – and apologised for the lack of mixers. I swigged mine neat, grimacing, glad that it would wipe out any residual garlic taste in my mouth. My heart was thudding still, loud as a bell tolling the hour.

Mike sat down on his desk chair. I realised our moods were out of step. He was tired, bookish, where I was wild and off-kilter. 'What did you do tonight?'

He stretched. 'Hung out with Kar a bit. We got a pint in the King's Arms.'

Jealousy stabbed through me. I'd been trailing my parents round Christ Church, dutifully pointing out the historical bits, while they'd been drinking and hanging out. *Kar.* I swallowed it down with more rum. I had to find a way to change the trajectory of this. I got up and went to him, leaning over his desk to look at the pictures he'd stuck there. His parents looked distinguished and indulgent, both things I wished for fervently. I wondered if I'd always be jealous of everyone else here. If I'd ever make it mine. Deciding I'd act more drunk than I was, I sat down heavily on Mike's knee.

'Oof. Hello.'

'Hello.' I ran my fingers through his hair. Shaggy and full back then. 'You're nice, aren't you.'

'I'm not that nice.' His gaze wandered but he didn't push me off. His fingers began to stroke my nylon-clad thigh. I wished I'd taken the tights off.

'Can I tell you something?' Hard not to adopt a little-girl voice. Karen would never do that. She'd just march in there and take what she wanted.

'Sure.'

'I'm ready. For – you know.'

'What?'

'You know. For . . . that. What we haven't done.'

'Oh.'

'And I want it to be you. The first time.'

He paused. 'Ali, are you sure? I mean, it's kind of a big deal, isn't it, the first time.'

'I know it is. That's why I want you.' I fixed my eyes on the picture of his mother. Would she like me? Would we become friends? I couldn't imagine her meeting my own mother, what they would ever talk about.

Mike took this in for a few moments that seemed to last years. What I was really saying. How I was laying myself before him, to be taken, to be hurt as he chose. And he made a decision.

The next day we were in Hall together for brunch, holding hands in public, wearing matching college hoodies as the sun came in the window, and I can honestly say I've never before or since felt happiness like that, so pure and shining. So full of hope.

◆ ◆ ◆

'I suppose you heard what happened.'

Mum read the papers every day, she knew everything that went on. Almost a week now since it happened. It was hard to believe.

My mother's voice was hard. 'I saw it in the paper.' A long silence stretched between us, so many things to say that saying anything at all felt insurmountable. I hadn't spoken to her in – oh, it was almost five years.

'He's been suspended from work. Until the trial. But that won't be until he recovers.' And he wouldn't recover without a transplant, and that meant sending Cassie under the knife. I felt trapped by choices, all of them bad. 'What I'm saying is – I need the money. The money Dad left.'

She was silent. I remembered how I'd screamed at her, after the funeral. That I didn't need his money – not even that much, a few grand – that I didn't want anything more to do with her. That she should have walked years ago, the moment he first hit her. The moment he first hit me. And here I was crawling back.

Then she said, 'It's your money, Alison. I always said you could have it. I'll have them draw up a transfer.'

'Thanks. I – I'll send the account details.'

Another long silence. 'It must be hard,' she said, and I heard a crack of sympathy in her voice down the line, from her dingy little semi in Hull, and my heart threatened to crack open the same, and I could not bear to let it in, so I hung up, and found myself with tears scorching my throat.

'Ali?'

Bill was in the doorway, bags of shopping in his hands. He'd been gone when I came in from the hospital and forced myself to call my mother. He was always washing up, or cooking, or even doing laundry and making beds. As if he had to earn his place here, as if I wasn't totally reliant on him already. I imagined what my mother would say about that – or what Karen would say, for that matter. I was being weak again. Replacing one man with another. And although it was nice, to have him do all this, it only made the house feel even less like my own. He did things differently, stacked the dishes in the wrong cupboards, bought the wrong brands of cleaning products. Everything had changed.

'It's fine,' I said. 'It's nothing.'

'Did something happen at the hospital? Is Mike—?'

'No. Well, he's not good, but no change. The police came.'

'Why?'

I searched Bill's face, his dark eyes. I tried to think of a time he'd ever hurt me, or been cruel, or neglectful, or failed to consider me. I couldn't. Bill would not have told the police about Martha. He wouldn't do that, not to me. He'd promised me as much, because to tell the truth would be to bring me down as well, and I believed Bill would never do that, even though I hadn't seen him in almost twenty years. No, it must have been Karen.

Bill was still watching me, the bags weighing heavy on him, and I wondered why he didn't put them down. 'Well, what happened?'

'It's Karen,' I said. 'She's fighting back.'

Chapter Twenty-Five

I remember the first time I ever saw the spires of Oxford. Unlike most people in my year, I hadn't been before I came down for interview. My school didn't bother running outreach trips; none of us were expected to go to university at all, let alone here. I got off a coach on the high street on a freezing December evening, my breath streaming into the cold air. There was no one around. I struggled to follow the map I'd drawn myself from Dad's road atlas, and when I walked down a small alley into Radcliffe Square, there it was: the dome of the Radcliffe Camera, its lights blazing against the cold starry sky. When I reached college a few streets later, it was like something from Narnia or Tolkien, the tiny gate set in the stone walls, the hidden garden with touches of snow round the edges. And it had me then – I started to want what I'd never even known I was allowed to before. I knew, too, that I would likely not get in. Everyone else on interviews was so loud, so confident, and I shrank back as they hit balls on the pool table in the common room. In the centre of them all, her eyelinered gaze taking everything in, was Karen. I would not have dreamed that we'd both get in, and more, that she'd become my best friend.

More than three years later, Martha Rasby would lie dead behind the same walls. And now I was here again, finally, to try and find out why.

◆ ◆ ◆

'Ali!'

Victoria had aged, I saw with a shock. I remembered her as a posh, horsey twenty-year-old, but her hair was touched with grey and her eyes disappeared behind severe glasses. She'd put on weight, too, and the vanished years hit me. We were women in our forties now, as Martha should have been, but she was gone.

Victoria Adams, who'd surprised everyone by being quietly excellent at Chemistry, when we'd all thought she only knew how to ride horses and buy clothes, had become Dean of Admissions at our college five years ago. I'd messaged her on Facebook, pretending I was scoping out a college for Cassie, and she'd warmly invited me to visit. It occurred to me that maybe people in my year had had these same entry points. Ways of being ushered in, of making things easier. That was what privilege meant.

I knew that college would have been winding down at this point in the year, some students busy with Finals and the others slacking off ahead of the summer. The place seemed quiet, no one revising on the lawn like we used to. When I knocked on the door of her office – her name, Dr Adams, painted in cursive script – she came to meet me. 'Oh, you didn't bring your daughter?'

'She's in the middle of exams. Between you and me, she hasn't made her mind up about applying yet.' Poor Cassie. She was unlikely to get in, with her mediocre mocks results. I remembered how Mike had turned to me, bewildered that we hadn't turned out another top-hitter, and I'd felt, obscurely, that it was my fault, with my lower-class genes.

'Well, it's lovely to see you. How's Mike?' From the way she said it, I could tell she didn't know. Maybe the news didn't penetrate these walls.

'Ticking along,' I lied.

'Coffee?'

I let her make us some, filling a little kettle from a sink hidden away in a cupboard. The walls were hung with pictures of Matriculating classes going back years. I got up and scanned them, looking for ours.

I found it, searching for us among the scrubbed, moon-faced first years in our black and white garb. There I was, with my unplucked eyebrows and ratty hair. Karen in the back row, wearing too much eyeliner. I remembered she'd turned up in fishnets that day. And Martha, standing out with her shining pale hair.

Victoria had come up behind me. 'Seems like a long time, doesn't it.'

'Eons. But this is great, you're working here!'

She sat down at the sofa area, placing the two mugs on the coffee table and indicating for me to join her. 'Things have changed since our days. I don't know if you've seen the brochure, but we have a new boathouse, a new common room—'

I had to play this carefully; I didn't want her to throw me out. 'Victoria – something odd happened the other day.' I'd already decided not to mention the rape. If the college didn't know, I wanted to keep it that way. 'The police came to see Mike.' I left out the part where Mike was unconscious, sinking further every day. How easy it came to me, all these lies.

'Oh?' She was frowning.

'They were asking about – Martha.'

I saw her jump at the name, as if I'd slapped her. Martha had been her best friend, and I tried to imagine how it would have been to lose Karen back then.

'What?'

'Do you remember, after the ball, they interviewed lots of us?'

Her hands were white around her coffee mug. 'Yes. It was so horrible.'

'They had this idea that Mike – that maybe Mike had been with her. I think he helped her sit down or something. You remember, she was – she'd been drinking more than usual.'

'I tried to stop her.' Victoria's voice had dropped. 'I said I'd take her home, but she – I couldn't get her to leave.' Guilt saturated her tone. It had been our creed back then – make sure your friends get home safe.

Call them a taxi. Always our responsibility to keep ourselves safe, never the men's not to hurt us.

'It wasn't your fault. The thing is, the whole business seems to be surfacing again. I guess because they never caught the guy.'

'Why now?' she frowned. I knew that, as soon as I left, she would likely Google Mike and find out the whole thing. Word of it would spread through our college network, over email and Messenger, whispered in City wine bars and at sporadic birthday meetups until everyone knew: I'd married a rapist. Unless I could turn this all around.

'I don't know. A cold case thing, maybe.'

'And what can I do?' Her manner had cooled so much I felt chilly.

'I just need to see what you remember. Try to – piece it all together, I guess. It's so hard to recall every moment.'

She relaxed a fraction. 'I know. I find myself reliving it all the time. How did I manage to lose her for so long? You know, you're drinking, you're having fun, and before you know it three hours have gone by.'

I nodded. 'It's all such a blur. When did you last see her?'

She squinted. 'I guess it was in Main Quad. She was dancing with a whole crowd of people and I saw her stumble, so I said maybe get some water, yeah, but she wouldn't. You know, Christian had broken up with her that week and I think it was the first time she'd ever been turned down for anything. You remember Martha, she was so lovely, but nothing bad had ever happened to her. It was a shock. So she was drinking – a lot, for her.' She glanced at me. 'I did see her with Mike at one point, in there – the Fellows' Garden. I remember because – well, he was usually with you.' She would have noticed, as others did, that Mike and I weren't together at the ball. She'd maybe have seen our altercation on the lawn. Perhaps she'd even have speculated as to what Mike was doing with me in the first place, when I'd give up and realise it was just a dalliance for him. I didn't ask if it was Victoria who told the police Mike had been seen helping Martha into the garden – any number of people might have done that.

'How was she then?'

'Pretty drunk. I tried to take her home but – she wouldn't. She wanted to stay.' Victoria shrugged, but I saw the weight of guilt on her. If only she'd insisted harder, Martha would maybe still be alive.

I picked up my coffee and sipped. 'He said he took her there to sober up – that she wanted some peace and quiet, so he left her there, and then a while later someone ran up to say she'd been found.' That someone had been Jodi, of course, always first with bad news, but I shied away from revealing I could, in fact, recall many details of that night verbatim. 'Then the police talked to all of us and it seemed like they'd made their minds up about Mike, because he'd been seen with her.'

Victoria traced absent-minded circles around her coffee cup. 'Martha was an only child,' she said. 'I suppose that's why her parents spoiled her a little. They were just broken when she died. It ruined them.'

It had ruined a lot of things, her death. And yet the six of us had managed to walk away unscathed. Or so I'd thought. 'It was so awful.'

She frowned at me. 'You saw Mike after he left her in the garden?'

After so many years, it came smoothly into my mouth. 'Yes – he said she was fine then. It was just – bad luck. Wrong place wrong time.'

Her frown deepened. 'Worse for Martha.' I wondered if I hadn't played it right after all, if I'd made things even worse.

'Of course.' I set my cup down, leaned forward earnestly. 'Victoria, I think about Martha all the time. I know we weren't that close, but she was so lovely, so pretty. But I'm just trying to help my husband. None of it was his fault.' But was it, was it? Could I be so sure now? I held her gaze, steady.

'What do you want from me?'

'Oh, nothing. Just giving you a heads-up, in case the police start looking into it again. I didn't think the college would be happy.' It would be bad for them too, to have it all dredged up again, the death of a student within its walls, the suspicion that another student had strangled her, left her spread out on the cool green lawn with her white silk dress torn and rumpled, her skin even paler than the fabric. No one needed that image in their minds. Martha was dead, and that was a tragedy, but there was nothing we could do about it now.

Victoria nodded, and although I knew now we'd never be cordial again, I also knew I'd got what I came for. 'Of course not. I'll just tell them what I did back then. That she was drunk, and Mike took her to sit down.'

◆　◆　◆

It's funny how, at times like this, words take on so much weight. How many I've spilled over the years, careless, like pocket change, but in the two times in my life where I've been close to a crime, every one is like a landmine. Victoria had said, *I did see her with Mike.* Mike had never told me Victoria saw him with Martha. The way he'd described it, he'd just left her in the garden then gone right away. Helping her out. Not lingering in a dark, perfumed garden with the most beautiful girl in our year, drunk and willing.

My taxi reached the train station, having passed so many familiar landmarks it made my heart ache, and I climbed the steps. It was then that I finally thought to take out my phone, and there they were: three missed calls from Cassie's school.

Chapter Twenty-Six

'I don't understand,' I said once again. 'How can you suspend her when it's not her fault?'

Cassie was outside the office of the deputy head, Miss Hall, in the waiting area. I could hear her ragged sobs through the walls. They were different from the ones she'd cried when her father was stabbed. More broken. Like she'd given up already. A crying jag, my mother used to call it.

'We believe she sent the image to Aaron. And unfortunately it seems a few other boys were – exposed to it.' As if Cassie was at fault, contaminating them. Miss Hall was a sporty, inscrutable type, wearing a grey trouser suit. I saw a cross peep out from around her neck. What must she think of us?

'So what? It's of her, she's entitled to if she wants.' I was trying to sound reasonable, sex-positive and forward-thinking, as if I truly believed in the right of my fifteen-year-old daughter to photograph herself topless, her bra and vest top huddled shamefully around her waist, and send it to her boyfriend.

'Technically, Mrs Morris, it's illegal to send sexual images of anyone under eighteen.'

'Even of herself?'

'Even of herself, yes.'

'So let me get this straight. It's not illegal for these boys to share a picture of her . . .' My vision popped around the edges, thinking of them, those disgusting animals, walking tubes of semen and sweat, scrolling their fat dirty fingers over their phone screens. Leaving smears on her face. '. . . but it's Cassie getting in trouble for taking what she thought was private? Why aren't they being punished? Why isn't Aaron suspended?'

'Unfortunately, we can't prove Aaron sent it on.' She was twiddling a pen between her red, dry fingers and it was starting to get right on my nerves. I wanted to punch it out of her hands.

'Of course he did, don't be ridiculous . . .'

'He claims a friend stole his phone.'

'What friend?'

'He won't say.'

I stared at her over the desk. 'I suppose it's just a coincidence that Aaron's captain of the rugby team, and his father paid for the new sports centre?'

'I'm not at liberty to discuss other pupils with you. This is about Cassie. We really feel it would be best for her if she was removed from school for a few weeks.'

'She has exams!' She'd only managed to go to school twice, and both times I'd been called to pick her up.

'There's a centre. Many students aren't enrolled in school and . . .'

That was just great. Cassie, shunted off to the special centre with the home-schooled weirdos and the kids who'd been excluded for setting fire to things. Away from her friends, her routines. Just because some sleazy boys had looked at her picture. And how had Aaron got it? Had he forced her into posing? I felt my blood boil in my ears and I was worried, I really was worried for a minute I was going to hit the woman.

'I honestly believe this is the best outcome,' she said smoothly. 'As you know, technically we aren't required to let her sit exams anyway because of the fees issue.'

I stood up. I didn't really know why but suddenly I was on my feet and leaning on her desk. I'd knocked over a pot of pencils and I didn't apologise or move to pick it up, and it was intoxicating. 'You should be ashamed of yourself, Miss Hall. A student suffers a terrible loss – her father could die – and then she's humiliated in front of the entire school, sexually abused really, and all you can think about is punishing her, making her suffer even more. I imagine the media would love to hear about this – a young girl bearing the brunt of what a boy did. Not a word about punishing him for passing on a picture of her, oh no.'

She didn't even blink. They probably trained them at teacher school. She just looked at me as if I was the enemy. As if I was the classless mother rolling up to school in my Juicy Couture sweatpants yelling and screaming about their darling little thug getting into trouble. Threatening to sue, go to the papers, have her fired. Because I was. I was that parent. She just said, 'Mrs Morris. I really wouldn't advise any further media intrusion into your life. You must think of Cassie.'

I gaped at her. All the words I wanted to hurl back like grenades, they were suddenly gone and my mouth was empty. She was right. I'd lost my moral high ground. I could no longer talk about these things – revenge porn, the sexualisation of young girls, rape culture – I couldn't say a word about it because I was the woman who'd said her raped friend was drunk, wearing a short skirt, flirty.

She seemed to realise she'd bested me, and briskly put Cassie's file away. 'Alright. I think you should take her home now, and I'll arrange to have her sit the exams elsewhere. We will of course try to get to the bottom of the matter, but once these things go viral . . .' Viral. Like a disease. My Cassie. 'And if I didn't say so before, please accept my best wishes for your husband's recovery.'

Outside, Cassie's ragged sobs went on and on, a sound as repetitive and deadening as the hum of air conditioning. I had to leave now. I had to take her and slink away, ashamed, dirty. Beaten.

◆   ◆   ◆

'Sweetheart, I know you don't want to talk about it, but we have to.'

Cassie slumped in the car beside me, weeping. Her face was red and swollen, her hair limp.

'How did he get the picture?'

I wanted her to say, *He made me*. It was how I pictured it. Aaron, wanting sex, putting pressure on. Making her send him a photo to prove her love, then sharing it round his mates in the locker room. Disgusting.

'Cassie, if he took it, that's a crime. We can go to the police, get him to stop this. Have it all deleted.' Although I knew it didn't work that way, that the picture had already spread from phone to phone like cold sores, that it was maybe even on one of those websites I'd written a piece about. That it would never truly go away.

Her sobs had subsided now, and she hitched in breath. I thought how much she'd had to deal with in these short weeks. Her father on trial, then bleeding in the street. Finding out her best friend was her brother. And now this.

'Please, honey. Just tell me your side, and I promise I'll make it go away.'

Cassie took in a long breath. Her eyes stared dully out the window and when she finally spoke, her voice was cold. 'He didn't make me, Mum. He dumped me. So I – I wanted him back. I didn't know it was against the law to send it.'

It took me a few long moments to understand what she was saying. 'You took it yourself? You sent it – he didn't ask you to.'

'No.' She stared at her hands. 'He doesn't want anything to do with me.'

In that moment, I could have killed Aaron. Already so self-assured, confident of his trajectory to Oxford, then some City law firm. How dare he make her this sad, force her to these degrading lengths. I thought briefly of myself, offering my virgin body to Mike, trying to hang on to him with all I had. Pathetic.

'Did you see it?' Cassie pleaded.

I started the car. 'No, darling. I didn't see it. Let's go home.' I only saw the picture once, in the blink of an eye. I'd pretend I hadn't until my dying day, because I knew it would kill her, to know I'd seen her like that. It wasn't so much her exposed breasts, small and delicate. It was the look in her eyes. A million miles from sexy – the eyes of a cornered dog, a trafficked sex slave, a girl forced into something she had no wish to do. And I found myself wondering if that was how Karen's eyes looked now as well.

Cassie said, in a small voice, 'Mum? Can we go and see Dad? I – I want to see him.'

Mike

The world had been grey for a long time. It wasn't gone exactly – he could make out vibrations, sounds, flashes of light – but it was behind a thick grey curtain. His head hurt, a lot. His body felt numb, shot through with points of pain. At times he was confused, thinking he was diving, the surface a bright-lit oval far above. Whenever he approached it, the realisation came – something bad had happened. Shame. Guilt.

Karen.

It wasn't true. What she'd said. It was all such a jumble. Sex that day, in the hot stuffy room above the garage, her familiar smell, the pull of desire and shame. Telling her *it's over, we can't do this to Ali*. Seeing the snap of pain in her eyes. Impossible not to care for her, after years of intimacy. Missing her, even, on nights beside Ali on the sofa, watching yet another Scandi drama with subtitles.

What did he remember of that night? So little. The dinner in the garden, Ali going off to bed, mealy-mouthed, and pregnant, puffy Jodi. The four of them, Karen always one of the boys, laughing too loud, resting her feet on Bill. Trying to make Mike jealous maybe, and perhaps it had worked. The soft caress of the night air, the beautiful house and garden he'd worked so hard for, he'd earned.

After that it was a blur, with large spots that he just didn't remember at all. The weed, the alcohol, it was all such a bad idea. Feeling ashamed about Karen, maybe, wanting to drown the guilt and the tick of anxiety that he'd slept with her in Ali's house, that she would find out, that their shame would ooze somehow between the walls of the building. Wanting to impress Callum, and show Bill he was still young and cool. Aware that Bill had wanted Ali for himself, more than Mike even, and a vague sense of shame there too, that he'd known he was leading her on at university, should have let her go. That he'd stood in the way of her and Bill. And he'd have ended it too, that night of the ball, or he'd have let it fizzle once he moved to London, knowing Ali didn't have the money or connections to get there right away. Everything could have been so different, if he hadn't needed her that night. If Martha had lived. Or who knew. She'd seemed to like him that night, laughing at his jokes, tossing her white-blonde hair. Maybe she'd have been his wife instead. Everyone would have seen him with this beautiful glowing woman. A different life. No Cassie or Benji. He couldn't imagine that.

Voices above his bed. 'I'm afraid—'

'No change—'

'Transplant list—'

He knew he had to wake up, but also that what he'd wake up to was not his life. Not the life he might have had, not at all. That had died over twenty years ago, on the lawn of an Oxford college.

Chapter Twenty-Seven

'Mum, of course I'll do it! God, do you mean all this time I could have helped Dad and you didn't tell me?'

My heart sank. There was no getting away from it – Mike was getting worse. I could see that even without the doctor's grave words. His skin was the colour of ash, stubbed-out cigarettes. His eyes were shrunken in his shrivelled face; he'd aged twenty years in a week. Something had to be done – and that meant testing Cassie. When she saw him, she had started to cry, hunched over his bed.

'I said I hated him.'

'I know you didn't mean it.'

'I don't hate him – I just, I don't understand how he could do all these bad things.'

'Neither do I. I think – we can't know until he wakes up, and can explain it to us himself.'

'But what if he doesn't wake up?' Her face was red and shiny. 'That could happen, right? He's really sick!'

I thought about it for a long time, resting a hand on Cassie's head, which for once she didn't shrug off. 'There is a way we can help him, darling.' And so I'd told her. I'd tried to make the liver donation sound awful, painful and bloody, but I'd forgotten who I was dealing with. Cassie, who, when she'd sliced her toe to the bone as a child, wading into the sea where some idiot had smashed a beer bottle, had set her chin in determination. *Mummy, it doesn't hurt.* Although it must have, a lot. It seemed this news had lifted her from the slump she'd been in since Mike was injured. Cassie was fifteen. She'd had a sheltered life until now. The chance to be part of the drama, to gain a scar, maybe even atone for her suspension from school, for saying she hated her father – of course she'd take it. I'd handled this all wrong.

'Dad wouldn't want you to.'

She gave me that look, like I was the most stupid person in the world. 'He wouldn't want me to save his life? Sure, he'd rather just die, never see me or Benji again.' She made a loud noise. 'Benji. Christ, what would I tell him? He'd never forgive me if I could save Dad and I didn't!'

'It's not as simple as that!' I was getting angry with her too, with the US-teen-soap way she saw the world. Where everything was a story, where you offered a sacrifice and it actually made any difference at all. 'It doesn't always work, his body might reject it, and you might not be a match anyway . . .'

'But we can find out! We have to at least find out!'

'You could get sick too—'

She made the noise again. Half-anguish, and half a kind of fevered excitement. 'Mum!' I tried to understand how she was feeling. The loss of control that I did – all these things happening, Mike arrested then almost dying, Jake in prison, Karen weeping and bloodied, her own nude picture shared around school – but worse, because she was a kid in a woman's skin, who couldn't even vote or drive or drink. The rage that must have been in her, with nowhere to go, like a body hurtling forward in a car crash, stopping fast against a wall. 'We can find out! I'm going to find out. You can't stop me. You just said that we won't ever know what happened unless he wakes up – he has to wake up!'

I could stop her, of course, it was just bravado of Cassie to say that. But I wouldn't. I couldn't take this away from her. 'Alright. We'll get the test.'

All I could do was pray it wouldn't work, that they wouldn't be a match. That this wouldn't be the way my husband was saved.

◆ ◆ ◆

'He's dying.'

Bill watched my face, trying to read me. It was so long since Mike had properly looked at me that I found this strange, part intoxicating, part suffocating. 'It won't come to that. They'll find a way.'

Briefly, I rested my head on my arms as I sat at the kitchen table. It was late; it had been such a long day. Thank God again for Bill, making dinner, taking care of Benji. 'Slicing up Cassie? I don't think he would even want that.'

'The transplant list, then. It's designed to save people like him.'

But I knew people died all the time, waiting for organs. 'I'm sorry,' I said. 'I shouldn't dump this on you.' I'd no idea what Bill must be feeling, watching me fight for my husband. 'I have to do everything I can for him. He can't speak for himself and – for Cassie, Benj . . .'

Bill made an impatient gesture, as if to say I'd no need to explain. I felt he was waiting for something from me, the same feeling I'd so often had in college, when the frazzle of dawn would interrupt our long nights spent talking over cheap red wine or Nescafé. Back then I'd always ignored it – always gone running when Mike called. I couldn't do the same again. We hadn't talked about what was happening with us, the nights we'd spent together in the same bed, the fact he was now ensconced in my house, cooking my meals and caring for my children.

I looked up; Bill was standing in front of me with the air of a man about to say something important. 'If Cassie's not a match, I think you should ask Jake to get tested.' I blinked. He said, 'I know it's crazy, but Mike is going to die without a donation.'

'Jesus, Bill. Are you serious?'

'I mean, the circumstances aren't ideal. But Jake's looking at some serious prison time, and if he donated to Mike the CPS might go easy on him, or even drop the case. I've been looking into it. He was under eighteen when it happened, so with time already served and various pleas, he could end up doing no time at all. And Karen – I know you two had words, but she can't have honestly expected you to support her over Mike. You were in an impossible situation. I think you did the best you could. She'll see that eventually, I think.'

How I wished that was true, that I'd risen above the tidal wave that had engulfed us all, handed things over to the courts to decide, done my best for Mike while at the same time sending all my good wishes to Karen, who was clearly suffering, even if she hadn't told the whole truth. But I hadn't.

'That's not entirely true,' I said.

When I finished telling him what I'd done, Bill was staring at me. His skin had gone pale and his hands were shaking. 'Ali, are you serious? You – you told the police Karen slept around? That she lies?'

'She does! Bill, you've been away for years, you don't know. You remember how she was in college – well, it never stopped. There've been so many men. Married ones, even. She slept with my husband for twenty-five years!'

Something had frozen between us. That feeling I'd always had, that Bill saw me as good and beautiful and important, it had receded.

'Ali. You saw her. The blood, the way she was – shit, can you really believe she wasn't attacked?'

'We don't know anything for sure. She was drunk . . .'

'Ali.' He almost didn't believe me, the way he said it. 'Listen to yourself.'

'She's trying to destroy us! He ended things with her, she was hurt, so she made it up. That's what I think. I know it doesn't happen all that often, a false accusation, but it *does* happen! Why not this time?'

Bill was shaking his head. 'I've never seen anyone in such a state. I don't think I'll ever get over it – hearing those screams, then going downstairs, and the blood on her – the look on her face. She was broken.' He stared at me. 'Ali. You don't mean it? Tell me you didn't do this.'

But I couldn't. And I knew then that this thing between Bill and me, it had not escaped the slow erosion of everything, and that even when you think you've lost it all, there is still more that can be taken from you.

Chapter Twenty-Eight

'Where's Bill?' Benji woke me at seven, bleary-eyed, his hair sticking up in the exact configuration of Mike's. 'He didn't make breakfast.'

Bill had left in the early hours of the morning, the roar of his bike no doubt waking the elderly neighbours. I didn't know where he'd gone. Maybe to Karen. Maybe back to Leeds. There it was. I'd done a terrible thing to Karen, and he couldn't feel the same about me any more. 'He's gone, honey.'

'What?' Benji gaped and I felt a surge of irritation. How entitled were my children, that they took it for granted a total stranger would move into their house and wait on them hand and foot?

'He's gone. He was only visiting! We have to manage on our own now, so I need you to be a grown-up boy and get dressed for school, OK?'

'But Bill makes eggs.'

'Benji! Now isn't the time for the spoiled little brat routine, OK? Make yourself cereal. You're ten years old, for God's sake – I was cooking dinner at that age.' A small exaggeration – at the most I'd heated spaghetti hoops – but I was sickened with myself for making my kids so dependent, so lacking in resilience. And me too. After my childhood, you'd think I would have been prepared for hard times. I'd been spoiled, and blind.

I got up, knotting my towelling robe around me, bundling my hair above my head. What had I been playing at, wafting around Bill in perfume and silk? It was pathetic. We had things to do. I hammered on Cassie's door. 'Get up!'

'I'm suspended!' she yelled. 'Why would I get up?'

'Because, we have to go to the hospital. And you're going to study. You'll be taking those exams, sooner or later.'

Benji had followed me out into the hallway, bewildered at the loss of Nice Mummy. 'Mum, it's not fair!'

I could feel the phrase rise in my throat, and I leaned into it. 'Life's not fair. Now stop whining and get your uniform on.' And it felt good, to yell at my children, to stop treating them with kid gloves. This was the real world, and it was time they learned about it.

'I'm so sorry. Cassie isn't a match.' There it was again, that doctor's sorry. Sorry-not-sorry, as Cassie and her friends would say, with the cruelty of teenage girls. Cassie was crying again, a harsh sobbing sound coming out of her mouth, her hand pressed in front of it but doing nothing to keep the noise in. The doctor had to raise her voice over the din. '. . . We'd have had to go to court anyway to get the permission so it was a long shot . . . he'll go on the transplant list now. There's always the chance of altruistic donation and . . .'

'How long does that take? Waiting for a donor?' I was watching Cassie from the corner of my eye, the way she was doubled over. The front of her white polka-dot top was already wet. She loved her father, despite what he'd done, despite declaring she hoped he went to prison. I'd forgotten what that could feel like, the kind of love that isn't even dented no matter what someone does to you. The kind that, it turned out, I did not have for Mike.

'Four years is the average.'

'Four years? Can he . . .' Could Mike survive that?

Cassie got up and ran out, slamming the door behind her. A thought was forming in my mind, cold and heavy as a bullet. I hadn't wanted to let it in. There were other options – the transplant list and . . . But four years. Jesus Christ.

The doctor had looked at the wall clock several times. She was coming to the end of her 'compassionate time with the family'. She had other people to see, other lives to glue back together. 'So those are the options, I'm afraid. Unless a family friend wants to donate, it's wait for the transplant list. And they might not match, of course. We're out of blood relatives, I take it?'

Mike was an only child, his parents too old to help. I would have to call them, tell them to come from France. They hated doing anything last minute, they would be upset and flustered. Our children were the only possibility for donation. Or at least, that was what I'd thought until a few days ago. 'There is another option,' I said, leaning forward slightly, lowering my voice. The doctor frowned, as if she understood. 'A . . . blood relative.'

'Over eighteen?'

'Just.' By three days. Jake had celebrated his coming of age in prison. I hadn't bought him a present, and even with all this happening that felt wrong. Stupid.

'And would they give consent?'

'I . . .' I thought of everything we'd gone through in the past two weeks. Jake stabbing Mike, the blood pooling on the pavement. The look on Mike's face as it ran over his fingers. The pictures I'd handed to the police. *I need you to know who Karen really is.* 'I really don't know,' I said.

◆ ◆ ◆

Cassie and I drove home, my head throbbing. I was surprised to see a car in the drive, a people-carrier. My mind ran through possibilities – the police with yet more bad news, reporters, bailiffs – before realising it was Jodi and Callum's car. What were they doing here?

Callum was standing on the drive as we pulled in, a hand raised in greeting. He wore a work suit, and looked tired. I rolled down the window. 'Cal!'

'Sorry to barge in. I was just in the area. Thought I'd check on you.' That was strange – Callum worked in the City, and I couldn't think of a reason he would be in this part of the country – but I led him in, sending Cassie upstairs with stern instructions to study.

'Tea? Something stronger?'

'Tea would hit the spot – got the wheels with me.'

'How's Jodi?'

'Oh, you know. In the home stretch. I think I'm just getting under her feet.' He barked a laugh, sitting down at the kitchen table. 'How are you coping, Al?'

'Oh . . . Not so well.' I found myself spilling out selected highlights of the story. Cassie suspended (I glossed over why). Our money problems. Mike in hospital, needing a transplant.

Callum looked grave. 'Bugger, I'd no idea it was so bad. Ali, I'm sorry. We've been rubbish – it's just Jodi can barely leave the house, and I'm so slammed at work. I'll call in and see him, shall I?'

I shook my head. 'He won't know you're there. Thank you, though.'

'Wish I could do something to help.'

'The main thing you could do would be help me figure out these payments.' I shuffled among the papers on the table – clutter that would never have been there before all this – to find the financial statements Bill had been going through. 'Bi – er, I managed to find out it's some kind of shell company, but I don't know which, or why Mike would be paying money to it.'

'Hmm.' Callum took the papers, frowning. 'I can take a look, sure. These things can be tricky to decipher though.'

I popped teabags into mugs and poured the water on. As I carried them over, Callum said, 'Heard you went to Oxford.'

'Oh?'

'Victoria and Jodi keep in touch. She's very good at that, keeping in touch.' Jodi was good at everything. 'Why did you do that, Al?'

'I just . . . they've reopened the case. Martha's. They might charge Mike with it.'

He looked incredulous. 'After all this time?'

'Maybe. Cal, did you . . .' I hesitated. 'You've told me everything you remember about the ball, right?'

He was thoughtful. 'He was with her. You know that.'

'For a while?' I held his gaze. Had Mike lied to me about this too?

Callum screwed up his face. 'Yeah. I saw them together, in the garden. Kissing.'

'And then?'

'I left them to it. I was – well, I was bloody angry, to be honest. That he'd do that to you.'

'So it wasn't the truth – that he just took her to the garden and went?' He told me he'd left her there and immediately gone back to the ball, looking for me. But that wasn't true.

'I don't think so. Sorry, Al.'

'He lied to me.' That explained Mike's panic after Martha had been found – he knew he'd been with her much longer than he'd said. That people could have seen them. That maybe his DNA was even on her, if he'd kissed her. 'Jesus.'

'I wanted to tell you but – well, let sleeping dogs lie, that's what they say. I thought it was best. I'm sorry.' Callum closed his hand over mine, and I was grateful for it, but at the same time I couldn't believe the way everyone had kept secrets from me all these years, covered for

Mike and his indiscretions. Although, of course, I'd kept secrets of my own as well.

1996

'Hey,' said Bill, as I reached him on the lawn.

'Hey.' I downed my drink, feeling it pour through my veins. 'Bill, let's get drunk, want to?'

'Aren't you already drunk? I am.'

'Drunker then. Please. I want to watch the sun come up with you.' The sky was lightening, showing the remnants of the party, everything a bit tattered and stained. I began to screw my eyes up.

Bill hesitated a moment, as if he knew what I was really asking. 'What about Mike?'

'Who knows. Who cares?'

He watched me. 'Ali.'

'Please, Bill. It's the last night. Our very last night.' I threaded my arm through his, tossing my plastic cup on to the lawn. He followed it with his eyes but said nothing. The place was a mess, what difference would one more cup make? I bunched my dress into the hand with the shoes. I imagined how we'd look, a girl in crumpled silk with bare feet, a boy in an outdated tux and floppy hair, on the lawn as the sky streaked pink. I bet we looked beautiful. Powerful, young. Sexy. Suddenly I was in love with the idea of Bill and me. Of course it made sense. He'd been there all this time, waiting, carefully not asking for more, while I ran about after Mike, making a fool of myself. Karen was blue in the face telling me he didn't love me, he used me, he'd never settle down with me. At last, I knew she was right.

Bill hesitated. 'Wait here a sec. I saw some bottles of champagne no one's opened.' He dashed across the lawn with his loping stride, and I waited. As I did, someone else lumbered up to me – Callum. 'There you are!' I said. 'Jodi was looking for you.'

'Oh.' He seemed vague. He was very drunk. 'Al – wanted to say. You look good tonight. Beautiful, really.'

'Thank you.' I smiled at him.

'Heard about your dad, earlier. My old man, he's the same. Always saying Callum, do better, Callum, you've messed up again.' He wiped a hand over his mouth. I began to feel worried I would get stuck there, that because Bill was nice, he would stay and try to listen to Cal's drunk ramblings. I wanted to go, be out of here, alone with Bill.

'Thanks, Cal, I appreciate it. But I'll be OK.'

'You ever need anything . . . I'm your friend, you know?'

'I know.' I looked around me; where was Bill?

Callum put his hand on my arm. It felt hot, heavy. 'He doesn't deserve you.' His words ran into each other. 'Mikey-boy. Al. You don't even know what he's . . . he's not good to you.'

I didn't want to hear about what Mike was doing – a vague sense it would be something I didn't want to know – so I pulled away. 'It doesn't matter. I'm fine. Listen, Cal – I think I just saw Jodi in the next quad.' I hadn't, but I wanted him to go, I wanted out of this situation.

His face looked woebegone, and I didn't understand why. Again, he put his hand on me, this time around my waist. The other too. *Oh no*, I thought. 'Cal – I have to go.'

'He doesn't deserve you.' His breath was boozy, and for a second I panicked that this was all going to go wrong, but then Bill was there.

'Everything OK?' There was a bottle of champagne in his hands.

'Fine.' Callum released me and I stepped back. 'Cal's just a bit drunk. He's going to find Jodi now, aren't you?'

Cal nodded, sadly. 'OK.'

'Come on, Bill.' I felt him hesitate, knowing he should stay, that something was going on that needed to be smoothed over, but I pulled him on and he came, and we walked out of the quad and through the lodge, into the street.

'We could go to the park,' he suggested. 'See the sun rise there. Come back for breakfast.'

'Let's do it.' And we left. I'm not sure of the timings for that night. I've always wondered what difference these small interactions on the lawn made – if they made any difference at all. If by arguing with him I'd kept Mike back for a crucial moment, allowing someone to slip into the garden and hurt Martha, or if Martha was already dead by then, behind the wall in the Fellows' Garden, while the rest of us danced and drank and kissed just metres away.

Chapter Twenty-Nine

I kept checking my suitcase obsessively. Did I have my purse, my phone, my charger? It was so long since I'd spent a night away. 'You will be good?' The pleading note was back. 'I mean, you better be good.' Could I really leave, when Cassie was in such a slump, hardly getting out of bed unless dragged? I'd even seen her leave her phone switched off, which was unheard of. Probably the picture was still circling. Maybe it would never truly go away.

'But where are you going?' Benji still looked confused, standing in the doorway of the bedroom as I crammed clothes in my case. I'd shouted at him so rarely in his ten golden years on the planet. 'And who's going to mind us?'

'I'm – I have some things to sort out. To help Daddy.' Although it seemed like such a long shot that my breath bunched up under my ribs.

'But who's going to mind us, Mummy?'

'I – I'll explain when they get here.' If she got here. I'd taken her long silence, the request for my address, as agreement, but I wasn't at all sure. 'Benj, let me past.' I lugged my case into the hallway, catching sight as I did of the mess in his room. I knew what she would think. She wouldn't say anything, but that didn't matter. 'For God's sake, can you tidy up? Is it too much to ask that you keep your own room clean!' I saw him flinch again, and remembered it. Remembered that a rain of criticism, of shouting, can feel like blows as a child. 'Oh come on, let's just get these out of sight.' I dashed into his room and started picking up Lego and Minecraft toys, lifting the lid of his chest-shaped toy-box to chuck them in. Something was in there – a flash of red. A whiff of smoke.

'Mum—'

'What is this?' But I knew what it was. I recognised the bright colour. I'd finally found Mike's missing jumper. My heart began to race. What did this mean? 'Benji, where did you get this?'

He squirmed. 'Don't know.'

'Tell me!' My voice cracked like a whip.

'It was in the rubbish pile. Mummy, I'm sorry! I didn't want Dad to get in trouble so I – put it here.'

Benji's head hung, the picture of guilt, but I didn't have time to take it in, because there was a sharp rap at the door, and Cassie was running to answer, the one time I would have wanted her to be lazy and inattentive. 'Mu-UM!' Confusion in her voice. The sound of another low one, which struck me to my core.

I hissed to Benji, 'We'll talk about this later. Go down.'

I shut the toy-box and steered him in front of me like a human shield, and when we rounded into the kitchen there she was, with one small bag at her feet. She looked old, her clothes cheap and unfashionable, bought in Tesco or Asda no doubt. My heart ached to see her, to feel all the things her face made me feel. But like it or not, I needed her here.

'Cassie, Benji – you remember your grandma. Mum. Thank you for coming.'

The kids gaped at me. We did not hug, my mother and I. I think both of us knew that the two foot of kitchen between us was an insurmountable distance to cross.

◆   ◆   ◆

It was a long, sweaty train journey. I'd been lucky to get a seat, but the aisle was so crammed, people sitting on the floor, that there was zero chance of making it to the loo or buffet car. Instead I sat and brooded, unable to focus on the magazine I'd bought. All those things I used to care about, like matching tableware and new face creams. I felt torn in all directions. Cassie, weeping. Mike in hospital. That jumper in Benji's room. Someone had hidden that in the garden waste heap, likely hoping it would get destroyed. Did that mean it was someone who knew about Andrej and his bonfires? I sat and thought about it all. About Bill, the look on his face as he left. Karen. Her white face, her shaking hands. And long ago, Martha, dead in her silk dress under a moon as pale as bone.

I almost turned and ran at the base of the street. I could only imagine DC Devine's face if he knew I was here. It might even be a crime of some kind. I didn't know. I'd come anyway – I had no choice.

I'd got it out of a reluctant Jodi that Karen had gone home to Birmingham. Probably, the police housing budget had run out, so they'd sent her back to her old life. It was a long time since I'd visited Karen here – had it always been this shabby? The kind of road that made me pull my handbag closer to myself, walk stiff and fast. Bins in what had been front gardens, litter in the gutters, a house boarded up and graffitied. The last time we'd come, I remembered, we'd swooped Karen and Jake off to stay in a cottage in the Cotswolds with us. Thinking we were being kind, giving Jake a glimpse of fun and wealth. Not realising that maybe we were being cruel. I put my hand on the gate then pulled it back as if it was hot. The paint was rough and peeling, and someone's takeaway sprawled across the pavement like a crime scene, chilli sauce ebbing against my loafers. I tutted, wiping it off as best I could, and rang the number for Karen's flat. It was a lifetime since I'd lived somewhere like this – right after uni I'd floated along with Mike to a Clapham houseshare with Callum. Even that had been nice, the boys' salaries propelling us right through the scuzzy broke stages of life, scraping together coins for a gas meter, living off brown rice till payday. For the first time, I registered that maybe this wasn't right. At least it told me one thing – if Karen and Jake lived like this, they were unlikely to be getting money from Mike every month.

I rang the bell. A large part of me was hoping she wasn't home. But where else would she be? She hadn't been able to work, she'd said. Leaving the flat was too much for her.

There was a moment of silence, and I heard feet scuffling in the hallway. Karen stood in her doorway, the communal hallway behind her littered with pizza leaflets and dead leaves. She wore too-large jeans and a baggy sweatshirt I registered as our college hoody. It was the first time in my life I'd no idea what was going on behind her eyes. Her daily hopes and dreams. Her wish list, who she hated most at work, which particular quirk of Jake's was causing alarm. She was like a stranger. She was wearing glasses. I tried to think: had I known Karen wore glasses? She said, 'Oh.'

'Hi.' Would we ever be like we had been, words tumbling over each other, carrying on five conversations at once? Mike had always shaken his head. *How do you keep track of it?* And we'd smiled indulgently over his head. Because what we had was special. And look, that was gone now. Every memory involving Mike was spoiled like a sheet of paper dropped into water, a dull stain spreading through it. 'Can I come in? I need to discuss some things with you.' Business-like. That was the best way.

A flicker of anger crossed her face, and she went to shut the door on me. I held it open. 'Please, Kar! Please. I need to talk to you.'

'You shouldn't be here.' Her voice was low.

'I know. But you came to me. I'm doing the same, OK? Please.'

As she led me upstairs, saying nothing, I tried not to look around me. I wasn't sure I could control my face at the smell of cooking and the dirt on the stair carpet. The loud noise of CBeebies blared out from another flat. Karen and Jake's was nicer, prints hung on the wall, stacks of second-hand books, a throw on the sofa. But there was no disguising the mould on the wall or the stink of damp in the corridor, Jake's room little more than a cupboard. She stood in the living room with her hands on her hips. No offer of tea. I sat down on the old brown sofa. I realised suddenly it was the one we'd had in our first London flat. Handed down.

'How are you?'

She ignored my question. Just as well really. I wasn't ready to hear the answer. Instead she crossed to the mantelpiece and took a cigarette from a packet of B&H. Karen hadn't smoked since uni – not until the night it happened, of course. She saw my look. 'It's either this or vodka.'

'Right. Sure.'

'What do you want?'

'I think we need to talk. Mike and Jake are . . . we have to do something.'

Karen's eyes were blank. I couldn't read her at all. 'He won't get a long sentence. It was too much for him, finding out who his father was.'

'You told him before the attack?' I didn't believe this for a second – why would she tell him something like that at such a moment? But there was no way to prove it and Karen didn't bother answering again. She lit her cigarette, sucking deeply; for the first time, I saw her as someone I'd cross the street to avoid. A poor woman. A woman who drank too much, smoked, had a kid with no father. Like mine, Karen's family were not wealthy. If I hadn't hitched myself to Mike after college, this could have been me.

I said, 'He stashed the knife beforehand. That looks bad – attempted murder.' It might be actual murder if she didn't agree to help me, if Mike died. 'I know you're angry but surely you don't want Jake in jail? He could be tried as an adult. It's at least five years, probably more. It'll ruin his life.'

'You've got some nerve,' she said quietly, dragging on her fag. 'Telling me how to raise my son.'

'I'm trying to help.' There was a snap in my voice. 'He stabbed my husband. I don't have to help him. But if I were to put in a word – say he's a good kid, we know he didn't mean it and so on – it might make a difference. Or I could say maybe he just wanted to scare us with the knife – it wasn't meant to go in.'

'I asked you to do that and you said no. Why the change?'

I took a deep breath. 'Because Mike will die if he doesn't get a liver transplant. It's too long to wait for a donor, but if a family match were available . . .'

She stared at me. 'Please tell me you're joking.'

'There's no other option. The transplant list will take too long, Cassie's not a match, Benji's too young – it has to be a relative.'

She laughed, a short bark. 'I have to hand it to you, Al. You found a backbone after all these years.'

'I don't have a choice. He'll die otherwise. And if he does – well, Jake could be looking at a murder charge. Manslaughter, at least.'

She leaned forward to stub out her cigarette, but I could see that had struck her. Mike was her son's father, if nothing else. 'Why should we help? You think that's all we are, poor relations you can harvest for body parts? Christ, Ali, it's like *Never Fucking Let Me Go*.'

We'd have laughed at that, once. 'I'm trying to keep your son from years in prison.' As if her son was all Jake was to me, as if I hadn't practically raised him when he was a child. 'And to stop Mike dying. If he dies he won't go on trial. Is that what you want?'

'He might get off anyway.' She toyed with her cigarette. 'It's only my word it wasn't consensual. And the prior . . . relationship. The police seem to know all about that, not to mention my previous boyfriends.' I said nothing. 'I need someone to say they saw what happened. Or he confessed to them. Someone who spoke to him right after.'

She'd explained it as if to a child, but there was no need. I knew what she wanted as soon as she started talking. I'd forgotten how clever she was. How she'd powered through Oxford barely even trying, which was why her failed degree was such a shock. 'I didn't see it. You know that. I'd have . . . you know I'd have said.'

She didn't say: do I? But I heard it in the air between us. 'I need to be believed, Ali. If this doesn't work . . . if those people in court say I lied or they don't believe me or that maybe I wanted it . . . it will kill me. I really think it will kill me. I can't sleep, I'm all alone here. Every time there's a noise outside or downstairs I find myself standing in the middle of the floor, and the adrenaline, it's drowning me, like I literally can't get a breath in and it feels like I'm going to die.'

'A panic attack.' The women in the refuge often had them.

'Yes. You know, sometimes I even ask myself – well, we did it before, so could it really be that bad if I didn't want it this time? Could it really make so much of a difference that I can't sleep, can't eat? I tell myself to pull it together. Is it really worth all this, you hating me and Jakey in there and Mike . . . but I can't help it, because this is the truth and this is how I feel. It is different. It's the difference between hugging me and choking me. I can't explain it but until you've been held down like that . . . until you know how weak you are as a woman, how help-less, you'll never understand.'

'I don't hate you,' I said, and even to myself it failed to convince. Hadn't I wanted to kill her just days ago? Hadn't I fantasised about punching her over and over in her lying face? Hadn't I told the police all her secrets, the ones she'd trusted me with, her worst moments and darkest deeds? 'I wish I could help. But I didn't see it. He didn't say anything to me when I woke him. He was passed out cold.'

'But he could have. No one else was there. No one else would have heard. He might have said, I'm sorry, or, I didn't mean to hurt her, or she wanted it. Something like that.'

I couldn't imagine Mike saying any of those things. He wasn't usually one for apology or pleading. He didn't see the point – what was done was done, no sense in dwelling on it.

She said, 'Maybe you didn't remember right away. In the shock. Or you didn't want to believe. But maybe you'll go away and think about whether you heard anything that night, anything to back my story up, and if you do you'll go to the police again.' She looked me in the eyes. 'After all, it wouldn't be the first time you've lied to them.'

She had me there. The implicit threat, the knowledge that this line was one I'd crossed before. I couldn't say I was too moral to do it. I wasn't.

'And if I do that?'

'Well. Maybe then I could talk to Jakey and explain the situation.'

I understood her perfectly. There was no need to say anything else. After all, we'd been best friends for over half our lives. 'If I do . . . No one can know I was here today. It's a crime.'

'Right.'

'Your neighbours?'

She shrugged. 'Bunch of potheads and sleep-deprived mums. They don't even know my name. I can always say I didn't let you in.'

It was shocking, how easy it was, when it came down to it. To lie. To break the law. And what a choice to make – saving Mike's life, lying, committing a crime myself. I could go to prison for something like that. Both Mike and I could end up in there, if I did what she wanted. Saving his life so he could go on trial and probably be convicted. 'Can I think about it?'

'Don't take too long. Sounds like Mike's in a bad way.' Had she no feeling left for him, after all those years of being together? I nodded, then I got up and went out, down the smelly stairs, leaving her standing in the doorway with her too-big sweatshirt wrapped around her bony body.

Chapter Thirty

DC Devine had this way of looking at me, a long slow blink, that I found very unnerving. I'd always struggled with eye contact. It wasn't encouraged in my family. You kept your head down, got on with things. I'd gone to see him first thing in the morning after getting back from Birmingham. It had been a long sleepless night, wrestling with myself. But, in the end, I knew I was prepared to do it. Why else would I have gone to see Karen? She was always going to ask for something in return. 'You said you saw nothing that night. That Mike said nothing to you.'

'I – I was in shock, I think. I didn't realise the significance. Karen was in such a state and I didn't understand what was going on at first. I couldn't make sense of it.'

We were in the nasty interview room, the one where one side of the table had the veneer all picked away, leaving a rough surface that caught at unsuspecting fingers. He had a notebook in front of him but hadn't written down anything I was saying. Instead he leaned back in his seat.

'Tell me again what happened.'

'Well, I went outside to see where Mike was. Karen was screaming and crying, a real state, and I thought maybe there'd been some kind of accident.'

'This was after Ms Rampling came into the kitchen and said, *Mike raped me*, yes?' How could he remember these facts off the top of his head?

'Yes, I suppose, but I couldn't – I didn't take it in right away. Mike was on the swing seat, and he was slumped over, and I thought he was asleep, but then he said, *I'm sorry. I didn't mean to hurt her.*' That was the phrase I'd come up with as I lay awake last night. Ambiguous, slightly, but hopefully enough to appease Karen.

'Meaning Karen, as you interpret it now?'

'I suppose so. I don't know for sure.'

Another slow blink. 'You didn't mention this at the time, Mrs Morris.'

'No. As I said, it was all such a jumble. It just came back to me and I thought it might be . . . relevant.'

'Because it suggests he did attack her?'

I put my hands on my knees to stop them shaking. I had to keep it together, hold on to all the bits of my life that were flying out of control. 'I don't know. It could do.'

'Which you were previously sure could not possibly have been the case.'

I stared at the damaged table. They should throw it away, get a new one that wasn't so scarred. 'He's my husband. I just wanted to protect him, I think. That's natural, isn't it?'

'Meaning you lied to protect him. You do know it's a crime, to obstruct a police investigation?' I thought of the jumper I'd found in Benji's room. I'd taken it out, bagged it up and put it in the garage, unsure of what to do with it. If I destroyed it, that was a crime. But if they searched the house again they were sure to find it. What did it mean? Had Mike put it there himself? Or perhaps someone else had found it, discarded, and thrown it away on the rubbish pile, not knowing what it was. I tested myself to see if I could believe that. I couldn't.

My heart began to race. 'No! No, not at all, I just didn't remember. That must happen all the time. Right? You don't remember and then suddenly a bit of time passes and the shock eases and it comes back. Isn't there . . . I remember reading some research about witness interviews, how unreliable they are.'

He tapped his notebook. 'Mrs Morris. Back in 1996, when Mike was interviewed about the murder at your college, you also spoke to police, correct?'

'Yes. They spoke to all of us.'

'And you gave him an alibi. You said he'd been with you all night.'

'Yes.' How had I been able to do that, a callow twenty-one-year-old looking a police officer in the face and lying? Driven on by love of Mike, or at least what I'd thought was love; by the need to 'get him' before it was too late. By the need to not go back to my old life, fearful every moment of my father's rages, his flying fists. Fearful of turning into my mother, diminished, defeated. 'Well, not all night, obviously. Most of it.'

'Is there anything about *that* night you find yourself suddenly remembering?' I was foolishly stung by his tone, as if I'd thought we were friends. Tears pricked my eyes. Stupid. He was never my friend.

'Nothing. It was such a long time ago.'

He straightened the papers in front of him, with neat, careful gestures. In another life, if I was younger or he was older and we weren't in this situation, I might have found him attractive. 'Rape trials are notoriously difficult, Mrs Morris. The conviction rate is terribly low, even if the woman calls us right away, and even with forensic evidence. Having a witness to the assault can often swing the balance.'

It took me a stupidly long time to realise what he wanted from me. When I did, I almost laughed in confusion. 'But you can't – I can't do that. Surely you can't – make a wife testify, against a husband?'

'You can't be compelled to testify, no. But you could do it voluntarily. To put right a wrong. It would – send a message.' It was so close to what Vix had said, what seemed like a lifetime ago, but wasn't even weeks. I wondered what she would think of me now.

'I can't.' And yet I kept butting up against these barriers, these lines I said I wouldn't cross, only to be pushed over them. Life skewing wildly to the left.

He looked at me over the table for a long time. Then he stood up. 'I'll be in touch, Mrs Morris. If you change your mind, or you remember anything about Martha's death, do let me know.'

◆　◆　◆

I'd never been to a prison before.

I repeated that to myself with something like amazement. How lucky I'd been, to be able to say that. I was forty-three and I'd never been to a prison before. I looked around the waiting room at the other women – younger than me, I was sure, many of them, yet some were here with grandchildren. Waiting to see their sons, the children they'd birthed and raised who were now behind bars. I tried to imagine Benji here, in this room with flickering fluorescent lights, and vending machines that were sticky with fingerprints, and the sad box of toys in the corner. I couldn't. Benji would never be anywhere like this – that was the point of all those piano lessons and bedtime stories and dentist visits. But then, I'd never have thought Jake would end up here either.

Karen's text had come in shortly after I'd spoken to DC Devine. Payment for services rendered. *He'll see you*, was all it said. She wasn't going to make it easy for me, and why should she? I'd have to convince him myself.

At least it wasn't an adult prison. I didn't think it had sunk in what that meant, the difference in a few weeks' accident of birth. Jake was in a glorified school, where they'd rap his knuckles and give him tough love. Not a grown-up jail with the rapists and thieves and killers. But maybe he would be, if convicted. He was over eighteen already, and I knew the boys in this place were at most twenty-one. He'd stabbed Mike in the liver. He almost killed him. It was planned, it was intended. The sentence for that would surely be long, unless I intervened.

The other women were on their feet, as if by some signal I couldn't hear. I stood up too, painfully conscious of how much my shoes cost. As if they'd notice, or care. Oh God. I was sweating. My throat was dry. I felt trapped, even though when this was over I could leave. Jake couldn't. We all shuffled into a line as the door opened, and a bored-looking female guard passed a wand over us. It was like the airport, only with less sense of urgency. I shuffled forward with my plastic bag clutched like a baby, having left my expensive handbag (£600) in a locker. The woman in front of me was wearing what looked like pyjama bottoms, printed over in puppies, and a sagging vest top showing her breasts, which hung down almost to her waist. Her hair was dyed with streaks of red and purple and she could have been any age. Thirty? Fifty? I was horrified by this place, and by my reaction to it even more. Her huge gold earrings set off the wand, and she was pulled to one side. I took her place, assuming I'd zip through as I always did at airports, and I actually jumped when the detector went off.

'I don't . . . sorry . . .'

The guard sighed, so disinterested she could hardly look at me, and patted me down. Under my arms. Round my breasts. Between my legs. It was humiliating, and I stood spread-eagled in my Toast dress (£160) and felt her rough hands roving over me, and I was horrified to find tears in my eyes. What would Karen say? She'd be disgusted with me. She must have been here so many times already, despite living miles away, despite having no car. There was no way she'd leave her boy in here alone. She'd done everything she could for him over the years – working for idiots, grinding her teeth and getting on with it, demanding the extra funding at his school and the tutors and the support. Fighting to keep him in his father's life, even though no one but Karen knew it. I used to admire that. Before I knew I was the duped wife in it all.

I wasn't going to think about Karen.

I was waved through, feeling shrivelled and fearful, like I'd done something wrong, and the room was huge and noisy, waves of sound crashing against the walls like in the canteen at school. The boys were so big, in their yellow tabards, with their tattoos. Meaty hands resting on tables. Shaved heads. Bulging muscles as they hugged the women, their mothers and girlfriends and the children brought to see them, already semi-hysterical with fear and joy. And in the middle of them was Jake. He was sitting at the table looking thin and hunched, like a wartime evacuee. The tabard was too big for him. *He's only a kid*, was my first thought. Not much older than Benji. Hardly older than Cassie at all. Imagine Cassie in a women's prison. She had, after all, broken the law by sending that picture, though she didn't realise it. Perhaps breaking the law wasn't such a big transgression as we thought. All too easy to cross that line. I made my feet walk towards him and then I stood in front of him.

He looked at me. His hands were neatly folded. Such delicate hands. Mike's hands. Why did I never see it before? *Because you didn't want to, Ali.* I wanted to reach out and flatten his hair, as I had when he was little. Again, I felt tears rising up, in my eyes and nose. I couldn't cry in front of Jake.

'Hi,' I said, and my mouth was so dry I could hardly speak. He looked at me. 'Can I sit, please?'

He jerked his head in assent.

'Um . . . I can get you a tea, or . . . a soft drink or something? Food?'

He looked towards the vending machines. A flicker on his face. 'Juice. I don't drink that caffeine crap.'

The walk to the vending machine was welcome, a chance to compose myself, fumbling change until my fingers were metallic. The juice box tumbled out and I scrabbled for it in the bottom. I used to give Benji these. I still did sometimes. Jake was only eight years older. How could he be in here, when he drank the same drinks as Benji? Benji had believed in Santa Claus until two years ago. Asked to write an essay in class on how they'd learned there was no Santa, that was how he learned the truth, and he had to bite his trembling lip all day. Maybe I'd babied him too much.

Jake stabbed the straw in and drank without saying thank you.

'How are you?'

He shrugged. 'Alright.'

'The other guys, are they . . . is it violent or anything like . . .'

Shrugs. 'The guards stop anything like that. They leave me alone mostly.'

'Oh. Good. That's good.'

We faced each other. This boy had stabbed my husband, almost killed him. And yet I felt guilty. 'Jake. I want you to know that I – I understand why you did what you did. You must have been very angry.'

He said nothing. The slurping of the juice was rude, childish, and I tried not to let it annoy me.

'But you hurt him. He's really sick. Jake, he's – the doctors say he needs a transplant. His liver.' I didn't know how to talk to him. I was speaking to him like a child, like Benji, and here he was in prison. 'Jake . . . do you see what I'm saying? Mike is really, really sick.'

He didn't react. Did I expect him to be sad? He tried to kill Mike. Perhaps he was sorry Mike wasn't dead. I couldn't believe that of sweet, sensitive Jake, who'd cried so hard that day I told him we were leaving town. 'I know you didn't mean to hurt him like you did,' I risked. My throat felt like it was closing over. 'Jake, I – I know we let you down. Moving out of London. We didn't see you enough. I'm sorry. I wish I could change things, but I can't.'

Jake just looked at me, his head cocked slightly to one side. Finally he said, 'Why are you here?'

'Because he's very sick. He needs a transplant, but you know it takes for ever to get donor organs, and there's no guarantee – we can't wait that long. The other chance is a living donor, when you give a bit of your liver. You know, our livers can grow back. It's pretty clever really. But, you see, it has to be a match. A relative. I can't. And Cassie . . .'

Her name at least got a reaction from him. He turned away slightly, folding his arms. They were smooth, unmarked. I imagined them covered in prison tattoos. I knew he loved Cassie, even if he hated me, and Mike even more. 'She can't,' I said, my nose filling up again with the unfairness of it, with the sound Cassie made sobbing. 'She tried but she's not a match.'

I had been hoping that by now Jake would have understood my meaning and jumped in. But he just sat there, his eyes as flat as a shark's. I decided to just say it, all in a rush. 'The thing is, Jake, you might be a match. I realise this is all a shock and you're very angry and betrayed, and you lashed out, but I'm sure you didn't mean to really hurt him, and if he does – if the worst happens, you could be in here for a long time. If you do this thing – if you help him – it would help you too. With sentencing. You know.' I couldn't believe I was saying these words, so cold and clear, and yet there was a certain relief in it too. To finally say what I really meant. To say, give me a piece of you, cut yourself open, bleed, and atone for what you did and maybe I'll help you get out of here. 'So. Think about it. You'll have questions, I know. We can . . . a doctor can call you, or come to see you and explain. But it has to be soon.'

I didn't know if visiting time was over, or what the protocol was at all, but I knew I couldn't spend another second in this room, so I stood up, scraping the chair over the floor. 'Just think about it.'

He stared at me, unmoving. But he hadn't said anything. He hadn't laughed in my face, at the idea that he would give a part of his liver to the man he'd tried to murder. To his father. A father who'd abandoned him, who'd possibly raped his mother. It was small comfort, but I had to take what I could get. But I couldn't leave without one final thing. Without pleading my case one last time. 'I want you to know that I . . . I had no idea. That Mike was. That your mum. I really had no idea.'

He stared at me for a long time. His eyes were so blue. Just like those of my own kids. Karen had once hinted his father was foreign, Scandinavian maybe, someone she'd met on a night out and never seen again, but I could see now his eyes were Mike's, clearly Mike's. I'd been blind all these years when the truth was sitting right in front of me. 'Then you're a fucking idiot, Ali,' he said, clearly. He'd never called me Ali before, not like this. And before I could go he stood up and walked away, towards the bowels of the prison.

I sat in my car outside the prison, tears running down my face. Maybe it was the shame of asking him to do what I couldn't bear for Cassie. Slice into his smooth unmarked skin. Offer up bits of himself to a father that didn't deserve it. How had Mike never suspected? He must have. He'd turned his back, as I had.

I wiped my tears, ashamed of breaking down, and remembered to turn my phone on again from where it had lain in the prison locker. Immediately the ding of alerts. Missed calls, messages. I was so tempted, for a moment, to ignore it. The human nervous system can only handle so many shocks and disasters, before we become numb to danger. I was beginning to feel that way. As I considered putting it away, it began to ring again. The house. I answered, and heard my mother's voice on the end.

'Alison?' High and wavering. I knew that tone. She was scared. I was already putting the car in gear as she told me what had happened.

1996

'We should get back,' Bill said. 'We'll miss breakfast otherwise.'

I was longing for that – the decadence of Buck's Fizz before noon, the burnt-out sexy exhaustion of it all – but at the same time I didn't want to break whatever this was between us. We'd walked around the university parks for hours, crossing bridges, me lifting my skirt over puddles, watching the river and the early-morning rowers go by, coxes shouting. It felt like a film about Oxford, about being young and glamorous and privileged. I had my usual stab of jealousy at the over-educated kids being propelled around by punctilious parents. What could I have been if I'd had that kind of upbringing? Someone who knew Latin, for a start. Then I had what I recognised as a more mature thought than I was used to. It didn't matter that my childhood had been ordinary, even embarrassing. I was here now, in a silk dress, with a man in a tuxedo, and we'd stayed up all night talking about books, and music, and life. I felt huge and hollowed-out with the talk we'd had. The kind that changes your life. It was tomorrow now and I wasn't going to be the same. I didn't have to be the Ali I'd been born and brought up as – I could be anything.

Bill and I were walking back now, my skirts swishing round me. He'd given me his jacket, because he was the kind of boy who'd do that, and I thought we must make quite a sight, traipsing down the street on a weekday morning, his hands in the pockets of his oversize trousers, my hands lost in the sleeves of the jacket. I kept turning to look at him. 'What?' he said.

'Nothing. I'm just seeing you.'

'Seeing me.'

'Yeah.' And I was. The way his hair fell over his forehead. The braces, so cool and understated. The way his sleeves turned up over his slim dark wrists, the loveliness of the bones there. His eyes screwed up against the blood-red morning sun. The way he held back at road crossings, waited for me to be ready to go over. Mike always dashed ahead and it drove me mad. It seemed natural to slip my hand into his and keep it there. Neither of us spoke. I could almost feel him turning it over in his head – to say the wrong thing now would shatter it all.

'I've always seen you,' he said finally.

'I know.'

I didn't look at him, just straight ahead. It was forming in my mind. When we reached college, we'd have our first kiss. The one we should have had three years ago. The one that would erase Mike, and start everything properly. I'd go travelling with Bill, and it would be so simple, falling into step beside him as I did now. I wouldn't have to choose, or decide, or ask Mike if I could move in with him in Clapham and look for a job. It would be as easy as choosing one crossing instead of another on a path.

So this was how we were, Bill and I – hand in hand, his fingers stroking the inside of my wrist, me in his jacket – as we approached college. Immediately I could see something was wrong. There were too many people gathered outside on the pavement, spilling out of the lodge and on to the road even, girls wearing jackets as I was or hugging bare arms to themselves, and there was a hubbub of voices, but in the wrong key for the fuzzy-headed joy we should be hearing. And parked by the railings was the yellow and green of an ambulance. I think it was then that I dropped Bill's hand.

'What's going on?'

He said nothing. He was good like that. When there's nothing to say, and you don't know the answer, just keep quiet. I saw Karen, her face streaked in tears, which was so unlike her I felt panic gnaw at my stomach. 'What's wrong?'

'Someone's been hurt.' Her voice was dull and flat. 'Something happened. We don't know. They said to come out here.'

Rumours were flying. James Collins, pale as his shirt, said: 'They found something in the Fellows' Garden. Someone.'

'Who?' No one answered, but I asked again. 'Who?' Mentally I was scanning the crowd. Where was Mike? And I hated that my first thought was of him, but it was, with a sick inevitability. I stood on my tiptoes and scanned for him, a strange sort of passion erupting in me when I saw him and Callum in a tight knot by the railings, whispering to each other. 'Mike!' My voice was loud and I knew Bill had turned to look but I couldn't stop, I went on barrelling through the crowd. 'Mike! What's happening?'

Jodi, I remembered too late. I should have thought to check. What if . . . but she was there too, standing a little away from Callum, her head bowed and her arms wrapped over her pashmina, hugging it to herself. All of us were fine. But all the same I knew something terrible had happened, and I knew it had something to do with us as a group, as sure as the ground I stood on.

Mike's eyes were wide, and I realised he was scared. That was something I'd never seen before. Usually it was me vibrating with anxiety, knowing how few minutes I'd be allowed of his attention, doing my best with them like someone on a variety TV show, just waiting to be shouted off stage. 'Ali,' he hissed. 'You have to help. Shit, this is a disaster.'

'What's going on?'

'They know I talked to her and now she's . . . shit. You see how it'll look.' He said this last to Callum, who nodded silently. Sneaking a look at Jodi. Then Mike moved close to me, so I could feel his panicked breath on my neck, and he started talking very fast. How he'd been with her, just chatting, she'd been really pissed and they'd never talked much and she was sad, so he just cheered her up. That was all, honest, he got her some drinks and they chatted and then she wanted some quiet, she wasn't feeling well, so he walked her to a bench in the garden, and then, swear to God, he left her there. Didn't he, Cal? Yes, he left her there and maybe he should have put her to bed or something but she seemed OK, just a bit pissed, and he thought she wanted some time alone and no one was meant to be able to get in there, were they, the whole ball was meant to be private, those security staff must have fucked off early and he hoped the police were going to look at them not the students.

My head swivelled back and forwards, but all the same I was aware of another feeling building in me. Power. I had power here. 'Who are you talking about?'

It was Jodi who answered, arms still folded, in a tight bitchy voice. 'Martha. Martha Rasby. Mike was with her.'

'We were just having fun,' Mike pleaded to me. 'I looked for you, after. You were off . . . I couldn't find you.' He was talking like he even owed me an apology, and that was something new, to have any rights at all. I thought of how I'd seen him on the lawn, getting gin, how he'd rejected me. Already he was rewriting the truth.

I looked round at them all. 'But I don't understand. What's even happened? Why does it matter?'

'Because, for fuck's sake . . .' Mike drew in his breath, as if frightened by his own burst of temper.

Again, it was Jodi who could say it, while Mike and Callum stared at the ground, and I realised they were both white and shaking. 'They're saying she's been found dead,' Jodi said. 'In the Fellows' Garden. Martha.'

'Oh my God.' Finally, I grasped it. 'And you were with her.'

'No! I mean, yes, but before. I left. I left, didn't I, Cal? I swear it. You saw me, after.'

Jodi said: 'I was with Cal. But I didn't see you, Mike.'

Callum cleared his throat. 'You see the problem, Al. Mikey-boy was seen talking to her and if she's been . . . hurt . . .'

'And I was looking for you,' said Mike. 'I looked all over. Cal said you were with Bill.'

Bill. Where was Bill? I looked in the crowd but couldn't see him. Karen was there, staring into the lodge, her face strained and terrified. 'I was, yes,' I said, not bothering to apologise. Another new thing. I still wasn't quite taking it in, the connection between the boys' pale faces and the ambulance and Martha. I'd seen her only hours before, beautiful and laughing.

Again, Jodi. Dry and practical. 'You need to say you were with Mike,' she said. 'All night.'

'Why?' I was bewildered.

Jodi looked at me like I was stupid. 'Because, this is everything, Ali. This is the future. Don't you get that? It's our lives.'

'But . . . I was with Bill. Everyone saw us come back.'

Mike spoke urgently. 'Say you were here until an hour back. That's when . . . someone first called the police then. Say I was with you and then you and Bill just went for a walk. OK?'

'But . . . I don't understand. Couldn't someone else say you were with them? Where were you?'

Mike hesitated, just a second. 'Looking for you, like I said. Moving all round the place. You see the problem.' *You see the problem.* That seemed to be a phrase they had agreed on, he and Callum. My head spun slowly, taking in the way the balance had shifted beneath my feet. And where was Bill?

'But . . . she can't really be hurt, can she?' Stupid, but when these things happen our brain wants to reject it and does its best to.

At that point there was a commotion, and someone cried out – Karen, I think. I don't know why. She didn't know Martha all that well, none of us did. She was first-tier, we were second. Even in such a small college there were strata, rules, cliques. I followed Karen's gaze, all the way through the lodge, through the gate to the Fellows' Garden, which had just swung open. There were two male paramedics there, one young with a beard, one older with grey hair. A woman paramedic knelt beside them. They were working on something. A huddled heap. As they moved, from a distance, I saw something in my line of vision – a small white hand, which was already beginning to smudge with bruises. A woman's hand. A woman who was clearly dead. A flash of white silk, stained with dirt. And nothing was ever the same again.

Chapter Thirty-One

Here's what my life had become. My husband was in the intensive care ward of the hospital, clinging to life. And my daughter was in the psychiatric ward of the same building, having had her stomach pumped after my mother found her slumped in her bedroom, a packet of tranquillisers scattered beside her. The same ones my mother had been taking for most of my childhood. The ones that made it easier to turn a blind eye to what our home had become. There would be time for that later, to blame myself for leaving her with my kids, for not seeing anything sinister in the fact Cassie wouldn't leave the house or get dressed or shower. That she'd stopped even going online, so toxic had her life become. And it had poisoned her.

They told me she'd be alright. That she hadn't taken enough to do permanent liver damage – the irony of it, as if trying to destroy the organ she couldn't give to her father – that once she stopped throwing up black-coloured bile and grew a little stronger she could go home. But there was more to it than that, wasn't there? She'd tried to kill herself.

I'd always prided myself on my kids. Sure, Cassie wasn't as academically gifted as Mike might have wished, but she was pretty and popular and seemed happy. I was just now finding out what my mother had always said – pride was a sin. And the punishment was to learn how wrong I'd been about all the things I took pride in. My marriage, my long friendships, my house. That still stood, but tracked through with blood and dirt and now Cassie's vomit on the stairs where they'd carried her out. My mother had scrubbed it by the time I got back home on the Saturday morning, having spent the night in the hospital yet again, the dirty feel of unbrushed teeth becoming normal to me. She'd given me a darting, fearful look, one I recognised from my childhood, after my father had hit her, or me. Shame. I didn't say anything, just gathered what pyjamas I could find of Cassie's and threw them in a bag. Most of them skimpy and unsuitable for hospital. I'd buy her more, it would give me a thing to do while I waited for her to wake up.

As I packed in Cassie's room, noticing that she'd taken down all the pictures of her and Aaron, the ghosts of BluTack on the paint, my mother came up behind me, the drag and tread of her feet so familiar it set my teeth on edge.

'I didn't know,' she said stiffly.

'You left pills out where she could find them? You're still on that crap?'

'I – I haven't taken them in years, Alison. It's an old pack. I just thought – just in case it was hard. Being here.' She sucked in breath. 'She – she seemed alright. Quiet, but she would be.'

'There must have been something that wasn't normal.' I didn't look at her. A vast and unformed pool of rage was swirling in my stomach. For this. Not just for this. For everything all at once.

'I don't know what's normal for her,' she said quietly, without accusation, and I found myself weeping hysterically, a noise coming out of my mouth like the scream of ambulance sirens.

I was on Cassie's bed, or beside it, kind of kneeling. 'I can't do this. It's too much. I can't. I can't bear it!'

I felt her hesitate, then her cool hand – she always had such poor circulation – touched mine and I felt the cotton of the handkerchief she always carried up her sleeve. 'It's always hard to see your child suffer.'

So many things I could have said then. *But you let him. He hit me. You went out of the room and you let him.* Instead I took the hankie she offered, wiped my red face. 'Thank you for being here. I know it isn't easy.'

She hadn't expected that. Her own face crumpled in on itself. 'I'm so sorry. I've been thinking and thinking if there were any signs I missed. That she was going to do . . . That. I – I'm just glad Benjamin didn't find her.'

I shook my head, wondering how I'd find the strength to stand up. Looking up at my mother from the absurd vantage point of the floor. 'You can't really stop someone. If they want to.'

'I think she was just in pain. Something happened with her boyfriend, was that it?'

'Something.' I couldn't explain about the picture. For a moment, I saw myself strangling Aaron. Snapping his rugby-player's neck. 'She hasn't told me everything.' I was sure of it now. Something else had happened that night, the night everything unravelled in my hand like a cheap jumper. Cassie sneaking round the side of the house in her pyjamas. The blankness in her eyes when I asked what happened.

My mother took my arm and helped me up, like an old woman who'd fallen. 'It's terrible,' she said, firmly. 'With Michael, and now this. It's alright if you need help, Alison. Anyone would.'

'I do,' I sobbed, wishing the opposite was true, that I was able to soldier on, instead of drafting in old crushes and my estranged mother to help prop me up.

'Well, I'm here to give it,' she said, in the same resolute tone. 'It's what I'm here for. So no more thanks. If anything, I should be thanking you, for the chance to know your children. They are – a credit to you.'

So many more things I could have said, like why had she let our contact lapse, why hadn't she chased me down, so I could have spilled out how angry I was with her. But it was too late, and so I just cried some more, and for a brief second she squeezed both of my arms with her bony hands. The closest she came to hugs. 'You'll be alright, Alison. I raised you that way.'

◆ ◆ ◆

I made an excuse to go out not long after that, uncomfortable with the rawness of feeling in the house, and left Benji watching *The Lego Movie* while my mother polished glasses that didn't need it. It was a relief to throw myself into the shopping mall, the blur of faces, the cold sterile air, the tinny inoffensive music. I was queuing in Debenham's with some modest checked pyjamas for Cassie when I saw them. A family, choosing kids' clothes. The mother, the father, a baby in a buggy and a little girl of around three. I blinked and it was Julie Dean. I remembered her weeping and bruised in the police station, but here she was glowing with happiness, her laugh high and unfettered as mine hadn't been in years. The man beside her settled a heavy arm over her shoulder. It was him. The husband, the one who'd attacked the refuge, sending women and kids screaming into the night. Got Julie by her throat against the wall. Brought a knife. He looked like a nice guy. Maybe you never did know.

Julie caught my eye as I looked over, clutching the flannel of Cassie's pyjamas in my hands, and she turned away, into her husband's embrace.

Chapter Thirty-Two

Cassie was awake. I could see the peep of blue under her heavy, bruised eyelids, and as I went in, laden with clothes and flowers and treats, anything I could buy her instead of what she needed, she gave me the same look of shame my mother had.

'Oh darling.' I went to her, wanting to crush her in my arms, but there were too many tubes. I stroked her greasy hair from her face.

'Sorry.' Her voice was small, raspy from the stomach-pumping.

'It's alright.' I wasn't going to say how scared I'd been, or beg her not to do it again. I needed her to feel safe, not judged and ashamed. I knew now that shame could corrode a life right down to the bones.

'I was just – I felt so alone. I didn't know what to do.'

'Can you tell me what happened? I mean – the night of the party?' I felt her tense, and knew I'd got it right. It had been there in front of me – Cassie out of the house at night, her strange avoiding behaviour, the abrupt change in how she dressed – but I hadn't had the space to see it.

She sighed, deeply. 'Do I have to?'

'If you do, I might be able to help.' Though I could hardly promise that when I'd not fixed anything so far, only made it worse. 'I'll try at least. And you might feel less alone.' Another small sigh. 'Was it something to do with Aaron?' A tiny nod, her head shifting under my hands. 'He made you do something?'

Through her damaged throat, the words dredged up as if in deep-sea nets, Cassie told me what had happened. One more story of that night, the space of a few hours in which so many things had been broken for ever.

◆ ◆ ◆

It had been easy for Cassie to slip out. I'd gone to bed, her father was – preoccupied, and also very drunk, and Benji was fast asleep. A house of adults, full of their own concerns. She'd gone out the back door into the woods, in her flip-flops and pyjamas, a cardigan thrown over them. Aaron had been waiting for her under the trees. It was very dark, the streetlights on the main road hardly penetrating. 'I was scared,' Cassie told me, sounding ashamed. 'I kept thinking about that film, the Blair Witch one. It freaked me out.' She'd been pleased to see him, glad to get away from whatever strange tensions were in the house, but when she'd tried to tell him about it, her parents' boring, drunk friends, he'd stopped her words with a heavy kiss. 'Not even like a kiss,' she said, trying to work it out. 'Like he didn't want me to breathe.'

I remembered kisses like that. The kind that say, *shut up now, silly girl*. Then it was all going fast, and his hands were under her pyjamas and he was undoing his jeans and pushing at her. That was how she described it. 'Sort of pushing, and grabbing, really hard, so it hurt.' How I wished I'd taken the time to talk to her about sex. Not 'the talk', with all the distant biology of it all. About how it should be, that you shouldn't feel like you were fighting off a mugger or negotiating a contract with someone's hand down your pants. That it should never hurt, and that your own pleasure mattered. All things I had no idea of at her age. And beyond.

'He made you?' I asked quietly.

She screwed up her face. 'I told him I'd changed my mind. I wasn't ready. He – he was pissed off.' I wondered how I would act if I saw Aaron around town, his mother with her pinched lips and Prada hand-bag. If I'd be able to walk past without grabbing the little bastard.

'Sweetheart, if he made you – if you didn't want to – you know what that means?'

She went quiet, and I worried I'd pushed it too far with the feminist lecture. 'Jake said that too. On the night. He thought I shouldn't do it.'

Jake. Trying to protect her, only to stab her father a few days later. I couldn't make sense of it. 'So . . . ?'

She gave a small sigh that turned into a sob. 'He didn't make me. But I think that's why he finished with me. Like, what a cliché, you don't put out so you get dumped. I guess I like, "led him on" or whatever. I said I was into it.' She tried to do air quotes, but her hands were tangled in tubes. 'That's why I sent the stupid picture. I guess, if it meant I could have him back . . . I'd have done it the next time.'

And there she was, learning for herself what so many women had learned before her. That sometimes, you'd hide it so well that the man might not even know you hadn't wanted it. That it was hardest to admit this to yourself of anyone. And I realised what I ought to have known weeks before – I should have taken Karen's side. No matter who she accused. I knew her and I knew rape and if she had the courage to be that victim, to take on that role, I should have been at her side.

A thought struck me. 'Where did Aaron go, after you said no?'

'I don't know. He was angry, and I was crying. I went back round the side, and by the time I did, Karen was, like, screaming.'

I tried to add up the time in my head. 'How long did it take you?'

She shrugged, as best she could. 'I was upset. Could have been a few minutes. More maybe.'

So that meant Aaron had also been around the house that night. Another person we hadn't known about. Angry, rejected by Cassie. I leaned over to kiss her wan forehead. 'I have to go now, sweetheart. I'll back soon, OK?'

◆ ◆ ◆

I waited near the school until he came out. He was hard to miss – already over six foot at sixteen, broad-shouldered as a grown man, and the shine of his fair hair in the sun. My hands gripped on the steering wheel. Aaron. The other person who'd been at the house that night, who I hadn't even thought about. I couldn't believe I was even considering this – that it could have been Aaron who wandered into the garden, somehow getting there ahead of Cassie, and attacked Karen with no one else seeing him. Surely he was too tall, too broad to be mistaken for Mike. Maybe I was going mad. All the same, everything else about this was mad too. I thought about going to DC Devine, yet again, telling him there was another possible suspect. Even though my current position was that Mike had admitted he'd done it, confessed to me on the night it happened. DC Devine would think I was a lunatic. I thought about it all for a long time, so long the kids had all gone home, and the school gate was deserted. I started the engine, and swung the steering wheel around, away from the school. The sun was in my eyes, and for a moment I was almost blinded.

I drove to the police station, finding parking in one of the expensive bays outside. It was one of those annoying machines that you have to text payment to, so I fiddled about with that for a while, growing more and more impatient. Then I dashed inside, and asked to see DC Devine.

Back in that same room again, the one with the chipped table. Him and me staring at each other. I thought how this man had brought me so much of the worst news of my life, how even if this was all resolved somehow, I would never forget him. But for him I was probably just another member of the public, an annoying one who kept pestering him for updates, changing my story. A woman who'd choose a man over her hurt, abused best friend. He wrote down what I had to say about Aaron being near the house that night, but I could tell he was just humouring me. 'Don't you think it's worth looking into?'

'Mrs Morris. Are you suggesting this lad, Aaron, he might have attacked Ms Rampling?'

'I – I don't know.'

He put down his pen and looked at me. His eyes were tired. 'Mrs Morris. In cases like this, there's often not a lot of evidence. It makes it hard to convict. But this time – we have Ms Rampling's injuries. Your friend, Mr Anwar, he saw them on the lawn together. And we've had the DNA results back now. The semen – it was from your husband.'

I hated the clinical way he said that word, *semen*. 'But they slept together earlier in the day. Couldn't it . . .'

'There was no other DNA found. And you yourself said you thought he'd confessed to you.' He was calm, but I could feel tremors of irritation in him. I didn't blame him.

'I know. I was just . . . telling you what he said. I don't know what it meant.'

He said nothing.

'Isn't it good to know everything that happened? Everyone who was there?'

'Yes.'

'So you'll . . . look into this?'

'I'll speak to Aaron, take a statement.'

'OK.'

'You should go now, Mrs Morris.' I stood, clutching my bag, and he said, in a different tone, a kinder, more human one: 'Ali. I'm really sorry this has happened. No one ever wants to believe it, when it's them. But – it does happen. You know? It does.'

I didn't know what to say, and so I left, feeling deeply ashamed of the person I'd become. Or maybe it was even worse than that. Maybe I'd been like this all along.

Chapter Thirty-Three

'I could stay longer, you know. A few weeks, even. There's nothing for me at home now. The house is so quiet.' My mother was folding towels, which she'd taken and washed and hung out on the line, all without me asking. I could have been annoyed at the presumption, but instead I just felt a deep relief that someone else was there to manage things. Minus the slight guilt I'd had when Bill was around, the sense that I would have to pay it back at some point.

Mum was due to go home the next day. I hadn't heard a word from Bill since he'd gone. I didn't even know if he was in the country. 'It's OK,' I said. 'Mike's parents will be here from France soon, and . . .'

She nodded, understanding. Our parents had only met once, awkwardly, on the day of our wedding. Mum and Dad stiff and uncomfortable at the swanky hotel ceremony the Morrises had insisted on, Dad asking how much everything had cost, then raising his bushy eyebrows. *That's a terrible waste, Alison.*

'I'm sorry I haven't been up to visit,' I mumbled, seizing some laundry to avoid looking at her.

'We both said some things when your father passed.' That was an understatement. My father had died five years before, when Benji was five and Cassie was ten. Karen had come to stay to help Mike – and I could guess now what they'd done while I was gone, with my children and her son asleep in the house at the time.

It had been a small funeral. Dad and his temper had managed to estrange most of our neighbours in the small, dingy street I'd grown up in, and he'd never really had friends. It was only a few cousins, who'd barely known him, some people from the pub, a few old colleagues. The vicar had said some lies about him, how Dad was a loving family man, quick with a joke or a helping hand. He hadn't been any of those things.

After the funeral, helping my mother clear out his sad, worn-out slacks, the jumpers with holes in the neck, the oppressive smell of the house all around me, I'd come across his pipe, resting on the side of the armchair. Where he sat night after night, controlling the TV, shouting if anyone banged a door or talked too loudly. Mum had said something like, *he loved that pipe, make sure you don't break it*, and I'd exploded. Said some things – how could she pretend he'd been a good man, after all he'd done. How could she sit there in church as if he hadn't controlled our lives with his moods and temper, his quick fists. As if he'd never broken her arm, or kicked her when she lay winded on the floor. Never left slap marks on my face, or thrown a full cup of tea at me when it wasn't to his liking.

She'd fought back. How dare I, coming back here, turning my nose up at their life, dishonouring my father on the day we put him in the ground. When I stormed out, grabbing my wheelie case and rushing down the street in uncomfortable heels, not caring which of the neighbours saw my angry tears, part of me had felt relief. I didn't need to go back now, bring Cassie and Benji for awkward visits, watch Benji trip on the death-trap stairs or Cassie's bafflement at the tinned, sugary food my mother dished out. That part of my life was over.

'I'm sorry,' I said again. 'I shouldn't have said it. Not then.'

She waved a hand. 'Put it behind you, Alison. We need to get you sorted here now.' She was right – the mess of my recuperating daughter, now out of hospital but refusing to go anywhere or see anyone; my husband, who was set to receive a partial liver transplant in just a few days. He would be receiving it from Jake, and in return for ripping himself open, Jake would likely face a lighter sentence; and if Mike recovered, he would go on trial. Where I would testify and say I thought my husband had raped my best friend, in our garden, while I slept upstairs. I'd say he had confessed the truth to me, because it was the only way to save his life. I'd fought it for so long it felt strangely inevitable. I hadn't been able to stop any of it, and my efforts had only made things worse. It was time to just give in. I hoped Karen would never hear of my madness the other day, suggesting Aaron might be involved somehow. A last-ditch, desperate attempt. They had Mike's DNA. I had to face the truth.

'I'll put the tea on,' Mum said, and I dimly registered that not long ago I would have winced at this, snapping 'dinner' back at her. I'd worked so hard to shed those working-class tells. As she moved into the kitchen, the phone began to ring and I heard her answer it: 'Morris home.' I felt a brief stab of gratitude that she was here, that maybe we could salvage something from all this. And if it meant old Ali, working-class Ali, wasn't gone after all, perhaps it was good. Middle-class Ali hadn't got a clue, it turned out.

Mum appeared in the doorway, holding the wireless handset to her chest, looking troubled. 'It's a nurse,' she said.

'Mike?' I stood up too fast.

'No, in London. Something about a Mrs Mackintosh, having her baby?'

If Mum hadn't been there, I wouldn't have gone. I had too much to do to keep my own family together, never mind other people's. But Jodi was my closest friend now Karen hated me, and she'd asked for me. Mum had the house in hand, and knew to make sure Benji ate well and did his homework, to not believe Cassie if she said she was fine or wasn't hungry. And so I ran to catch the train to London. It was quiet, all the commuters going the other way. Within two hours

I was at London Bridge and swapping trains to Waterloo, and then to St Thomas's Hospital.

1996

The first time I lied to the police, I was twenty-one. It was two days after the ball, and I still hadn't been able to take in Martha's death. We hadn't been friends, but she was so alive, so young, and then gone. I think we all struggled, especially as everyone was due to go home over the next few days. There was a lot of crying and hugging in the lodge while confused parents stood by with overpacked cars. Mine had heard about it on the news, and my mother had called to say they were coming to get me the next day. No mention of my father's threats to kick me out, or that he'd slapped me, as was so often the way. Brushed under the carpet.

I wasn't even sure the police would interview me. They had a lot to get through, and I think we all had a certain awareness that once we were home for the summer, in our semis in Wales or mansions in Surrey, they wouldn't be coming after us. Martha had been killed by a stranger, of course. The security had been lacking. Someone must have got in. There was no CCTV in the garden and it would have been possible to climb over the back wall. The ball was so busy, no one would have noticed. None of us mentioned the fact that a stranger not in black tie might have stood out somewhat. So when it was my turn to present myself at the tutor's office, I didn't even think twice. I didn't see it as lying, just as helping out friends. Helping out Mike. And Jodi was doing it for Callum, saying he'd been with her all night, so it couldn't be that bad. All the same I was sweating as I waited outside, in a strange repetition of admissions interviews. In jeans and a She-Ra T-shirt, I looked very different from the night before. I was just Ali again, and all my problems and longings were there waiting for me like the socks I'd rolled on that morning.

Bill came out as I waited there. We hadn't really spoken since the morning after the ball. 'Hey.'

He just nodded. 'They're asking about Mike and Cal.'

'What did you say?'

'Are you going to do it?' He looked me in the eyes. 'What he asked?'

I didn't like the idea that there was an 'it' I was going to do. 'I mean – I'll just say we were hanging out, I guess.' I'd already spoken to Karen, telling her what I was going to say so she didn't contradict it. *So we're on the same page*, I'd said. Mike's words. She hadn't protested. I didn't know where she'd been most of the night either.

Bill looked down at the green carpet. Muffled sounds of college life came in from the quad, and the window cast diamonds of sunlight at our feet. 'We were away for hours, Al.'

'Oh, it wasn't that long.'

'We left at four. I heard the bells go.'

'That can't be right. I looked at the clock in the lodge when we passed.'

'Sure you did, Ali.' His voice was bitter. I actually stepped back.

'What should I do? They're our friends. I don't want to get them in trouble. Not when it's some stranger, some townie who's got in and . . .'

'She's dead, Al. Don't you think she deserves us telling the truth?'

'It is the truth. I don't know what time it was when we left, but I know it was late.'

He stared at me. 'You don't have to do this. I'll help you. I know you're scared about what's next, about him, but – you don't need to be.'

A long moment ticked by. I stared down at the carpet. It did occur to me to wonder why I was doing this for Mike, when all he did was mess me about. But I'd tried for so many years to make him want me, never having any leverage, never any influence over my own relationship. Now that I had some, it was impossible to let it go. 'I don't know what you mean.'

Bill sighed. 'OK, Ali. You do what you have to.'

'Wait! What did you tell them? The police?'

Bill was already moving away down the stairs, his face in shadow. 'Don't worry, Ali. I didn't say anything you can't contradict.' I hated the way his voice sounded.

He walked down the stairs again before I could say anything else, and I heard later on he'd left, catching the coach to Harwich and then a ferry out of the country, and I didn't see Bill again until Jodi and Callum's wedding. It was the last time until the night Karen was attacked.

'Do come in.' The police seemed kind. There was a younger woman with chestnut hair pulled back, and an older man who was grey-haired and paternal. Deliberate, maybe. A lot of us would be wishing our dads were on hand to sort things. Not me, of course.

I sat down, tucking my feet nervously under the wooden chair, feeling like it was a tutorial I hadn't done the reading for. They consulted their notes. 'Alison, I understand you left college at some point before the breakfast, when we discovered Martha.'

It wasn't Martha any more, I told myself. She was gone, and nothing would bring her back. 'Just for a walk. With Bill. My friend. The one who was . . .'

'With Bilal Anwar.'

'We all call him Bill.' And it had never occurred to me to ask why, why he felt he couldn't use his real name with us, his closest friends.

'Alison. We've had you in because I understand you're close friends with one of the boys we're looking at, Michael Morris.'

'That's right. We're all friends.' I rubbed my hands together; they felt clammy.

'And you and Michael are . . . together? Dating?'

It seemed very important I play this down; I didn't know why. 'Oh, not really. Now and again. Friends really.'

'So he wouldn't have minded you being off with Bilal.' This was the woman who spoke. It had never occurred to me that Mike would mind anything I did, but I suddenly wondered. Had he been angry, when he saw I was gone? Had he drunk more than usual?

'We're all friends,' I repeated.

'When did you last see Michael, before you left?'

I screwed up my eyes. 'I think he was on the lawn. Getting a drink. A whole bunch of people were there but I just wanted to see the sun come up.'

'You're sure you saw him?'

'Yes, I'm sure.' And I was sure. We'd had a row, even. I just wasn't sure what time it was.

'When was this, Alison?'

'I'm not sure. Maybe an hour before we got back and the college was shut down.'

They exchanged glances. 'Bilal seemed to think it was longer.'

'I don't think it was that long. It was almost light already.' Was that right? I told myself it was, probably. That I wasn't even lying.

They exchanged a look. My stomach sank. But really, how could they prove me wrong? I'd just said I thought it. Anyone was allowed to think something. I pushed down the thought of Martha, how beautiful she'd been in her white silk. Her hand, bruised and limp. 'Did you know Martha well?'

Safer ground. I felt it like when your feet catch the bottom again in the sea. 'Not really. She was nice. But we weren't friends.' I bit my lip. 'It's so awful. She was so lovely.'

'Ali, did you ever see any of your friends take drugs?'

'God no, we don't do that. I've never touched them.' That at least was true. Were drugs involved? Had Martha been given something, the thing we were warned about? Don't leave your drink unattended. Don't accept drinks from strangers. But there were no strangers at the ball.

Except the one who had somehow scaled the ten-foot wall and killed her. 'Did she – is that what—' A drug overdose was sad, but no one's fault. A chink of light opened up to me. Maybe no one did this after all. Maybe I wasn't doing a terrible thing.

The man detective looked at me. 'Martha was strangled, Alison.'

'Oh.' Bile rose up in my mouth. 'I – God, that's awful.'

The police seemed so tired, like they'd already given up. They asked me where I'd be over the summer – in bloody Hull, where else – and I got up to go. As I walked downstairs, into the sunlight, I could see Mike hovering anxiously. Waiting for me. I took my time coming down the stairs, slowly, like a queen. I had the feeling that the next few moments were going to be very important. That maybe they'd even determine the rest of my life.

'Well?'

'It'll be fine. I don't think they know what happened.'

'They knew I was with her. That I . . . that we were together.' I knew there was more he wasn't telling me, but what did it matter now?

'It's fine. I told them I saw you afterwards, not with her.'

He breathed out hard. 'Shit, thank you, Al. I just can't have this on my record if I'm going into law. You've no idea what you . . . thank you.'

I looked out to the lawn, my friends blurs against the sunlight. This was my last day here, my last time walking down these steps or crossing the grass. It was all ending. 'Can I share the house with you and Cal?' I said suddenly. 'I need a place. I can't stay at home. My dad . . .'

He paused. 'There's only two bedrooms, Al.'

'I know.'

That was it, the moment everything was decided between us. Almost twenty years of marriage, two kids, a ridiculous house. My whole life. His whole life. Turning on a small lie. Barely even a lie. Mike said nothing. I was asking so much that I should have felt sick and shaky, but I didn't at all. I felt strong. 'I'll talk to Cal,' he said. 'I guess it would be good to split the rent.'

Chapter Thirty-Four

Jodi was crying when I went into her hospital room. Lying on the bed, red-faced, her legs splayed out like a rag doll's. Crying in a low moan, like a baby left howling for so long it gives up. 'You're here,' she wept. 'I was all by myself.' There was blood on her clothes.

'It's OK,' I said, though it was about as far from that as it could be. 'Where's Callum?' He couldn't still be at work, could he, when his wife was in labour?

Jodi was groaning, her face grey and bloated. 'We had – row. Can't – reach him. Jesus.'

'You're OK.' I began to rub her back, in a way that seemed to be handed on in female DNA. Cavewomen had rubbed each other's backs in just this way, even though Jodi and I were never that close, even though we rarely hugged or touched each other's arms or kissed cheeks. Her back was in spasm, the muscles roiling in some disturbing way that made me think of a snake swallowing an egg. She was wearing a shirt, blue and white striped, and it was easy to see it was Callum's. Why? A self-conscious gesture, to show how much she loved him? To be close to him now she was in labour and he was gone? Or because she really did love him and always had? I thought about how long Jodi had waited for this moment, which Karen and I had experienced sixteen and eighteen years ago. We never knew why it had taken them so long – mutters about fertility problems, references to 'trying', followed by a small wry grimace, Callum's occasional little jokes about Mike being 'all man, mate'. Jodi's careful questions about acupuncture or diets, a group trip to Cornwall – 2007 maybe, or 2010? – stopping off at a Co-op and Jodi palming a small box, her face tight. A jumper tied tight around her waist. Refusing to swim although it was so hot, 27 degrees, and the sea blue and purple and green. The things we don't know about our friends. The things we don't ask.

'Where are the nurses?' I said, glancing about for a phone or call bell. 'They should give you something for the pain.'

She shook her head. 'No. Don't want anything. Christ! Does it always hurt this bad? Will it stop?' I could hardly remember, the exuberance of my children bursting from me, my own cleverness at producing them. Mike so proud. Proud of me, of what I'd done. Had I always known I needed to hold on to him? Had I seen his gaze tugged by Jake, ruffling his hair? Then I thought of Karen, only twenty-five, having him alone. How young and stupid we'd all been, gathering at the hospital like it was another party or holiday. Callum with a hip flask of whisky, passing it as we waited. Hadn't we jobs, responsibilities? How had we all been able to wait for Karen like that, as the sticky summer day turned violet and evening came? And I knew, when we were shown in, Karen scrubbed and raw in her hospital gown, the baby worrying into her with his crown of dark hair, I knew I had to have some of that too. The glare of success on her face, like she'd been in a different light to the rest of us. A journey she could send no postcards from. The ultimate 'you had to be there' moment. I tugged on Mike's arm, as he rushed over to her. Jodi already there exclaiming over the baby, probably thinking she'd have one herself in four or five or six years, no hurry. Callum soppy and tender, quite drunk already. 'Bloody well done, Kar, you trooper.' Bill not even there, far away in Sweden already.

I pulled on Mike as he strained towards the new life in the room. 'I want this,' I said. He looked back, confused – did he suspect this baby was his? On some level do we recognise our own blood? But no,

I had to believe he'd have done so much more for Jake if he'd known. 'I want a baby,' I said again. We'd been married four months, the ring still shining on my finger, and I'd been cross with Karen for spoiling the wedding by puking into a centrepiece, her belly pushing out the bridesmaid's dress I'd chosen. Not drinking on my hen do. Upstaging me, with all the whispers about who her baby's father was. She wouldn't say, hinted at some one-night stand. Maybe I'd been too preoccupied to really think about it. You aren't allowed to say it but your wedding is perilously close to a licence to let out the selfish little diva inside all of us. It says to girls – you won't matter any more, not after this, so for today you get to matter the most.

Now, out of nowhere I was blind-sided by pity for Karen. Giving birth alone, bringing home her baby alone. His father visiting but married to her friend. His eyes skipping over her like they'd never slept together. Like Jake couldn't be his, not even possible.

He must have known it was possible.

'We have to get Callum,' I insisted, as Jodi bellowed again. 'He has to be here. Where is he, for God's sake?' Was I really going to end up being Jodi's birth partner? 'Can you not reach him, is that it? He must be somewhere, I can call . . .'

She was shaking her head again, her knuckles white. 'He went off. Says – baby's not his.'

'*What?*' Jodi would never cheat. She just wasn't the type – far too much of a deviation from acceptable, Instagram-worthy behaviour.

'Donor . . .' she panted out, and it all made sense. Callum's comments on the night it all happened, about turkey basters and sperm machines. The sudden pregnancy after years of trying. They'd used a sperm donor.

'He's got a problem?' I shouldn't have asked, it was rude, but I felt so far past manners now. In a whole other country.

'Nothing . . . comes out. Nothing in it.' I was getting the picture but she felt the need to say more. Like she really wanted me to understand. 'Started . . . in his twenties. He can do it but there's nothing to come out.'

I thought about that for a minute, and then put it aside. Too much to unpack in there, Callum's hurt feelings, Jodi's happiness.

Jodi let out another cry, and I forced myself to focus. If I'd learned anything from these last weeks, it was that it wasn't possible to save everyone. You just had to pick someone, and save them, and let the rest drown. In the middle of it all, everyone I loved most going under, I had chosen Mike. I just had to hope that, with everything I'd sacrificed, it had been worth it. I just had to hope I had saved my husband after all. There was no room now for doubts and fears.

I made my voice firm and confident. 'I'll find him, Jodi. Where do you think he could be?'

She panted, 'Maybe . . . at home now. Don't know.'

'Then I'll go there. It isn't far. Will you be alright for an hour? I'll make sure they take care of you.'

'I already – called – Karen,' she panted. 'Sorry. I just – was panicking.'

So Karen might be on her way, and I would have to face her again. 'Never mind,' I soothed. 'We'll sort that out later.'

Jodi looked up at me, and I could see the relief on her face. All this time I'd been waiting for someone to take charge, and it seemed now that someone was me.

Chapter Thirty-Five

I knew Karen's mobile number by heart. After all, she had been my best friend. Was my best friend. I didn't know the right words to say it. All I knew was that she felt like a part of me. I knew she felt like my sister, if I'd had a sister. Closer than blood. All I knew was I had always turned to her when I didn't know what to do, and this was no exception.

In the lobby of the hospital, I dialled her number. It felt like a good place to wait while your life moved into positions you'd never imagined, the continental drift of your future. It was full of other people doing the same, waiting with twisted plastic cups between their hands, standing up and pacing, thumbing at mobile phones, staring blankly at the rolling news screens. The bright lights against the dark. I rested my head against the cool metal of the phone as it rang. I wondered if I'd ever feel happy again. Peaceful, and well, and hopeful. I wondered if I'd ever like myself again.

I thought she might not answer. I'd called from a payphone so she wouldn't recognise my mobile number. I was sure she wouldn't want to talk to me. But she answered, her voice low and wary. 'Hello?' Her voice that I'd once heard every day, first thing in the morning and last thing at night. We'd called each other 'wifey' back then, a little joke, but really it wasn't a joke and she'd been closer than that to me. Closer than anyone had ever been. I could hear a train announcement in the background; she must be on her way.

'Kar?' She'd know my voice. No need to say who I was. She said nothing, but I could hear her breathing on the line. 'It's me. I'm so . . . I'm so sorry to call. But something's happened. Callum's – well. He's gone AWOL. And – I've found out some things.' I didn't know how to explain it. Jodi's baby wasn't Callum's, and he was having some kind of breakdown over it. I had already tried his phone, and the house phone, but there was no answer. He wasn't picking up. Karen said nothing, but I could hear she was listening, so I went on, trying to explain as delicately as I could the startling thing Jodi had just told me. 'I think – I don't know what I think. It's sent him off the rails or something. Will you come straight here and be with Jodi? I'm going to run to theirs and see if Callum's there – I'll meet you back here.'

A long silence. Then she said: 'I'll be there in an hour.' And I knew that between us we would find a way to fix this. Then I went outside and hailed a taxi, thankful they took cards now, and directed it to Pimlico.

◆ ◆ ◆

The white stucco house glowed in the moonlight, and I couldn't see a single light on. I leaned hard on the doorbell. Nothing. Then I remembered the side return.

It was open, the gate unlatched. As I crept around to the back door, over their neat patio, I realised how easy it would be to just walk into most people's lives. We are too trusting. We think everything is locked up and safe and we take it for granted, until something goes wrong. The kitchen blinds weren't pulled and I could see into their home, their lives. The glow from the kitchen light showed me a bottle of whisky with the seal pulled off, standing on the counter. I turned the door handle and it opened.

'Hello?'

The kitchen looked neat as always, a rinsed mug sitting on the draining rack. I wondered if Jodi had gone into labour, then calmly cleaned up before taking herself to hospital. It was the kind of thing she would do.

I moved into the hallway; the place was silent. A dim light was on in Callum's 'den', a room he'd done up in leather chairs and books, like a drinking club.

'Cal?'

He was there, slumped in a chair, wearing a crumpled suit. He was drinking, of course. A large whisky. It seemed clichéd – as if even at that moment, Callum was concerned that someone would see him and know him for a man drinking the correct drink for a moment of emotional breakdown. I stood and let him see me, which he did slowly, blearily. 'Al.'

'Jodi's in labour. She's at St Thomas's.'

He nodded into the whisky, swirling it. I wondered if he even liked whisky or just pretended to. 'She'll be OK.'

'Well, she might not be. It's a high-risk pregnancy – she's forty-two. I can't believe you left her. What were you thinking?'

It was a larger question that I was asking, really, and Callum must have known this because he didn't answer. He seemed weary, beaten somehow. 'She'll be OK,' he said again. 'She hardly needs me.'

'Of course she needs you! She needs someone to advocate for her, make sure they keep to the birth plan, and . . .'

'I'd be no good at that. Don't know anything about kids. It's not even mine.' He slid the last in matter of factly, as if he thought I already knew this. And had I, before Jodi said? On some level, had I suspected? I seemed to remember Karen saying: *I guess they're doing something.* Something covered a lot. Interventions. Petri dishes. Donor sperm.

'Of course it's yours.' I sat across from him in the other leather seat, determined to be brisk and clear and not give in to the small pulse of panic at the base of my spine.

'I mean it. Got no lead in my pipe. It works but there's nothing. Tanks are dry.'

I winced. 'You mean you used a sperm donor.'

He drank some whisky and made a face. 'Some German fella. Imagine we'll have a tall blonde baby who's very good at cycling. At least we'll get sun loungers on holiday.'

'Cal . . . lots of people do it this way. It doesn't mean you're not . . . that it's not . . . anyway, Jodi needs you. She's in pain, and she's scared, and you need to go to her now.'

He raised his head. His eyes were bloodshot, piggy, as if he'd been smoking weed for hours or hadn't slept in weeks or both. 'She doesn't need me. No one needs me.'

'That's not . . .'

He sighed. Regretful, or maybe irritated with my slowness. 'Al. Ali. You know by now, don't you? You know and that's why you've come?'

It was almost a pleading. 'What do I know?'

Another sigh. His voice was small, like a child's. 'What I did. I kept waiting for them to come for me, but they never did.'

My heart was pumping very hard in my chest, like someone was pounding me with their fist. 'Cal . . .'

And I thought back to that moment in the kitchen, Karen stumbling in with blood on her thigh and my sense that this was it, the last moment before everything changed. I had that same feeling now, looking over the polished parquet floor at Callum, my friend of twenty-five years. I thought about the jumper I'd found in Benji's toy-box, scarlet red, now dirty with burrs and leaves, unearthed from the rubbish pile. They'd say Mike took it off that night, afraid of DNA or blood, then he hid it somewhere he knew it would be burned. But Mike had not been sober enough to think of something like that. I'd seen him myself. So someone else must have done it. The jumper had been left on the decking, carelessly dropped. It was the jumper both Bill and Karen had mentioned seeing in the dark of the garden. But Mike was in bare arms when I confronted him right after, on the swing seat. Someone else could have put the jumper on.

Someone else could have done this to Karen.

Callum

It was a strange thing, consciousness. He'd used the excuse before at uni – *I was so drunk, sorry mate, I can't remember.* To get out of bad behaviour, spilling someone's pint or staggering off home without them from Park End or groping a girl on the dance floor. *Sorry, sorry, I can't remember, all a blur, must have blacked out.* Back then, it hadn't been true. He'd never truly blacked out, the kind where you're walking around and talking and doing things but there's just a big black hole in your memory. These days, now he kept a vodka bottle in his glove box and one in his desk drawer and went to a bar for a whisky chaser every day before heading home, he'd learned the true meaning of that word. *Blackout.* And who could blame him if he needed something, when he was going home to Jodi, standing at the top of the stairs with her dressing gown done up all the way to the neck? Wrinkling her nose at him. *You stink of booze.* She could smell everything now she was finally, at ruinous expense, pregnant. Other things had changed too. When he reached for her, made sad and squishy by the booze, sad enough to wish they could bridge the space between them somehow, she turned away in bed. *I don't want to hurt the baby. I can't bear the stink. I'm too tired.* Reminding him, in a million subtle ways every day, that she was pregnant with another man's child.

Callum thought about the man a lot. He was German, that was all they knew. German and thirty-eight. Callum imagined someone tall and blond with amazing abs. He pictured him like he'd always pictured Bill, stripped to the waist hewing wood in a pine forest. Jodi had always liked Bill a bit too much. All the girls did. *He's so sweet. He really listens.* Easy to listen when you had nothing to say, no jokes, no banter. A man like this would be the father of his child. Callum would dandle a huge German baby, who'd grow up taller than him. He could picture the graduation photos, the strapping blond boy and his dark, five foot seven father. People would laugh. People would know he was not the dad. That he wasn't man enough to get his own wife up the duff. When the kid was eighteen he'd maybe be allowed to track the man down, his real father. While Callum would have spent years paying for him and changing his shitty nappies and picking him up from discos pissed. It wasn't right.

When he'd told his parents what they were planning to do, IVF with donor sperm – Jodi had told them, Callum hadn't wanted to, but she was excited, and he thought maybe she'd wanted to make the point that it wasn't her with the little problem, the issue – his mother had faltered, then gushed. 'Oh, how lovely. Isn't it wonderful, the things they can do these days.'

His father had said nothing. Later, in the garden, while Callum pretended he knew how to cut grass, he had said, 'I don't know how you can do it. Another man's bairn.'

'It'll be mine,' he'd said, wishing he felt it.

'You'll always know it isn't,' his father had said, and Callum felt it all well up in him, the years of rage, feeling so small and so stupid, even now when he could buy his parents' house twice over, knowing he'd never measure up to his father, because he couldn't fix things and build things and ejaculate working sperm. He'd said nothing, but it was in there, moving under a thin layer like an iced-over river. Getting restless.

Then, that night. Karen so hot and flirty, her legs bare. Sexy still at her age, when Jodi was a whale and Ali was so prim and proper. Ali had always been the good girl. Even Jodi, quiet as she was, had once had her wild side too. Before the lack of babies had soured and killed it between them. Before she realised his cock was no use to her for what she needed. When she'd lumbered up to bed that night, she'd hissed at him. Actually hissed with disgust. 'You better not come stumbling in to bed pissed like that. It's not good for the baby if I get woken up.'

'But where am I meant to sleep?' He'd heard his own little-boy voice, pathetic and whiny. His father would have hit him for that.

'I don't care. Sleep on the sofa. Sleep in the garden.' She'd thrown him a contemptuous look over her shoulder. 'Sleep with Karen. Seems like that's what you want. Not that she'd have you.'

It was the *not that she'd have you* that rankled. Even his pregnant wife, leaking and enormous, wasn't worried other women would want him. No one wanted him. Even the women in the office and the hotels, they'd been paid, hadn't they? One way or the other.

He'd suspected about Karen and Mike in college, of course. They didn't even try to hide it, and Ali was the only one who didn't see or want to see, locked up with her books and student activities while Karen and Mike dry-humped in the corner of clubs, disappeared off at bops for an hour only to come back five minutes apart, glowing and dishevelled. Callum burned with jealousy. There was Mikey with both the sexiest girl in their year and the nicest too. It wasn't fair.

He'd thought it was over, of course. Just a college thing, all in the past. Then that lunch, the one where he'd sweated right through his shirt thinking he had to explain to Mikey he didn't have the money. The cash Mike had lent him to shore up the mortgage, after one year and then another he hadn't got his yearly bonus. Booze on his breath at work. One girl and then another paid off, disappearing from the office. No surprise. He kept hoping it would right itself, the money would start flowing again, and he'd be able to pay Mike off. But it never did.

Then, a miracle. Mike had a new phone, hadn't set it up right yet. He went to the loo during lunch and it went off, flashing up Karen's name and a query about meeting later. Terse, but Callum knew the rhythms of an affair text. There'd been a few girls. Interns mostly, a leg-over for a leg-up. Everyone knew the score. When Mike came back he'd said lightly, 'You want to change your privacy settings, mate. Don't want Al seeing that, I guess.' And watching Mike turn pale and stammering, how lovely it was. 'Don't worry mate, I won't tell. We're pals.' And not bringing up the money he owed, and instead letting Mike pick up the tab for lunch, it was glorious. It really was. He'd even asked for more, nice and neat every month, slipped into an overseas savings account he'd set up through work. It wasn't blackmail, of course it wasn't! They were old mates. He just needed it, and Mikey had it, so what was the harm?

The night of the reunion had slid by in a smear of old jokes, recycled until the juice was wrung out of them. He'd felt old, and tired, and a strong sense that this would be the last time for all of them. The six of them who had remained friends when so many others weren't, shored up by the two marriages in the group, and Karen who never went away. He understood that now, and in a way he felt sorry for her. Having to watch as Ali swanned about, gabbing about her kids' achievements and the price of her new house. Giggling behind her hands. 'I shouldn't say, and I hate to brag, but isn't it just mad? Almost a million? Can you believe it?' Karen smiling thinly, probably thinking of that hole she rented in Birmingham. Everyone – well, Jodi – had tried to push Karen and Bill together at uni. As if it was some stupid American sitcom where everyone had to pair off in the end. Almost Shakespearean, almost incestuous, as if there was no one else in the world but the Group. The blonde Swedish bird of Bill's, she'd been sexy, if a bit older, but Callum hadn't liked the cool appraising way her eyes passed over his face, the few times they'd met. And she'd been four inches taller than him. It wasn't right, in a woman. And Karen had some fellas over the years, some builder or something, slumming it with manual labour. It had amused him and Mike to ask the guy his opinion about the tax system, see him stumble. The lecturer was smarter but wasn't ageing well, already grey and cracked round the eyes, and you could tell Karen wanted something else. She wanted Mike, and she'd never get him. Callum had known before her that Mike was ending it. Poor bitch. Poor stupid bloody bitch.

It was maybe this that had made him follow Karen into the garden. He'd gone to the loo – Bill was in bed already – and when he stumbled back out Mike was passed out in the swing seat. Pathetic bastard. It was dark, a pitch-like dark you never got in London, and turning cold.

Mike's jumper was on the decking and without thinking he'd pulled it on, rubbing at his arms. It was soft and expensive, Mikey flaunting his cash again. And Karen, poor cow, had gone wandering across the lawn wringing her hands, pissed and sobbing. His heart broke for her and without really thinking he was lumbering after her, to hug her or share something, share their pain – *Hey, Kar, I know how you feel, Mike's a bastard, a bastard who always comes up smelling of roses no matter what he does, and my wife is up the duff with some German sperm and I'm obsolete. I have to pay women to fuck me.*

And maybe the thought was there, that Karen was sad and desperate, and she'd had some shockers in the past, as they always liked to remind her in their bantz. Maybe that thought was there as he put his hand out to steady her, on the back of her neck, like a frightened horse. He didn't remember what happened after that, not until he was lying on the sofa and everyone was shouting and Karen was screaming in the kitchen. But he had a feeling that the memories were there inside somewhere, like the bugs that scurry and run when you disturb a woodpile. And he didn't want to see those bugs.

In the car the next day, going home. Jodi driving, by tacit agreement, as he was still surely over the limit. She was mad at him, he thought, for getting drunk again, but that happened so often it was hardly worth mentioning. No discussion about what had happened all the way home to Pimlico, a silent drive without even the radio on. Afraid to hear news bulletins. *Man arrested on suspicion of rape after Bishopsdean party.* Karen was sure it was Mike, positive. She'd been so drunk.

Mike was his friend. But Mike had shagged Karen, over and over, and got away with it, hurt her, hurt Ali, and all Callum had done was a silly misunderstanding. That was all. Reached out to hold Karen, and then she'd seemed to want him, but then she'd changed her mind and he'd just tried to make her be quiet and listen, understand what they both had to lose if she kept screaming. But she'd been so pissed she couldn't tell one man from the other. And wasn't that her fault too?

It was easy in the end. He kept waiting for Jodi to bring it up, tell him she knew something, but she never did, and neither did he, and they slid back into their lives, work and the baby and the house, so easily it was like dropping into a moving stream of cold clear water.

Chapter Thirty-Six

He talked. He talked so much, in a stream of words that sometimes made sense and sometimes didn't, as if half the conversation was happening in his own head. 'She was so, you know how she was. Flirting her ass off. That dress. Throwing herself all over Bill and, and I was so drunk, Al, and I just felt . . . I'm not a man. I know that. I'm not a man because I can't make anything and Jodi knows I'm not a man and you know and. And. You see. She. How she was. You know? That dress . . . Al, I never meant to. I thought she wanted to. That dress. Flirting. Christ, she's such a tease when she wants to be. We called her that. Karen the Pricktease, back then, only, only, Mikey, she wasn't teasing him. Never told me. His best friend. Never told me. But I saw. I saw it on his phone.'

For a moment I thought he was going to cry with self-pity, poor old Cal, that no one had told him and he wasn't a man. '. . . I thought she wanted. She was so. So, so. You know. And I saw her on the lawn and her legs were all bare so I went up to her – I thought she wanted. And she didn't stop . . . she didn't say no. You know Kar. She likes rough. You can tell. Dirty, like. Tell from looking. So we . . . and I went over and I was so drunk and then I . . .'

I felt frozen. I could see the glass of whisky in front of me, diluted by melted ice cubes, but I didn't know if I could lift my hand to touch it. All I could see was Karen that night. Blood on her thigh. Callum.

Crashed out on the sofa in the living room, as if he'd been there for hours. But for Mike's sake, I needed to be clear. I needed to be very very clear, even if having this conversation felt like putting my hand into a flame. 'Cal. You're saying that you and Karen . . . that you had sex with Karen . . . that night?'

He nodded up and down, like the dog in that ad. 'Thought she wanted it.' Sorrowful. 'Feeling bad. Jodi up the duff . . . not a real man. Not mine.'

'So you . . . Cal, she was hurt. She was bleeding.'

He shrank, like a boy being told off. 'Thought she liked it. She didn't say stop. Was awkward though. She kept kicking, like kicking me, and I had scratches. Hurt. Wildcat.'

I had to be very very clear. 'Did you . . . when you were with her, did you . . . finish?'

He shook his head sadly. 'Can't. Couldn't do it.' Could there still be DNA though, from skin or hair or something? My stomach turned.

I wondered if the police and lawyers felt like this sometimes. If it was simply too exhausting to even imagine building a case again, and going through all the evidence, the pages of text and sad little bags of bodily fluids, if they ever wanted to just throw up their hands and say, *guys, you'll have to sort it out between you.* Because how did you solve this kind of crime, which when you open one eye is sex, two old friends having drunk sex on a lawn, a laugh and a shameful giggle, then you open the other and it's a terrible assault, it's years in prison. It's lives ruined. It's a woman who can't sleep in a room with a window any more. I tried to let it all sink in. This happened. Karen felt this. It was done to her. 'Cal . . . you have to tell the police,' I said, and I tried to sound reasonable, like I was talking to a sane person. 'Mike might go to prison.'

'But he shagged her! He shagged her for years! That day he shagged her! Saw it when we got there, look on their faces.'

'I know. But she . . . she wanted him to. It's not the same.'

He pouted. 'How was I meant to know she didn't? Never said so.'

And there it was – the attitude I'd been fighting so hard against for years. That it was on us to say no, even if we were too drunk to move or speak or too afraid or couldn't breathe. And for Karen, I'd been the one to say: she was drunk. And, look at her dress. And, well they'd had sex before.

'So – Mike didn't do it.' My voice was low, calm.

He shook his head.

'And – Cal, what about Martha? Did you – do you know what happened to her?'

He stared at the ground, and I thought he was going to say of course not, it was some stranger like we always thought. Then he made a noise, some kind of bellow of guilt and relief and exasperation. 'I never MEANT to! She was so pissed! They always get so pissed and then they scream and you have to stop them! Jesus, she made so much noise. Everyone would – people would hear. Had to stop her. Never meant to.'

I swallowed. My mouth was so dry. 'Mike wasn't with her.'

'Went to get drinks. Fancied his chances. Snogged her already. Not fair, is it? He had you and Karen already, then he wants to score with Rasby too? What's so special about him, for fuck's sake? What's wrong with me?' I could picture it. Martha, drunk and alone in the garden, waiting for Mike to come back. Callum creeping in, maybe after I'd spoken to him. Drunk, sloppy. Angry at Mike. His bear-like hands trying to quiet her. Around her slender white neck. Oh God.

I felt sick. And Callum, my old friend Callum, was sitting across the room from me, his face puffy and red, the skin dry and cracking, and I had to decide now what to do. There was Jodi in the hospital, having her baby, all alone.

I stood up, feeling my legs like jelly beneath me. What could I do? Throw Callum under a bus? Call the police down in Bishopsdean right now? They'd hardly arrest him, all the way up here. Would they send local officers? He'd been walking around for weeks now, free. I could tell Jake, but he was in prison, precisely to stop him attacking the man who he thought had hurt his mother. I realised there was one person who had the right to adjudicate over what happened next.

I spoke quietly. 'Cal, let me get you some water, OK? I know this is hard.'

He nodded, rubbing a hand over his face. He looked awful. Twenty years older than he was. Slowly, I inched past him to the door, then out into the kitchen. My sandals clattered on the floor tiles, the ones I'd envied just a few weeks before. My bag was on the kitchen island, and in it my phone. I held my breath – no sound from Callum in the other room. I turned on the tap to run, then took the phone out and started dialling Karen's number. I was just listening to the ring when a clammy hand closed over my mouth.

Chapter Thirty-Seven

I struggled away from him, repulsed by the meaty tang of his skin. His wedding ring knocked against my teeth. 'Cal – what the hell!'

He moved his hand from my mouth to my arm. I could feel the fingers digging in. 'Ali, you can't. Can't tell anyone. S'over now. S'done.'

'It's not over! Mike might go to prison and . . .'

'I'm not going to prison. You hear me! I'm not.' It was absurd. Here I was with my friend and he had wedged his body behind me, pressing me against the kitchen island. I'd never realised how powerful he was, the stockiness of his short body. He gripped the phone, squeezing it from my hand, smearing it with his prints.

'Let me go! Fucking hell, what are you doing?' I pushed back hard against him, and understood, with horror, that I could not move. I couldn't stop him from doing whatever he was going to do.

I think that was the moment I fully believed it. Callum had raped Karen. In my garden. It had really happened, and it had started as this did – a woman slowly realising that her supposed friend had her trapped, and she could do nothing about it. He had raped Karen and he had murdered Martha, all those years ago. And Mike had borne the blame for both.

I lowered my voice, tried to sound friendly. 'Cal, come on. It's me, Ali. I wouldn't call the police on you! I just wanted to check on Jodi.'

'Jodi.' The pressure released a little. He was hurting my hand, so I let him take the phone. For a moment I thought he was going to smash it on the tiles, but he laid it on the counter. 'Having the baby.'

'That's right. So why don't we go and see her, OK?' If I could get out of this house, get him to the hospital, well, they had security guards. Other people around. 'We can call a cab, what do you say?'

He considered it for a moment, made slow and clumsy by drink. 'You told the police on Mikey. Didn't you? Told them he admitted it. You lied, didn't you?' How did he even know that? The lines that ran between us all, from Karen to Jodi to Callum?

'I – I had no choice. I needed Jake to help Mike, donate his liver.'

Callum was shaking his head. The pressure on my body was back, his hips and chest against mine. 'You've no loyalty, Ali. I don't trust you. Mikey gets in trouble and what do you do? You turn your back. Shack up with ol' Bill five minutes later.'

'I . . .' It was true. I didn't know how to justify myself. 'Please, you're hurting me. Let me go.'

'Oh Ali!' He made a noise like a sigh and sob. 'What am I going to do?' His clumsy hand pushed the hair back from my face. Somewhere between a slap and a caress. I hadn't been this close to him for so long and it felt all wrong. My blood was roaring in my ears, all my senses on fire. *Get out. Get out. This isn't safe.* I raced through scenarios of what to do, all the while holding on to how crazy it was. He was my friend. I'd trusted him. He pulled my face around to look at him, twisting my neck. 'How come never me, eh? You had a go on Mikey and Billy-boy. Why not me?' His plaintive tone made me want to vomit.

'You were with Jodi.' I tried to sound light but my voice sounded scared and strangled. I hated that.

'No. You never wanted me.' I could feel his boozy breath on my face, and his rubbery wet mouth coming at me. A shot of pure panic went through me. He wouldn't. It was madness! After everything? But my body didn't understand it was impossible, and I whimpered in fear.

'Don't hurt me, Callum, stop it. Stop it!'

I was fixated on his face, his body against mine, one hand in my hair and one trapping my waist, but then I was aware of movement in the room, and the sudden crack of something like pottery. A look of confusion crossed his face, and I saw red blood trickle down over his eye.

Then I saw Karen standing there, the remains of a pot plant in her hand, trailing soil and blood all over the floor, and on her face the grimmest expression I'd ever seen.

◆   ◆   ◆

'How did you know to come?'

She shrugged. 'I don't know. When you told me that – that he can't finish – I just – it was like something went off in my head. He said it that night. The man who – hurt me. He said, *Sorry, I can't*. I was just so – I didn't understand, couldn't take it in. But when you told me, I couldn't stop thinking about it. I was in the cab to the hospital and I sent it to their house instead.'

'Thank God you did.'

She nodded, unreadable. Despite the context, I was glad we were having this conversation in the police station. It felt neutral, bright lights blasting everything and laying it bare. Neither of us would make a scene here. She sat opposite me in the waiting room, the lights of cars passing outside in the road. They'd left us there, I think unsure what to do with two nice middle-aged women, covered in a man's blood, who'd rung them so calmly and told them what had happened. I remembered Karen's tight voice as she spoke to them. *A man was attacking my friend, so I hit him with a plant pot. He's bleeding.*

She'd called me her friend.

Callum was in hospital with a head injury. The same hospital as Jodi, and what did that mean? I didn't know. The facts seemed to elude me, like flies buzzing round my head. How would we tell Jodi what we knew now about her husband? Her son was only hours old and his father was a killer and rapist. What would it be like to find that out, when you'd just brought a child into the world?

Karen said, 'Tell me again what he said.'

I had told her already, what I knew, and watched it seep through her like water into rock. Her face didn't move as I repeated it. 'He said . . . he'd seen you outside on the lawn and thought you . . . he thought you'd been flirting with him. It was rambling. But he more or less – he did it, Kar.'

Her jaw set. 'Him.'

Timidly, I said: 'Do you . . . is that something you think might have happened?' I meant, was it Callum who had sex with you on the lawn, not Mike? *Had sex with*. That was not the right phrase, but I still didn't know how to say it. 'Did he – attack you?'

Karen thought about it. 'I wasn't lying. The aftershave, the jumper. They were Mike's.'

'The jumper was in the rubbish pile.' I explained that Benji found it, shoved right to the bottom.

'So someone wanted to destroy it? Wanted it burned?'

'I guess so. Mike had taken it off, before dinner. It was so hot during the day, remember. It was lying on the decking. I was cross because he never put things away.' Using the past tense to speak of him, my husband. Because I was afraid he would die, or because I knew things would never be the same again?

Karen's mouth was pursed. She was hunched over, and the hands that held an empty paper cup were shaking. 'He put it on. So I'd think it was Mike.'

'Maybe he was just cold or . . .' I stopped. I didn't know why I was defending Callum. Why I was still, after all this time, trying to ease the brutal facts of what had happened. Trying to spare myself, when it was Karen who'd had this done to her, to her body and her mind.

'He knew. About me and Mike. Mike said he thought Callum suspected.'

Me and Mike. It was a knife in me, but I was so numb I couldn't feel it now. Later, sometime, all these wounds would make themselves felt, I was sure of it. 'He did, yeah.' Would Callum ever have told me? Did all our friends know, everyone except me?

'He knew I'd think he was Mike, and I'd want to . . . that I'd not put my guard up. I was drunk. I was really really drunk. You don't know what that feels like, when it's being done to you, and you can't get away, you can't even move . . . he was kneeling on me, Al. On my . . . my legs. My back. I couldn't breathe. I couldn't see him. It was so dark. All I could see was the jumper, and there was the smell too. The aftershave.'

It was all making sense to me now, so much so that I didn't know why I hadn't seen it before. Blind, distracted, dazzled as I had been all the way through. Looking at the wrong thing all this time. Mike had doused himself in aftershave that night. Of course – he'd wanted to shower before dinner, and I'd nagged him not to, because there wasn't time, not knowing he'd been with Karen just minutes before I got back. He'd been trying to cover up the smell of her, of sex. His jumper would have reeked of aftershave, obliterating any other smell. And it had been sitting there, conveniently, on the decking, in a discarded heap.

'What now?' I risked. I didn't know what to do. I didn't know how to be with her.

She shook herself all over. 'I feel like I'm going mad. I was so sure. So sure it was Mike.'

I had felt that way too at times. 'I'm sorry.' My voice cracked under the weight of it, how inadequate those syllables were for everything I had to say sorry for. 'I should never have said those things. I should have believed you.'

She lifted her chin slightly. 'But it wasn't true, Ali. What I said. Was it?'

I swallowed. 'Maybe not. But you didn't . . . you thought it was him.'

'I did. I hope you understand that.'

'Of course. I should have – well, it was unforgivable, what I did. I'm fired, basically. My career's over.'

'What a mess.' Karen was strangely detached. 'What a bloody mess, eh. What will I do?'

'We should tell the police everything. Callum confessed to me, I don't think he'll fight it. Tell them you remembered the truth, and then they can drop the charges against Mike.'

'But Mike's sick. Right?'

'Yeah. He's very sick.'

'And Jake is the only donor.' She sounded like she was puzzling it all out in her head. 'OK.' She pushed her hands off her thighs lightly, as if getting organised. 'I'm going to tell them. That it wasn't Mike, it was – him. Then you and I are going to see Jodi. She's all by herself, and you shouldn't be alone when you've had a baby. We just aren't meant to do it.' Maybe that was a dig about all those years ago, the day Jake was born, when I'd dragged Mike away from the hospital to immediately have sex and try to get my own baby. Had I known, on some level, that Jake was his? Or was I just so selfish I didn't care? I'd never know. What a store of hurts we had from each other, Karen and me. Like a set of scales that were balanced with stones.

Karen stood up. 'Will you come with me?' she said. 'Will you help?'

'Of course,' I said. And I stood up too, and we walked to the door, shoulder to shoulder.

Epilogue

The For Sale sign swung in the breeze that had picked up round the house. The summer was on its way out – in a week or two Benji would start school, and Cassie sixth-form college. Neither of them in Bishopsdean, however. We were leaving the town behind, and hopefully, with the proceeds from the house, we'd be able to buy a more modest flat or terrace before Christmas. For now we were moving into a rented flat in London, not far from the one Cassie had been born in. Benji had grumbled about leaving his friends, but he understood, I think, the need to get away. For Cassie it would be life or death. A chance to start again, to outrun that picture and the pills she'd swallowed. A place where no one knew what kind of family we were.

She came up behind me as I stared out the kitchen door at the sign, past the spot where Karen had been assaulted. 'Are you sad we're selling?'

'Not really. I don't see how we can live here now.' My dream house – a pipe dream, one I never truly thought I deserved – was tainted for ever by what happened to Karen here. And Cassie, swallowing those pills. By everything.

I had given up my dreams of Aaron ever being punished for spreading the picture. I knew he wouldn't have thought he even did anything wrong, and lots of people would agree. Even Cassie wasn't convinced the whole thing hadn't been her fault – she'd sent it in the first place, after all. At least if we left town I wouldn't have to bump into him and his awful mother in Waitrose. The more I thought about it, the more I marvelled that I'd ever lived in a place like this.

Cassie nodded, and let me slip my arm around her shoulders without pulling away. 'Will Granny come and stay when we move?'

My mother had stayed for a month in the end, and although it was too simplistic to say we'd put the past behind us, she'd grown close to Cassie and Benji, and seemed able to show them affection in a way she never had with me. Guilt, maybe, had shadowed all of our encounters. I didn't forgive her entirely for never standing up to Dad. But I would try to understand, now I had faced the lengths a person would go to so they could hang on to their life.

Mike had already moved back to London. After the transplant, he'd made a good recovery, and woken up the next day lucid and remorseful, but we'd agreed our marriage was one more thing that could not be saved. Like with the house, there was no way back from everything that had happened. He was living in a flat not far from where we'd be, back at his old job. His boss seemed rather embarrassed that they'd ever doubted him. Karen and Jake were back in Birmingham and I didn't know when I'd see them next. I'd heard Jake wasn't getting over the transplant so well, that he'd been in and out of hospital a few times. He was on bail now until his trial, and I hoped his sentence would be light, given what he'd done for us. I tried not to feel guilty.

As for Callum, his trial was coming up in the autumn, not just for the rape of Karen, but for killing Martha too. Since it was a murder charge, he hadn't got bail and was currently on remand in a London prison. I'd have to see him, and Karen, in court, and I was steeling myself for that. I'd been lucky not to face charges myself, although DC Devine had made it clear he knew I'd deceived him with my ever-changing story.

Jodi had named her son Eric – a Teutonic name – and cut herself off from all of us. My baby gift had come back return to sender. I wasn't sure if I would ever see her again. I wanted to tell her I didn't blame her, that none of us had seen what Callum was. But I wasn't sure she'd listen.

I gave Cassie a squeeze. 'Have you started packing? The van will be here soon.'

She gave a small eye-roll, and I was happy to see it, a trace of her old self. 'We've ages yet.'

'Not really, it'll take hours to sort this place.' There was a crunch of gravel in the drive, and I looked up to see the large moving van manoeuvring in, and beside the driver, waving to us, was Bill. 'He's here,' I said to Cassie. 'Come on, let's get ready.'

Jodi

'Shh, shh, baby. It's OK. Mummy's here.'

It was early – before 5 a.m. still. Time had lost meaning now it was just her and the baby in the house. Her son. Finally, after so many years. At the sound of his snuffling cries, she eased him from his crib, so close to her own bed she could feel his breath on her outstretched hand, and put him to her breast. A smile broke over her face as he tugged, and latched. Her baby. Fifteen years after she'd expected him, here he was.

As she touched his downy cheek in the grey morning light, she found herself wondering once again had she done the right thing. If she could go back to that night, the night of the party, and make a different choice, was there a way to change the outcome? Maybe not. She lay back against her pillows and let herself remember what she'd been suppressing ever since it happened.

Something had woken her. It happened all the time since she'd got pregnant, shooting awake in the middle of the night, every hair on her body standing on end, her heart trying to pound right out of her chest.

And there was always nothing. A shadow across the bed, maybe, or a car passing in the street outside. Her body was on red alert for any danger to the child in her belly. Now, disorientated, she took a few minutes to understand where she was. Ali's spare room. The unfamiliar smell of her washing powder. The silence of the country, the dust under the bed where it wasn't vacuumed properly. Except it wasn't silent. There'd been a noise. Her ears might not have known but the nerves in her spine were sure. She got up, lumbering to the window that looked over the vast, dark garden. It wasn't fair. Her own London house had only a small patio area, despite costing close to a million pounds. Anxiety pounded through her as she passed a hand over her stomach. To soothe the baby, or soothe herself, she wasn't sure. It would all be OK. Cal had escaped all that nasty business at work, the girl had been paid off, and he'd promised Jodi it would be fine. Jodi wanted to give this child everything, and that included a mother who didn't work. Ali hadn't worked. She could do the same.

The lawn was illuminated by a ghostly half-light from the kitchen, and she thought again how dark it was. In London, a street light outside made their house as bright as noon sometimes. Here there were shadows deep as ink, and she could hardly make out the figure on the lawn. A flash of bare leg told her – Karen. Jodi made an audible tut with her tongue. Karen had been ridiculous this evening, in a dress that would have been too short for Cassie, throwing her legs up on Bill's knees. Poor man. Anyone could see he'd never been interested in Karen. Bill wasn't like that. He was quiet, kind. He'd offered Jodi his arm to cross the lawn to the table they'd eaten at, made sure she was OK.

What was Karen doing? She lifted the curtains aside to watch. Karen seemed to be weaving across the lawn, feet bare on the grass, a bottle dangling from her hand. Jodi had seen her this way before. That night. The ball. A burst of anger flared up under Jodi's solar plexus at the memory. Maybe someone should go out to her, put her to bed.

Karen was in her forties now, her son almost grown and gone, and still this was how she acted.

Jodi caught a glimpse of the clock on the bedside table, an irritating red glow in the dark, interrupting her REM cycle. 3.12 a.m. Christ, where was Cal? Passed out, most likely. Jodi made her way on to the landing, and if someone had asked her, she couldn't have said why. Only that a beat of panic ran down from the base of her skull to her feet. The house was quiet. Ali's door was ajar and in the gloom she was hunched under the blankets, almost foetal. Bill was in Benji's room, the door shut. She wondered why Ali would have put him in there, and Karen in the garage. It seemed the wrong way round for some reason. Cassie's room door was open too and Benji was asleep on the camp bed, trusting and limp in sleep, a child still. Cassie's bed was empty. Where was she? In her head she was counting everyone. Bill and Ali and Benji asleep. Karen on the lawn. Jake was in Mike's office over the garage, maybe asleep by now too.

Where was Callum?

Feeling the familiar pressure on her bladder, she went first to the loo, noting the rust around the old pipes. Ali would have chosen the house for the shabby chic appeal, but likely they'd have to remodel at some point. Better to have a modern build. She finished, and washed her hands, looking at her own moon face in the mirror. Not long now. Soon this would be over and she'd have her baby, she could get to the gym and recover the body she'd been working on her whole adult life. It would all be worth it.

Back out on the landing, and still no sign of Callum. She was tempted to let him suffer it, sleep it off wherever he'd fallen, but what if the kids found him the next day? What if he'd taken his trousers off or even wet himself, as had happened a few times? She'd put him to bed more than once, washing his clothes, never mentioning it.

She went down another step, and another. Clinging to the banister because the weight of her body was all wrong now, and she was so afraid all the time, afraid of falling, afraid of hurting the baby, that it was like walking around with a bomb strapped to her. The panic hadn't dissipated. Moving downstairs, Jodi noticed the back door, the one that gave out to the woodland path, was off its chain. Strange. She moved through into the kitchen, strewn with dirty dishes and half-drunk wine bottles, corks and foil crumbling on the worktops. It would take hours to clear this. The front door was open and something made her move out, her feet in her Uggs hot and muffled. Someone was on the swing seat – she saw the white oval of a face. It was Mike, his eyes closed and mouth open. Out cold. She tutted again to herself. They were too old to behave like this. She and Ali were the only ones who seemed to know it, the ones who thought about meals and dishes and locking up the house before they were all robbed in their beds.

There was movement on the lawn. A sensation of figures moving, as if dancing or wrestling. Her heart fluttered in her chest. She stopped at the edge of the lawn, feeling the damp seep into the edge of her boots. She would have called out, but who was it? 'Karen?' Her voice was low. 'Are you OK?'

The movement stopped. There was an impression of shaking free, of someone lumbering back over, zig-zagging like a drunk. She shaded her eyes for some reason, as if this would help her see out of the light and into the dark. The person approaching wore a red jumper. Mike's jumper. But Mike was in a polo shirt, bare arms stippled with goose-bumps. Why was Callum wearing his jumper?

'What's going on?'

He couldn't meet her eyes. He was horribly drunk, not the worst she'd ever seen but bad, his face piggy with it. 'Jod. S'OK. S'OK.'

'Was that Karen? What's going on?' She looked past him – Karen, or whoever it was, seemed to be lying on the ground, unmoving.

'Nothing. Nothing, nothing. Go back to bed.'

He tried to move past her but she caught him firmly by the elbow – smelling the aftershave that wasn't his, that must be Mike's – and propelled him into the kitchen and through to the living room, forcing his shoes off him at the door. They were stained and clumped with grass. Something was compelling her to act, and act fast, before the thought had even crystallised in her head. The same feeling she'd had so many times – cover up for him. Don't let anyone see. Get him *away*. Because if anyone knew the truth, it would all come tumbling down, the life she'd spent almost twenty-five years building and perfecting. 'Lie down,' she hissed, forcing him on to the sofa. 'Just lie there, for fuck's sake. Take this off.' She pulled his arms out of the jumper, his head getting stuck in it. She guided him free like a child and looked around her, then quickly stuffed the jumper down the back of the sofa. Later, she could deal with that. There was a pile of rubbish behind the shed, and she remembered Ali saying the gardener would burn it on Monday. For now it just had to be hidden. There wasn't time to think, but all the same she was very sure what had to be done. It was the same as all those years ago, the night of the college ball. Hearing that someone had been hurt – seeing Callum weaving across the lawn, a drunk dazed look on his face. Just knowing she had to hustle him, say he'd been with her, get his clothes into the college laundry room as soon as possible. Just to be careful. Just in case he'd done something that might ruin it all, the life they were about to embark on in London, both successful lawyers, with money and prestige. A holiday home. A new car every year. All the things Callum had taken for granted growing up, but which Jodi had never had. Back then she'd known she had to protect the future she was building, and tonight was the same. Her baby was due so soon. She so very nearly had everything she wanted. And so she had to tidy up, tie up loose ends, just in case. Maybe it was no surprise she'd gone into criminal law. She had that sort of mind. Testing for holes, looking for details.

That night, Callum lay down obediently on Ali's sofa, throwing his arms over his head. She could see sleep was already taking him, he was that drunk. 'Sorry,' he mumbled. 'Sorry, Jod. She wanted to.'

Jodi filed those three words somewhere deep down in herself, along with all the other things she had to sit on day after day, and went to the door. She had to be quick now. She could hear footsteps from upstairs. *She wanted to.* 'Go to sleep,' she whispered urgently. In the kitchen she looked out the window – was someone moving out there? It was so dark. Was it Karen, and if so, why hadn't she come in? Moving fast, she snapped on lights, like someone with nothing to hide. At the top of the stairs was Ali, in her white virginal nightgown. Quickly, Jodi grabbed the cafetière as an excuse for being up, dumped it into the sink, though it pained her to make such a mess. And that was when she first heard Karen scream.

◆   ◆   ◆

Her son lost his latch, squawking, rooting blindly, and she transferred him to the other side, feeling a burst of joy. How easy this was. How clever of her body to do these things. Watching him feed, she wondered why she'd been so sure she needed Callum. Just fear, perhaps, of how she'd manage alone with a baby, how she'd pay the bills when she'd already given notice at work. Of failing at her marriage, being divorced, a single mother. Less than perfect. She needn't have worried. What use would he have been anyway, drunk and maudlin, whining that Eric wasn't biologically his child? She should have done this by herself years ago.

Even a few days before she went into labour, the idea of Callum confessing to Ali would have horrified her. It was the reason they hadn't seen Ali much since the party – keeping a low profile. Except for Callum going round to Ali's, trying to find out what the police knew. Stupid. Careless. She'd been so angry at him then. Her first instinct had always been to cover up his mistakes, tidy his mess – something you got used to when you were married to a functioning alcoholic. That's what she'd done the night of the party, not even knowing what she was covering up at first. Then Karen had accused Mike, and Jodi had simply held her breath, said nothing, waited to see how it all fell out. Knowing as only a criminal lawyer could how unlikely a conviction was anyway. But as the weeks went on and Callum's behaviour got worse and worse – sent home from work, collapsed on the floor drunk, official warnings, threats of a sacking – she'd realised she'd been wrong. There was no future to protect except her own, and her son's. She and Callum had no future together. She could do this better alone than with him. So when Ali had said she would go and find Callum, Jodi could have stopped her. It was a safe bet that Callum, drunk and off the rails as he was, would tell her everything. But she hadn't. She'd let Ali go there. And now Callum would go to jail, and the house and baby were Jodi's alone, and no one would expect her to see him ever again. Not after what he'd done.

Jodi stroked the baby's cheek, smiling as he unlatched, a windy smile beaming back at her. Really, it had all worked out as well as she might have hoped.

ACKNOWLEDGMENTS

A big thank you to everyone at Amazon Publishing for getting behind this book in such an enthusiastic manner – I couldn't have asked for more support. Special thanks to Jack Butler, and to Ian Pindar for a surprisingly enjoyable edit, and to Jenni Davis for a great copy-edit.

Thanks as always to superstar agent Diana Beaumont and everyone at Marjacq, to Graham Bartlett for police advice, and to all my crime-writing pals for ongoing advice and plot fixes, as well as my university friends for not being like the ones in this book.

If you enjoyed this book, I would love to hear from you! You can find me on Facebook and Instagram, as well as on Twitter as @inkstainsclaire.

ABOUT THE AUTHOR

Photo © 2017 Jamie Drew

Claire McGowan was born in 1981 in a small Irish village where the most exciting thing that ever happened was some cows getting loose on the road. She is the author of *The Fall*, and the acclaimed Paula Maguire crime series. She also writes women's fiction under the name Eva Woods.